SILENCIO!

Second Edition

SILENCIO!
Second Edition

Mike Faricy

Published by

MJF Publishing
https://www.mikefaricybooks.com

Acknowledgments

I would like to thank the following people for their help and support:

Special thanks to my editors, Kitty, Donna and Rhonda for their hard work, cheerful patience and positive feedback.

I would like to thank Ann and Julie for their creative talent and not slitting their wrists or jumping off the high bridge when dealing with my Neanderthal computer capabilities.

Special thanks to Ann for her patience.

Last, I would like to thank family and friends for their encouragement and unqualified support. Special thanks to Maggie, Jed, Schatz, Pat, Av, Emily and Pat for not rolling their eyes, at least when I was there, and most of all, to my wife Teresa whose belief, support and inspiration has from day one, never waned.

Prologue

As I held the door Melissa Donnelly said, "Oh thanks." We were leaving Starbucks after our first meeting. We'd corresponded back and forth a few times on a dating site. She seemed about as bored as I was on the internet, and after three texting sessions, we decided to meet for coffee. I thought the in-person meeting had gone pretty well. She was an attractive blonde, liked to smile, and had a delightful laugh.

"Thanks again for making the time, Melissa. It was great to meet you. You're even nicer than you seemed online if that's possible."

"You are a really good liar, Dev Haskell. Believe me. The pleasure has been all mine. It was wonderful to meet you. No pressure, but I'll leave it in your court if you want to get together again."

"You free Friday night? I'm wondering if we could maybe meet up just for a beer or a glass of wine. There's a place just across the street from my office called The Spot. I pop in there once in a while," I said, thinking there was no point in mentioning I was in there just about every day.

"The Spot? That sounds so cute, but I don't know where it is. Across the street from your office?"

"Yeah, on Randolph Avenue. You can't miss it. It's on the corner of Randolph and Victoria. Just a small little neighborhood local."

"I'd love it. You name a time, and I'll meet you there."

"Why don't we meet up around six. We can have a glass of wine and maybe grab dinner somewhere. How about you pick the dinner place?"

"I'll put my thinking cap on," she said and gave me a peck on the cheek. She squeezed my hand for a moment then crossed the street to her car. She waved, blew a kiss, climbed in, and drove down the street.

That was great, I thought, as I climbed into my car and headed home. I'd dropped off Morton, my golden retriever, at home before meeting up with Melissa. I figured right about now he was probably due for a walk. I pulled in front of my place ten minutes later. I planned to grab Morton. We could take our walk down at the office and then head over to The Spot just for one.

I hurried up to the front porch, placed my key in the lock, but the front door wasn't locked. You gotta be kidding me. I always lock the front door. Was I that focused on meeting Melissa in person that I forgot to lock the door? Get a grip, man.

At first, I thought the noise was from my radio, but it seemed to be coming from the front room. Then there was the pizza box on the floor, and Morton was stretched out, dining on pizza crusts.

"Morton, where in the hell did that—"

"It's about damn time. Get your dumb ass in here," an unfortunately familiar voice called.

Fat Freddy Zimmerman was stretched out on my couch, oozing over the edge. Another pizza box rested on his lap. He stuffed the last half of the final piece into his mouth. "You better pat down douchebag," he said to the muscle-bound thug watching the cartoon on my TV.

"What the hell are you guys doing in my hou—"

"You heard what he said. Shut the hell up and assume the position," the thug said. He spun me around, pressed the side of my head against the wall, shoved a foot between my legs, and kicked them apart.

"Nice to meet you, sir. I can tell you right now I'm not carrying," I said as he reached between my legs none too gently, causing me to jump.

"Relax, Haskell, that's probably more action than you've had in months," Fat Freddy said and laughed.

"He's clean, boss," the one-watt thug said and stepped back.

I remained pressed against the wall. "Is it okay to move? I'm not going to scare you if I turn around, am I?"

"I hope that wasn't meant as an insult, Haskell. Austin might take that the wrong way, and then there's no telling what could happen."

"Oh, no, not an insult. I just didn't want to get on the wrong side of Austin."

"Much better, Haskell. Turn around so I can see your smiling face."

I turned around, careful not to rub Austin the wrong way. He was a good six inches taller and maybe a hundred pounds heavier than me, none of which was fat. Even his muscles had muscles. He glared down at me. I stepped to the side so I could see past him and focused on Fat Freddy, who was in the process of licking his fingertips. There was half a crust in the pizza box, and as he set it on the floor, Morton hurried in. He let Fat Freddy scratch him behind the ear and then snatched up the crust.

"Dog after my own heart. God only knows why he's still with you," Freddy said.

"Why are you guys here? How did you get in?"

"Your dog Morgan let us in. Not that it's important," Freddy said and laughed. Idiot Austin let out a fake laugh and then stopped a half-second after Freddy stopped. "Mr. Gustafson would like a word with you, now, Haskell. Let's go, Austin."

"First of all, my dog's name isn't Morgan. It's Morton, and just what does Tubby Gus- err, umm, Mr. Gustafson want with me?"

"I guess you should probably shut the hell up and come with us to find out. Look, Haskell, you're starting to be difficult again. Need I remind you that never, ever goes your way. Hey, I've got an idea. Maybe just get your dumb ass in the car, and then once you see Mr. Gustafson, if you still want to be stupid, you could ask him what he wants. Or, maybe just once, you could keep your trap shut, and he'll tell you what the hell he wants. Now, for your own good, please, don't say another word. Austin, if Haskell says anything, you have my permission."

"Permission to do—ooff," was all I could get out before Austin hit me in the stomach, lifting me off my feet. The room was suddenly spinning. I saw stars as I leaned against the wall and attempted to get back to whatever 'normal' had been just a moment before.

"See you later, boy," Fat Freddy said as he patted Morton on the head. "Bring Hassle out to the car, Austin. Be careful. I don't want him throwing up in the back seat."

One

S lowly but surely, I began to recover. I knew where Tubby Gustafson lived, I knew the route they probably took, but lying face down on the floor of the back seat in Freddy's Cadillac Escalade, it was impossible to determine where exactly we were. By the time we pulled through the wrought iron gates and onto the circular drive in front of Tubby Gustafson's mansion, I was pretty much back to normal, except for the dull pain where my stomach used to be.

Austin was driving, and he pulled to a stop at the front door. He hurried out of the car and opened the passenger door for Fat Freddy. As soon as Freddy's door closed, my door opened. Someone grabbed me by the ankles and yanked me out of the door, stopping at the very last second before I dropped at least two feet head-first onto the pavement. Instead, I landed on my knees, tearing both knees on my trousers. Idiot Austin grabbed the back of my collar, popping two buttons on my shirt as he yanked me on to my feet.

"Better pat him down again, just to be on the safe side," Fat Freddy said and headed into Tubby's mansion.

"When in the hell could I grab a gun?" I called after him. Brainless Austin gave me a look. "Okay, okay, sorry, just asking."

Fortunately, one of the thugs stationed by the front door stepped between Austin and me and began to pat me down. I raised my hands over my head and leaned against the car. He gently patted me down, then stepped back and shouted, "Clean."

"Let's go," said some other guy, who'd been leaning against the front of the house, and held the front door open. I hurried toward the door. At that point, I would have done almost anything to get away from psychopathic Austin. The door closed behind me, and I stepped into the entryway. Another thug was seated just inside, attempting to read a comic book. He gave me a look suggesting I was interrupting an important part and tossed the comic book onto the end table next to his chair.

"I know, I know," I said and assumed the position again, leaning forward with my legs spread and my hands above my head resting against the wall.

"Okay, good to go," he said a half-minute later. I stepped into the large entry with the staircase running up the side of the wall and the gilt-framed painting of Tubby Gustafson holding a bunch of rolled documents pretending to be someone who had done something noble in his life.

Fat Freddy tossed what looked like a chocolate into his mouth and headed down the hall. We passed the dining room and Tubby Gustafson's library, then stopped at the heavy oak door to Tubby's office. Fat Freddy gave me a quick look, knocked on the oak door, and pushed it open. "Greetings, sir. Sorry it took so long. We ran into a bit of difficulty along the way."

Tubby Gustafson stood at the opposite end of the room, on the far side of his desk. Usually, when I had been summoned, I found him stretched out on a massage table with his fat oozing over the side and his privates covered by a white towel. Two scantily clad women would be massaging his hairy, dimpled shoulders.

Today, he stood wearing a pair of red plaid boxer shorts and black knee-high stockings held up by black leather sock garters. He wore a strappy t-shirt that had to be a triple extra-large size. He leaned forward with his head down, holding a golf putter. With his large stomach protruding, it had to be damn near impossible to see the golf ball. He studied something a few feet away, then seemed to concentrate and putted. A moment later, he groaned, "Damn it," and tossed the putter onto a brown leather recliner.

He turned, stared at the torn knees on my trousers, and shook his head. "What have I done to deserve this?" he said as he pulled back the leather desk chair and sat down. "Well, now what is it you want, Haskell?"

"Actually, Tub, err, umm sir, I was under the impression you wanted to see me."

"I believe the politician, sir," Fat Freddy said from behind me.

"The pol…oh, yes, yes, with everything we've had going on, I almost forgot. Thank you, Frederick. Haskell, I want you to look into something for me, actually someone," Tubby said. He opened a drawer along the side of his desk, pulled out a manila file folder, and set it on the desk. "Hmm, another failed attempt to look trendy?" Tubby asked and nodded at my torn trouser knees. "Get over here and sit down."

I hurried over to one of the client chairs in front of his desk and sat down.

"I'm interested in a gentleman by the name of Casper Trickle. I need you to take a look at him and see what you can find. He's involved in—"

"Pardon me for interrupting, sir, but as I think you know, politics, financial dealings, taxes, and the like are really not my strong suit."

"Please, stop right there, Haskell. Have I asked you to think? Do I appear to be the kind of individual who would want you to examine financial records? Do you even have a strong suit? Good lord, you probably still have a piggy bank in your bedroom."

"Only for quarters, sir. I find—"

"Silencio," Tubby shouted. "God save me. I'll want a full report on the individual mentioned in this file. You may read the file while you sit there. I do not want to hear from you until you are finished, and then I only want to hear you say that you have read the information and will proceed with an investigation. Do I make myself clear?"

I nodded and pulled the file across the desk to me. Tubby returned to his putting.

Casper Trickle appeared to be involved in acquiring companies that ended up in bankruptcy. His name sounded familiar, maybe, but I couldn't recall why, exactly.

"Would you mind if I made a few notes, Sir?" I asked just as Tubby putted.

He was quiet for a long moment and then said, "Damn it, Haskell! You made me miss. No, I don't care if you make notes. I never expected you to be able to remember what you read."

I wrote down Trickle's name and his address along with what appeared to be a business and private phone number. I paged through the file until I came to what looked like a tax form. I quickly went through the remainder of the documents. With the exception of a half-dozen grainy images, it was all financial information. I closed the file and sat quietly, watching and counting as Tubby missed one putt after another. I was up to eleven when he swore and tossed the putter back on the leather recliner.

"Finished, Haskell?" he said.

"Yes, sir, I've his name and home address, along with his office address, business phone number, and—"

"I don't give a damn about his professional life. I know the man is successful. That's why he's thinking of running for governor. I want you to investigate his personal life. Find out his background, what his weak spots might be. This investigation is to remain private. Do not, I repeat, do not mention this to anyone. I'll want this information no later than a week from today. Do I make myself clear?"

"Yes, sir, very clear. I'll see what I can find out."

"See that you do. Frederick, get him out of my sight," Tubby said as he picked up his putter and focused his attention on his next missed putt.

Fat Freddy nodded toward the door, and I followed. Once out in the hall, I said, "I wasn't aware Mr. Gustafson played golf."

"He's just begun to take it up. Let's go," Freddy said and headed for the front door. As we stepped outside, Austin and the two individuals leaning against the front of the mansion stood and pretended to be focused on whatever they were supposed to be doing.

"Austin, get Haskell out of here and take his worthless ass back to that seedy part of town he lives in."

"Glad to, sir," Austin said and glared at me. He hurried toward the black Escalade and held the rear door for me.

"Why, thank you, Austin," I said as I climbed in.

He slammed the door behind me and hurried around to the driver's side. He started the car, slowly drove out through the gate of Tubby's mansion, and sped down the street. He hadn't driven more than three blocks when he pulled to the curb, turned toward me, and said, "Get out."

"What are you talking about? You know where I live. My house is four or five miles from here. I don't want to—"

"I don't care what you want, Hassle. Get your dumb ass out of the car. I've got shit to do."

"No doubt," I said as I opened the door and began to step out. I wasn't halfway out the door when Austin floored the vehicle. Fortunately, I landed on the grassy boulevard on all fours and gave him the finger as he sped down the street. Maybe it was a good thing I wasn't in the car with him. I stood, brushed the torn knees on my pants, and started walking.

It took me two hours, and I was starving by the time I made it home. Morton was asleep on the couch in the front room. As I stepped inside, he raised his head and wagged his tail. He'd torn up both pizza boxes and scattered the bits and pieces around the room. I went out to the kitchen, finished up pasta left overs from the refrigerator and then decided a nap might be in order. Morton woke me a few hours later. I grabbed his leash from the counter, and we walked around the block.

We passed a woman along the way that I'd seen before. She was walking a little furry white dog. She usually gave us a nod and a smile. Tonight she stared at the torn knees on my trousers and hurried across to the opposite side of the street.

Once we were home, I checked the locks on all the windows, wedged chairs beneath the front and back door, and stretched out on the couch in front of the TV.

I woke up a little after one. Morton had already headed
upstairs. I climbed the stairs, pulled off my torn trousers,
left them on the floor, and climbed into bed.

TWO

I was up before my alarm went off. I got the coffee going in the kitchen then hurried back upstairs to shower and shave. Morton was still asleep when I headed back down to the kitchen. I was on my second cup, going through email messages, when he wandered in. I gave him the proverbial head scratch and let him outside.

I took Morton out to my car and stopped. A half-dozen eggs had been thrown on the car sometime during the night. I put Morton in the back seat, turned on the garden hose, and removed most of the egg from my car. '*Damn kids,*' I thought.

We were in the office before Louie arrived. I turned off yesterday's coffee, dumped the remnants down the sink, and made a fresh pot. I was watching out the window when Louie pulled up and parked across the street behind my car. I filled his mug with coffee and set it on his picnic table desk. I listened to the stairs creak as he slowly made his way up to the office.

"Fresh coffee waiting for you on your desk," I said. Louie gave me a thumbs-up and settled into his chair. At the moment, I was looking into the apartment across the street through my binoculars. A woman in a black thong was standing at her kitchen counter applying makeup. Not a bad way to start the day, watching, that is.

"How'd your coffee meet-up go yesterday? Did that woman even bother to show?" Louie asked once he caught his breath.

I turned around in my office chair, put the binoculars in my desk drawer, and said, "To be honest, it went a lot better than I expected. Really a nice gal. We're going to meet up tomorrow night for dinner and see where things go. I'm not gonna put any pressure on her."

"I was wondering if everything worked out. Thought you might make it into The Spot last night and give me a full report."

"First off, nothing to report. We chatted for maybe forty-five minutes, and it went fine. I drove home to grab Morton and planned to head down to The Spot, only to find a couple of visitors in my place."

"Visitors?"

"Yeah, dumbass Fat Freddy Zimmerman and some thug named Austin, who punched me in the stomach."

"They were actually inside your house?"

"Yeah, and get this, they'd ordered pizzas and were giving Morton all the crusts."

"I'm sure he loved that," Louie said and slurped some coffee.

"God only knows what he left in the backyard this morning. Anyway, they drove me to Tubby Gustafson's place. He wants me to check some guy out. Then this Austin jerk was supposed to drive me home, but instead, he kicked me out of the car about three blocks from Tubby's, and I ended up walking home. I was so beat I fell asleep on the couch in front of the TV."

"Sounds like it maybe wasn't the best evening."

"The Tubby part sucked, but Melissa, that's the woman I met online. She was really nice."

"Who does Gustafson want you to check out?"

"Oh, vintage Tubby, he had me read a file while he practiced putting golf balls. I don't think he ever made a putt while I was there. You ever hear of a guy named Casper Trickle? Apparently, he's thinking of running for governor, at least, that's what Tubby said. Not sure how he makes his money. If he's interested in politics, he probably has some scam in mind. You ever heard of him?"

Louie seemed to think for a moment. "Now that you ask, something seems to ring a bell. I can't remember what, but probably nothing good. If I recall, and I may be wrong, I believe Casper Trickle was permanently dis-barred two or three years ago. He ran some shady 'loan modification' business. You know, for a price, he would get your mortgage company to lower the interest rate. He collected illegal advance attorney fees and, I think in a couple of cases, improperly borrowed money from client trust funds and failed to repay. He's your basic legal sleazeball, but then if he's going into politics, he'd prob-ably fit right in."

"Can you think of anyone who may have dealt with him?"

Louie shook his head. "Off the top of my head, nothing's ringing a bell. But just a word of warning. If anyone is linked up with Casper Trickle, they can't be good. I'm sure if you google him, things will come up. Does Tubby have funds somehow tied up with him?"

"Not that I'm aware of. He was pretty specific. He wants personal info on Trickle. He gave me a week to find out everything about the guy."

"Funny he wouldn't check him out on his own," Louie said.

"He's probably too busy, now that he's taken up golf. God knows he needs all the practice he can get. You in the office today?"

"Yeah, I think so. I may get a call from a new client. The guy was arrested for DWI yesterday afternoon and ended up in the drunk tank overnight. It depends on if he gets out today or they hold him for a second night."

Louie fired up his computer and began typing. I grabbed my binoculars and checked the apartment across the street again. Unfortunately, the woman in the thong was nowhere to be seen.

I fired up my computer and googled Casper Trickle. Not much came up other than he had been involved in the implosion of a hedge fund called Archegos Capital Management. He somehow seemed to escape without much damage. He was listed as a retired attorney, which was par for the course.

The three online images of him suggested a well-heeled sleaze bag. Light brown hair, slightly gray at the temples. He looked to be about fifty and apparently liked expensive clothes. He struck me as a guy who appeared to be very wealthy, and in case you actually wondered, he would somehow allude to that fact within the first minute of conversation. He lived in town on Summit Avenue. A pricey street populated by large mansions built at least a hundred years ago.

I checked the county tax site, got his address, and decided to check the place out.

"I gotta run a quick errand. You going to be around for maybe an hour?"

"Not a problem. Take your time," Louie said.

Morton gave me a glance as I headed out the door. He was more involved with the pork bone he was chewing on than wanting to get off his pillow and tag along with me. I made it through all five stoplights, so it was no more than a five-minute drive over to Summit Avenue. I took a right and headed down past the Governor's mansion. Today the protestors were waving signs about voting 'no' on proposition eleven. I had no idea what proposition eleven was. I drove two more blocks, pulled to the curb, and climbed out of my car. If what Tubby said was correct and the guy was thinking about running for Governor, I found it interesting he lived just two blocks from the Governor's mansion.

Trickle's mansion took up two corner lots. I slowed my pace as I walked past. The house was a three-story red-stone structure with a slate roof and there was a six-foot-high wrought-iron fence around the property. Three large oak trees were in the front yard. Four security cameras were mounted along the front of the house. I turned the corner and walked along the side of the house. I counted two more security cameras, one on either corner of the house.

I held my cellphone in my left hand and gave one and two-word answers to a fake phone call as I pressed the camera button and took pictures of the place.

The three-stall brick garage behind the mansion had a rental unit on the second story. There was a brick patio off to the side of the garage, and two muscle-bound guys were on the patio in gym shorts and strappy red t-shirts bench pressing some serious weights. One of the guys, blonde with a crewcut, stood as he spotted while the other was on the bench doing some serious lifting. The guy spotting gave me more than a casual glance as I walked past. I gave a simple nod, clicked my cellphone camera a few times, and kept going.

The back of the garage ran along the edge of the alley. The wrought-iron fence butted against the back corner of the garage. At least two more security cameras were mounted on the garage. Rather than walk up the alley, I went around the entire block and climbed back in my car.

I drove past Trickle's place, and now three cars were parked in front of the house. A red convertible, a black SUV, and at the moment, a white van labeled Duncan

Flowers. I slowed as I drove past the open gate, but I didn't see anyone outside. Rather than make a second pass and possibly attract attention, I headed back to the office.

Three

When I entered the office, both Louie and Morton were sound asleep. Morton slowly opened one eye, saw it was me, and drifted back asleep. Louie snorted when I closed the door and returned to breathing heavily. I drummed my fingers on my desk, wondering who I could call regarding Casper Trickle, when a light suddenly blinked on in my one-watt brain. Heidi Bauer. My on-again, off-again friend with benefits that I hadn't seen in several months.

I still had her number on speed-dial. I brought her name up, tapped the screen, and crossed my fingers, hoping she'd answer when my name appeared on her cellphone.

She answered after the third ring. "So, you heard. I guess the news is all over town," was how she answered. I'd been here uncountable times and knew exactly where this was going.

"Hi, Heidi. Just checking in to see if you're okay," I lied, having no idea who she broke up with this time. "I was more than a little surprised. Just for the record, I think the guy is an absolute idiot. The worst decision of his life. You doing okay?"

"What are you talking about?"

Shit. "I thought you broke up with what's his name."

"Cletus Devon? No, Dev, that was over two months ago. I was talking about my car getting totaled."

"Well, yeah, that was the other thing I was going to mention," I said, having never heard about it. "But you're okay after the car being totaled?"

"I'm fine, I guess. It's just a major pain in…well, you know. Of course, I'm suddenly getting jacked around by my insurance company. I'm driving a mid-range rental and wearing sunglasses, so no one will recognize me in the thing. I put Cletus's clothes in a box out in the garage six weeks ago, and he still hasn't picked them up. I tell you, right now, life is a pain in…So why did you call? I didn't think I'd ever hear from you again."

"You know that's not going to happen. I was thinking, if you're not too busy, I'd bring dinner over tonight, and we could catch up. No pressure, and if you don't want to, I get it, and I won't bug you anymore. Just thinking you could maybe use a night off, relax. I'd be happy to give you a back rub if you still like them."

"Yeah, right, like I would give those up. You know, Dev, this might be just the thing I need. I suppose you'll want something in return."

"No pressure, but there is something else I was thinking about."

"I knew it, typical."

"Sorry to disappoint, but I'm not talking about bedroom antics. I'm curious if you've ever heard of a guy named Casper Trickle. He's apparently thinking—"

"Casper Trickle? Oh yeah, who hasn't heard of him? I suppose I could fill you in, at least a little. Fortunately, other than investing in his stock, I've never had to deal with him. Let me do some checking and get up to date. What time were you thinking?"

"Maybe dinner time. I can bring dinner and a bottle of wine. Your only task will be to relax and take it easy."

"I'm sold. See you tonight, and thanks, Dev. It's nice to hear your voice again."

"Same here, nice to hear you. I'll see you tonight," I said, and Heidi disconnected.

"Was that Heidi I heard you talking to?" Louie asked, blinking his eyes open. He rolled his shoulders a couple of times, and I could hear them pop and snap all the way over at my desk.

"Yeah, I called to see what she knew about Casper Trickle and somehow got talked into bringing dinner."

"Oh, I think the evening will probably work out to your liking. It usually does when she's involved."

"One can only hope," I said. I took Morton for a long walk toward the end of the afternoon. We stopped in at The Spot for a minute just to touch base with Louie. He fed Morton two handfuls of pork rinds, and we headed out the door. I dropped Morton off at home, changed clothes, and grabbed two bottles of wine from Chuck at Solo Vino. I drove to Carmelo's and picked up two sun-dried tomato pesto dinners. Ten minutes later, I pulled in front of Heidi's. It was exactly 6:00.

She opened the front door before I even climbed the three steps to ring the doorbell. "Well, don't you look like you're on a mission."

"Dinner and wine, and I want to hear all about the car. First question, are you okay?" I asked as I handed her the bag with the two wine bottles. I followed her into the kitchen and set the Styrofoam dinner trays on the counter.

"Yes, I'm fine. I wasn't even in the car at the time. It's just frustrating."

"You weren't in the car? Who was driving?"

"Driving? No one was driving, Dev. This was that phone pole that went down when they were working on the lines."

"That was your car?" I'd seen it on the news, a red BMW 850 convertible, not exactly cheap. Somehow, the telephone pole had fallen on the car and crushed it. The local news station led with the story four or five nights ago. The vehicle looked like it was about six inches high, with the phone pole resting right down the center of the car.

"Yes, unfortunately, that was my car. A total loss, now we're arguing about what the value is, or rather, was. The good news is, I wasn't in the car at the time. The bad news is, I've been dealing with my insurance company ever since."

"Anything I can do to help?"

She looked at me for a moment, then shook her head and said, "Never mind, bad idea. So, what have you been up to for the past few months?"

We ate in the kitchen and chatted through dinner and a bottle of wine. Once the second bottle was opened, we moved into the den, and Heidi brought me up to date on Casper Trickle. The bottom line was he sounded like a well-connected guy who did all the right things until you really looked at the particulars. He was tied into the past and present mayors, the city council, a bunch of legislators, and a couple of judges. He donated to both political parties and all the sure winners in various campaigns. He would most likely be labeled as an independent.

"I've met him a few times, nothing personal, but deep down, I think he'd always make sure he came first in any deal. Kind of slimy was my impression," Heidi said. "I'll email you a list of people who are less than pleased with him, some former investors, a neighbor, and a couple of attorneys who dealt with him in court."

"Thanks, much appreciated. I'll take a look at that tomorrow morning," I said, hoping she caught on to my 'tomorrow morning' suggestion. If she did, she didn't react. "More wine?" I asked, thinking maybe another glass might loosen her up a little more.

"Oh, I'd love one, but I'd better not. I've got an early morning meeting with two potential investors, and I want to be at my best."

I was hoping that meant we might adjourn and head upstairs to bed. After a painfully quiet moment, I said,

"Well, I should probably take off and head home. Thanks for the info on Trickle."

She climbed off the couch, gave a revealing stretch, and said, "Oh, I think I'll sleep like a baby after that wine."

"Hey, I never gave you that back rub. I could—"

"That's okay, maybe some other time. Thanks for coming over with dinner and the wine. It's nice to see you again," she said and held out her hand.

I couldn't believe it, a handshake? From Heidi? You gotta be kidding me! She had really changed. I took hold of her hand and gently pulled her toward me for a kiss, hoping that might get her into the mood. She smiled as she drew close and then, at the last minute, turned her head, so I kissed her on the cheek.

"Good luck in your meeting tomorrow," I said as she gently pulled away and headed toward the front door. I followed reluctantly, wondering what I'd done wrong. She turned at the front door, looked at me, and suddenly laughed. "Oh, look at you. So disappointed. I love it. Come on, you big baby." She took me by the hand and led me upstairs.

It was still dark when she kissed me. My first thought was, *Really, again?* Then she said, "I've got to get down to the office early and prepare for this meeting. The coffee's on downstairs. Let yourself out and lock the door. Thanks for a wonderful evening and the back rub. I really enjoyed myself."

When I woke again, it was daylight. The digital clock on her dresser read just a few minutes after seven. My distant memory of the evening slowly came into focus, ending with her kiss and telling me to let myself out. I dressed, filled a travel mug with coffee, and drove home. Morton was just coming down the stairs as I stepped in the front door. I let him out into the backyard and went upstairs to shower. I pulled on a pair of jeans and a faded blue t-shirt with yellow letters that said St. Paul Police over the left breast. Once we finished breakfast, we headed down to the office. I couldn't remember if Louie was coming in or if he was in court this morning, so I made a full pot of coffee. He showed up about twenty minutes later.

"So, how'd your evening go?" he asked after a couple of sips.

"Nice night. I took dinner over to Heidi, and we caught up. She filled me in with some general information on financial deals with Casper Trickle, none of it very good."

"And?"

"And then I went home and came down here. She's going to send me a list of folks who aren't too thrilled with Casper Trickle, so hopefully, I can talk to some of them and have enough information to make Tubby Gustafson happy."

"And that was your night? You didn't, ahhh, you know…"

"Louie, it was more of a business meeting. I was interviewing her."

"Yeah, okay, but in the past, when you two got together, there was almost always fireworks."

"Sorry to disappoint, but we were both strictly business this time." He gave me a look that suggested he might not be buying my explanation, but there was nothing he could do.

Four

It was close to 10:00 before I began calling the names on the list Heidi sent me. I ended up leaving a message on the first four calls. I was prepared to do the same on the fifth call when a guy named Colin Demming answered after the third ring. "Demming."

It took me a moment to realize he was live.

"Hello? Anyone there?"

"Hello, Colin. My name is Dev Haskell. I got your name from a friend. I'm checking on someone I was thinking of doing some business with. He seems to have a somewhat mixed set of reviews and recommendations, and I wondered if I could get some input from you."

"Hmm, happy to help if I can. Who are we talking about?"

"A gentleman by the name of Casper Trickle."

"One piece of advice. Don't walk. Run in the opposite direction just as fast as you can. Get the hell away from him and never look back. Block any communications from him. In the end, he'll only do one thing, and that's Cost. You. Money. He'll be more than happy to take every last dime. He has ruined more than one life."

"That doesn't sound too promising," I said and chuckled.

"There is nothing funny about Mr. Trickle. All of us are surprised he's not behind bars. Virtually everyone I know who came in contact with him lost a substantial amount of money. A number of us are involved in a lawsuit that's bound to go on for eternity."

"The little information I have is that he was disbarred. Is that correct?"

"That's correct. As charming as he seems, the man is rotten to the absolute core. He'll be more than happy to lie to your face. Any financial figures he provides will, at best, be inaccurate, inflated, or outright falsehoods."

"What about more personal information? He seems to have a lovely home on Summit Avenue. Is he married? Does he have children? Is he involved in a church?"

"He's involved in all of the above, or at least he was at one time. He's been divorced for a number of years, at least eight, maybe ten. There were two children in the marriage. They must be college age by now, maybe even graduated. He's active in a church when it suits his needs. The saving grace for the man is the fact that he is politically connected to the powers that be. If you're running for office, he would be one of the first contacts you would make in fundraising, regardless of your party. He likes to back winners, and that seems to pay off."

I thought about the two guys lifting weights on the back patio of Trickle's home. "Are you aware of anything along the lines of, mmm, physical intimidation?"

"If you're referring to the two muscle-bound Neanderthals that have paid a visit to at least a couple of individuals, yes, I'm aware. But only on a second-hand basis. Fortunately, I've not had that experience. The three individuals I'm aware of who share that dreadful experience are not about to mention it to anyone. Suffice it to say, they were frightened to the point where one moved out of state, another hired round-the-clock protection. The third died of a heart attack about six weeks after his run-in with those two creeps. All three eventually dropped their legal proceedings."

"Would you be able to give me their names?"

"I'm sorry, but I won't. They've been through more than enough and not a reflection on you, but they won't talk to you or anyone else regarding this. They simply want to get away from Casper Trickle as fast and as far as possible."

"How does he keep doing what he's doing?"

"Trickle? Deep down, he's crooked as the day is long, and he's connected. I'm sorry, tell me your name again."

"Haskell, Dev Haskell."

"Forgive me, Mr. Haskell. I'll plead old age. I'm fifty-eight."

"Hardly old," I said.

"There are days," Demming said. "Mr. Haskell, as I said, the man is connected. I've seen it too many times and not just with Trickle. Things seem to be going well and then suddenly fall apart, whether it's the stock you purchased, the person he put you in touch with, or the great idea you ran past him for advice. You wake up one morning to find yourself suddenly screwed. Trickle's surrounded by a legal shield you're unable to penetrate. They don't take your phone calls. You end up having to close your office or let go of ninety percent of your staff. The gentleman you thought you knew, the guy you trusted and relied upon, he's off to Mexico, or Europe, or Southeast Asia, and you're left holding the bag. That's if you're lucky and haven't had a heart attack from stress."

"And then he starts all over again?" I asked.

"Like clockwork. If you watch and keep tabs, you suddenly realize that's his damn game. The information is out there. The problem is people always think they know better, and before they know it, they've been played. He's brought in a competitor, bid a higher price on the property, found someone to do the job for less. Whatever it is, you end up doing all the work, and Trickle seems to benefit."

"Incredible," I said.

"More like sinful and no doubt illegal, but I get your point. One of these days, someone's going to figure out how to deal with him, and I don't mean spending twenty years filing lawsuits. It will be swift and to the point."

"Do you know of anyone currently involved with him?"

"I'm not involved any longer, other than to be part of one of many lawsuits, which seems to be going nowhere, I hasten to add."

"Are you aware of a gentleman named Gustafson who is involved with him?"

"No, sorry, but that name isn't ringing a bell. Do you know someone involved with him?"

"No, I just heard a rumor about him looking into politics and wondered, is all. Would you mind if I contact you down the road with a question? Unfortunately, everything you've told me seems to match up with the little bit of history I'm aware of."

"Not a problem. Feel free to call at any time. But please, take my advice. If you're involved in some way with Trickle, get out. Sell at a loss if you have to but get out."

"Well, thank you for the information. I think we'll look somewhere else and keep our distance from Mr. Trickle."

"Believe me, that's the best thing you can do."

"Thanks again for the time, Mr. Demming. Nice chatting, wishing you all the very best," I said, but he had already disconnected.

Five

I talked to a half-dozen people over the course of the day. No one was quite as harsh as Demming, but their advice was basically the same. Get the hell away from Casper Trickle. I attempted to call a number of people back. Interestingly, three of the numbers I had left messages with had already blocked me. That suggested to me that those individuals had possibly had a run-in with Trickle or maybe his thugs and wanted nothing to do with anyone asking questions.

I kept thinking I was supposed to be somewhere or had something I was supposed to do, but I couldn't remember what it was. Even if I did remember, I never wrote a note to myself, which meant it couldn't have been too important.

Louie turned off his computer, stretched, and said, "I'm thinking of heading over to The Spot for one. You guys want to join me?"

"God, an entire day of folks telling me in no uncertain terms how awful Casper Trickle is. It's going to take more than one beer to get me thinking positively, again.

Let me take Morton for a quick walk, and we'll meet you over there."

"Enjoy your walk," Louie said.

As soon as I grabbed Morton's leash off the wall, he was at the door with his tail wagging. I clicked the leash onto his collar, and we headed down the stairs and out the door. We walked for a good twenty minutes. Morton investigated just about every fence gate and marked the two usual fire hydrants along the way.

I double-checked Randolph Avenue before we entered The Spot, just in case Fat Freddy Zimmerman or idiot Austin were around. Fortunately, I didn't see them. As we entered the bar, Mike, the bartender, gave me a nod.

"I'll take a Summit IPA and better refill Louie's glass," I said. It was Friday night, and The Spot was pretty full. A couple of the booths were empty, but most of the bar stools were occupied. It was the usual casual crowd, jeans, t-shirts, a few women in tank tops and cut-off shorts. Folks were ready to kick back for the weekend.

Morton charged along the length of the bar, heading toward Louie's permanent stool. The leash was pulled taut, and for a moment, I thought he was going to pull my shoulder out of joint.

"Well, Morton. Thank you for bringing Dev. It's his turn to buy," Louie said. As I followed Morton around the corner of the bar, Mike set a fresh glass in front of Louie and a glass of Summit on the bar for me. Louie bent down with a handful of pork rinds which Morton inhaled in about three seconds.

I took a healthy sip of beer and began to relax.

"You were on the phone for a good part of the day. Was that all about Casper Trickle?" Louie asked and took a sip from his fresh drink.

I took another sip from my beer. "I think your advice was in line with what everyone said. I find it interesting that no one mentioned any political aspirations. That said, a number of folks alluded to him being very well-connected. The type of individual always sought by people running for office from either party. Apparently, his contributions must be substantial enough that everyone has him on their list. My sense is that he expects special treatment in return, and apparently, he gets it.

"I'm afraid that's the world we live in," Louie said and took a sip.

"I think that's probably what it's always been like. But now, given the availability of all the information that's out there, sooner or later, even a dumbass like me finds some of this out."

"Maybe, it's just that it seems worse than we ever imagined," Louie said.

"Enough of my depressing day. Did you hear from your most recent DWI client?"

"Only that he's in the drunk tank for another night. Apparently not his first visit. He was in there in 2018, which is pretty much going to ensure extended time in the workhouse, maybe even a license revocation."

I shook my head. "What the hell is wrong with people that they forgot things didn't go so well last time they got nailed for DWI? At what point do you start paying attention? Louie? Hey, Louie?"

"What? Oh, sorry, I was just looking at that gorgeous thing that walked in the bar. I wonder if she's in the right place."

I glanced down the bar at the blonde standing just inside, scanning the crowd. She was dressed to the nines in a short, tight, black dress with a V-neck exposing a healthy cleavage. She held a pocketbook-sized black velvet purse with a gold clip in her right hand. Our eyes suddenly connected. She smiled, waved, and headed in my direction. Melissa. Yeah, that's what I forgot. We were going to meet here tonight for a drink and then go out to dinner. It all came back as she walked along the bar, turning every guy's head along the way. As she headed toward me in my faded blue t-shirt, dirty, wrinkled jeans, and worn running shoes, I tried to come up with an excuse.

Six

Heads turned as Melissa strutted toward us at the end of the bar. "Hi, Dev. I didn't know if I was in the right place. Wow, you were right. A great little neighborhood bar."

"Thanks for coming, Melissa. I wasn't sure if you were going to make it."

"Wasn't sure? You goofball. I think you said to meet around six, and I'm almost ten minutes early. I thought the traffic might be bad, so I left a little early. It ended up only taking me about five minutes to get here."

"Wow, you look great. How about a glass of wine?" I offered.

Louie cleared his throat a couple of times then extended his hand, pushing me to the side in the process. "Hi Melissa, I'm Dev's office mate, Louie Laufen. Dev has had nothing but nice things to say about you for the last couple of days. I feel as if I've known you for years. It's very nice to finally meet you in person."

She grinned and shook his hand. Once she let go, Louie signaled Mike.

He hurried over to our end of the bar, smiled, and said, "I'm sorry we're so crowded, ma'am, and this is the only available place to sit. If these two guys are giving you any trouble, just let me know, and we'll throw them out."

"I'll keep that in mind," she said.

"Melissa, this is Mike. Would you like red or white wine?" I said.

"I'd like a white. Do you have any Sauvignon Blanc?"

"I do, coming right up," Mike said and hurried down the bar.

"Oh, and this is Morton," I said.

"Morton, meet Melissa."

Morton stood with his tail wagging, and then, before I could do anything, he inserted his nose under her dress and between her legs.

"Oh, my God, cold nose, cold nose," she said, taking a half-step back. Fortunately, she was laughing.

"Here, hold out your hand, Melissa," Louie said. She had a strange look on her face but held out her hand anyway. Louie emptied the bag of pork rinds into her hand. A few of them dropped to the floor, and Morton inhaled them. "If you reach down and give those to him, you'll have a friend for life," Louie said.

"Sounds like a deal," she said and did just that. Morton immediately licked her hand clean.

"Here you go, ma'am," Mike said. "On the house. You're going to need it, hanging with these three."

"Thank you," she said and raised her glass toward Mike. Louie and I followed suit.

"Here, why don't you take this stool," I said. "I need to stand for a bit."

"You're sure?"

"Yeah, really. Did you, umm, decide on a restaurant for tonight?"

She flashed a half-second glance at my t-shirt and faded jeans and said, "Oh, not really. To tell you the truth, I don't really care. Whatever you feel like."

"Well, I have to drop Morton off at home, and I was planning to change," I lied. "I've had such a crazy day. I didn't want to miss you when you came in, so I just decided to come over here and meet you. Umm, I'll head home after this beer and change. If that's okay."

"Yeah, sure. Whatever works," she said, then took a healthy swallow of wine and looked like she didn't really believe me.

I finished my beer in about four minutes and waited another twenty for Melissa to finish her wine. Melissa, Louie, and I chatted all the while. As she drained her glass, I asked, "Want another?"

"No, I better not if I'm going to be driving."

"Well, I'm going to run Morton home, slip into some different clothes, and I'll be back in maybe fifteen minutes. Sure you don't want another glass of wine?"

"How 'bout I just follow you to your place, and we can head out from there?"

"Yeah, we can do that. Sure thing, where are you parked?"

"Just down the street," she said and nodded in the opposite direction of where my car was.

"Come on, Morton and I will walk you to your car, and you can follow us home."

She smiled at that, slid off the stool, and grabbed her purse.

"Very nice to meet you, Melissa," Louie said.

"The pleasure was all mine, Louie. Thank you and enjoy the rest of your evening."

She waved at Mike as we headed toward the front door. Morton and I held the door open for her, and as we stepped out, someone in the bar gave a wolf whistle.

"Sounds like you made quite the impression," I said. We walked to her car, a silver Ford C-Max. "I'm just parked in the next block. Wait here while I go around the block and pull up alongside you. It'll just take a minute or two."

"Okay, I'll just wait here."

"Yeah, see you in a bit," I said as she closed the driver's door and settled in. I signaled with my finger to lock the door. Once she did that, we hurried up to my car. I drove around the block and raced to the corner. I let a car pass, turned, pulled alongside her, and honked. She nodded and pulled out behind me. It was just a short drive. We were on the interstate for a quarter mile to the next exit. We waited for the stoplight on Ramsey, turned, and drove up Ramsey Hill. Three minutes later, I pulled into my driveway. I drove all the way up to my garage. Melissa pulled in right behind me.

I opened the gate and let Morton into the backyard. Melissa was out of her car and followed me in through the kitchen door.

"This is your house?" she asked.

"Yeah, I've been here for a lot of years," I said as I tossed my keys onto the kitchen counter.

"It's gorgeous. How old is this place?" she asked, looking around the kitchen.

"Built in 1885, like most of the homes down here. It was one of the earlier neighborhoods in the city. You want a quick tour?"

"I'd love one. Would you like me to take my shoes off?"

"No, not at all. You do whatever makes you comfortable."

"These heels are killing my feet. You have anything like a frozen pizza in your freezer?"

"Frozen Pizza? Yeah, I think so. In fact, I know I do. I've got a sausage pizza or one with everything and extra cheese."

"Would you think I'm crazy if we just ate that here and we didn't go out?"

"You kidding? You're a woman after my heart."

"Perfect," she said and gave me a peck on the cheek.

Seven

She chose the pizza with everything and extra cheese, which made her even more desirable in my view. I gave her a quick tour and then changed into clean jeans and a sport shirt. At the moment, we were finishing up the pizza in the kitchen. Melissa wasn't halfway through her first glass of wine, and I made a point of slowing down so I wouldn't pour a third for me.

"So you're always chasing bank robbers and murderers?" she asked.

"No, not exactly. I do a lot of work for a couple of insurance companies. You know, checking out work histories on people, arrest records, that sort of stuff. Occasionally, I'm taking pictures of someone supposedly having an affair. That's usually in a hotel parking lot, by the way, not in some room. I've dealt with a couple of criminals, but I like to avoid that whenever possible," I said as the image of Tubby Gustafson hitting golf balls in his office and wearing boxer shorts flashed in my mind.

"Sounds like you're always busy."

"Not really. It's more like feast or famine. Either I've got three or four things I'm trying to juggle, or I'm staring at my phone hoping it will ring."

"Did you check me out?" Melissa asked. She didn't appear to be joking.

"No, I didn't, and to be honest, I wouldn't."

"Not interested?"

"No, not that. I am very interested, as a matter of fact. But I think you have a right to your privacy. If we get along, we'll tell one another things at some point. No pressure, we only met the other day. After being the best-dressed woman The Spot has seen in a couple of years and having to meet up with one of the grubbier guys in the place, you pretty much hold the higher ground."

She smiled at that and took a healthy sip of wine. "Well, you should know I'm officially married, for the moment. I've been going through a divorce proceeding for the past seventeen months. I reverted back to my maiden name last year. I have a restraining order filed on my awful, soon to be, ex-husband. I have an eight-year-old son named Liam. I teach school, first grade, and I live in the Groveland neighborhood. But I'm thinking you probably knew all that."

"Actually, no, I didn't. I meant what I said. You have a right to your privacy. I work closely with the po-lice. I get along with most of them, although there is one guy who doesn't like me. I've dated lots of women, most of them were very nice, but for whatever reason, they decided they maybe wanted to go a different way. I've never had a restraining order filed against me, at least that I'm aware of. I was in the Army for a while. I took some college classes but never graduated, and I've been self-employed for a number of years, doing what I do."

"You sound really nice."

"You too. So tell me about your son, Liam."

"Oh, he's my darling when he's not driving me crazy."

"He's a boy. I think he's supposed to drive his mother crazy."

"Yeah, well, he's doing that. He's into sports, plays peewee football and baseball. Dealing with his father has been difficult. He's allowed to visit once a week for three hours provided there's an adult supervising the visitation. Word of warning, I've dated two other guys. One had his tires slit, the other had his car egged. I can't prove it, but I suspect it was idiot Jeremy."

"How's the visitation working?" I asked and decided not to mention the eggs on my car the other night.

She shook her head. "He usually cancels at the last minute, meaning I have to pay the supervisor. I've got an ongoing case requesting child support, but he's got some pro bono attorney fighting that. He's not a nice person, and yeah, I know, I married him, but I thought he'd change, and instead, he just got worse. A lot worse."

"What does he do?"

She drained the little amount of wine remaining in her glass. "Last I knew, he was working in sales for a company, medical products, I think. I don't know if he's still there. Lately, he seems to change jobs about every ninety days. I've really tried to limit my dealings with him."

"What's his name?"

"Jeremy Lawrence, he wanted to be called Crusher, but I wouldn't do that. Have you heard of him?"

I shook my head. "Jeremy or Crusher? No, never. Hey, how about another glass of wine?"

"I'd love one, but I better not. In fact, I should probably head home. I've got a sitter, and Liam has a football game tomorrow morning at 9:00."

"Would it be too much pressure if I showed up at the game? I'd like to meet Liam, and it would be nice to see you. I promise I'll behave. You wouldn't have to introduce me as the guy from the night before. We could just be two friends who bumped into each other."

She seemed to think about that for a moment before she nodded. "That would be nice. Thank you. To be honest, I wondered if once I mentioned having a child and the whole restraining order and divorce situation if that would be the last I'd see of you."

"That's not me," I said. "Where's the game tomorrow?"

"You know where Palace Playground is?"

"I do. I played many a hockey game down there as a youngster."

"Oh, God. Liam's latest obsession. He wants to play hockey."

"Can he skate?"

"That's the problem. He's never been on the ice, and then there's the whole thing about all the equipment and everything."

"Yeah, I know it can get crazy for parents."

"Especially if you don't know anything about hockey."

"I'll see you down at Palace Playground a little after 9:00 tomorrow. It'll be fun to watch a kids' game."

I walked her out to her car, got a kiss on the lips that lasted a second or two longer than just a peck. She waved once she settled behind the wheel, backed out of the driveway, and drove off. I watched her taillights disappear down the street and went back into the house.

Eight

I was up just before my alarm went off. I showered and shaved and was downstairs finishing my second cup of coffee when Morton wandered into the kitchen. I let him outside and filled his food and water dishes. Once he finished his breakfast, I took him on a long walk through the neighborhood. I was back online for maybe twenty minutes googling both Jeremy and Crusher Lawrence but never found anyone who resembled Melissa's brief description. At 9:10, I drove over to the Palace Playground, which was just five or six blocks from my office. All the parking spaces in the small lot and on the street were taken, and I had to park a block away. There were three different football games going on. I saw Melissa's Ford C-Max on the street and spotted her a couple of minutes later. She was standing on the sidelines next to a team in red jerseys. There were at least twenty adults on either side of the field yelling, clapping, and laughing as I headed toward her.

She gave me a little wave as I approached. "Hey, any trouble finding us?" she asked and then screamed, "Come on, let's go, Jets."

"Which one is Liam?"

"He's number 12."

"The tall kid? He's a running back?" I asked as they lined up for the next play.

"Yeah, I think that's his position today. It seems to change every week, so I'm never quite sure."

The ball was hiked. Liam bounced off a kid and kept moving, then ran toward the sidelines. The ball was passed to someone on the opposite side of the field, who missed it.

"That's okay. Let's go, Jets," Melissa yelled.

All three games finished up right at 10:30, and each team gathered around the respective coaches for a final round of positive thought. Fortunately, Liam's team, the Jets, had won, twelve to ten.

I was in the process of telling Melissa a story about Louie when she got a look on her face, and she stared over my right shoulder.

"Melissa, what's the problem?" I asked without turning around.

"It's Jeremy. He isn't supposed to be here. I don't know how he knew there was a game here today. Oh, God, umm, you better go. He's liable to cause a problem, and I don't want you—"

"Is he coming this way?"

"No, he's just standing at the end of the field. Watching me."

"Tell you what, you know where Nina's coffee is located?"

"Nina's, yeah, it's across from that hog restaurant."

"The Handsome Hog, actually. When the coach is finished talking, why don't you and Liam head to your car and drive over to Nina's? I'll meet you there. I know the folks that run the place. Mention my name, tell them I'm on the way, and I'll pay. I'll just be a couple of—"

"Dev, I don't think that's a good idea. Believe me, Jeremy has a temper, and I think it would be better if maybe I—"

"Look, Melissa, you take Liam to Nina's. We can have a nice chat there, and you won't have to worry about your ex-husband. I'll get to meet Liam. They have some great muffins, cookies, and cakes. Tell him it's his reward for a good game. Don't worry, Jeremy isn't going to follow you."

"You're sure? He can be a real pain in—"

"Just trust me. He's not going to follow you."

"Okay, we'll go. I'll be looking the entire way in my rearview mirror for that black Chevy Camaro of his. The thing just looks evil. It's so fitting."

"Don't worry. You just head up to Nina's. It looks like the coach is finishing up. Grab Liam, and I'll see you there."

"Okay. Thanks, Dev. I don't need Jeremy today or any day," she said and hurried over toward the group of boys beginning to drift apart.

I walked toward my car in the opposite direction. I glanced over at the end of the field. I was pretty sure the guy dressed in black jeans and shirt was the infamous

Jeremy. From a distance, he looked like a wanna-be tough guy. He was big, but it didn't appear to be muscles, just fat. If you passed him on the street, you'd have to give him some extra room. He didn't have a tattooed face. With the love handles and the gut hanging over his belt, he couldn't tuck a gun in there. His hair was shaved on the sides, long on top, and curly, but that was the style. His shirt was untucked, probably because he couldn't tuck it in. He wore what looked like a heavy gold chain around his neck, just beneath his three chins. I looked over a couple of times as I headed to my car. He was focused on Melissa, who was now talking to another woman as they walked toward their cars. Three young football players were swirling and chasing one another around the two women.

Jeremy suddenly turned and waddled across the field toward a side street. That was my signal to pick up speed. I jogged down the block to my car, a black 2009 Ford Crown Victoria Police Interceptor. I got the thing at a police auction almost two years ago. Anyone who saw me behind the wheel automatically figured I was a cop.

I was parked at the far end of the block. I climbed in, backed around the corner, and headed to where I last saw Jeremy Lawrence.

Nine

I spotted him attempting to hurry down the street. He wasn't running, not that he could, but he wasn't taking a leisurely stroll either. A sporty-looking black Chevy Camaro was parked almost at the end of the street. I drove past him, slowed as I approached the Camaro, repeated his license number a couple of times so I'd remember it, and pulled alongside his car. I left just enough room for him to walk between the cars, but he wouldn't be able to open the car door and get behind the wheel. I wrote down his license plate number on the back of an envelope and watched in the mirror as he approached and slowed his pace. If only I had a dozen eggs.

I figured there was a good chance he was either going to try to follow Melissa or, at best, maybe pull up to her car and give her the finger. Neither option presented a good alternative as far as I was concerned.

He stepped between our cars and had to turn sideways and sidestep to come alongside. His fat stomach brushed against the side of my car, rubbing the grime from the windows. He gently knocked on my passenger window, and I lowered it.

"Is there a problem, officer?" he said. He was red-faced, breathing heavy, and had droplets of sweat on his forehead from the one block walk.

"No, no problem. Is this your car?" As he nodded, his cheeks and chins jiggled. "Just admiring your set of wheels. What's the year?"

"It's a 2017."

"Very nice. You like it?"

"Yeah, yeah, it's good, great as a matter of fact."

"You like the way it handles?"

"Yeah, sure. Say, if you don't mind. I've got an appointment I'm heading to, and I don't want to be late. Would love to talk about the car, but I'm kind of on a tight schedule."

"Oh, yeah, sure, I get it. Didn't mean to hold you up. I just like to find out how people like their vehicles, you know, especially these really cool sets of wheels. I talked to a guy once, and he told me he'd taken his car all the way up to a hundred and twenty miles per hour out on the interstate at about three in the morning, just to see how it would perform."

"I'd never do that. Now, if you'd excuse me—"

"Oh, not suggesting you would. You know they're just such beautiful cars. Really, you're very lucky."

"Yeah, yeah, I am. Now, if you wouldn't mind, I really gotta get going. And I—"

"No problem. Sorry to hold you up. Have a good rest of the day," I said, then slowly pulled ahead. As I pulled ahead, he turned and stepped back to open the car door. He was mumbling something that probably wasn't very polite. I noticed the number thirteen on the back of his neck. Technically, that would mean the MS-13 gang, known for some pretty extreme violence, but somehow that didn't seem to add up.

I stopped at the corner, took my cellphone out, and held it against my ear. I watched as he backed up, pulled forward, backed up again, and finally cleared the car parked in front of him.

I had stopped, not quite in the middle of the street but far enough over, so he couldn't get around me. He pulled up behind me, waited maybe fifteen seconds, and politely honked. I raised my right hand and signaled 'one' with my index finger. He didn't honk, but I watched him in my rearview mirror swearing. Melissa was right. The guy had a temper. He backed into his former parking place, turned facing across the street, backed up again, and finally headed up the street in the opposite direction. The Camaro leaned to the left from his weight.

I pulled around the corner and drove past the park. I spotted his black Camaro going up the street, apparently looking for Melissa's car, which was now long gone. I headed over to Nina's Coffee and parked across the street. Melissa's car was parked in front of the coffee shop.

At no surprise, on a Saturday morning at a little after 10:30, the coffee shop was busy. I spotted Melissa and Liam at a table in the back. I waved and stepped in line to order a coffee. The line was moving pretty fast, and in no time, I was standing in front of the owner. I glanced back at Melissa's table and didn't see any sign of food.

"Hi, June, maybe give me four of those chocolate chip cookies, and I'll have my usual, a medium coffee. Did a woman mention I'd pay for her order?"

"No, Dev. Why? Are you in trouble again?"

"No, I just offered to pay. Her son is in the football uniform with a red jersey."

"Oh yeah, a decaf and a hot chocolate. She paid, never mentioned you."

"Probably a wise move," I said. She rang up my order, and I stepped to the side. I took my coffee and the cookies over to the table and said, "Hi Melissa, mind if I join you?"

"Please do," she said and laughed. "Dev, this is my son, Liam."

I set the plate with the chocolate chip cookies on the table and said, "Nice to meet you, Liam. You hungry for a cookie after your game? Go ahead and grab one."

He gave his mother a pleading look. She nodded. He quickly grabbed a cookie and took a large bite. I pushed the plate a little closer to him.

"Any problems getting here?" Melissa asked.

"No, no problems at all. So, Liam, your mom told me you're playing football and baseball. You like that?"

He took another large bite of his cookie and nodded.

"I played a little bit when I was your age but spent most of my time playing hockey. I really enjoyed that."

"You played hockey?"

"Oh yeah, me and all my friends. We had a great time. I still see a bunch of guys who were on the team."

"Do you still play?"

"Not too often. I just don't have the time anymore. But it was really fun. A lot of work but fun."

"I want to play, but, well, I can't skate."

"You could always learn."

"Mmm, I don't have any skates. I'd have to take lessons, and Mom says—"

"Mom says you have enough to do with football and baseball," Melissa said and moved the conversation to another subject. We chatted for a good half-hour. Liam ate three cookies, and then Melissa said, "Well, we had better get going. Thanks, Dev. It was nice to see you."

"The pleasure was all mine. Besides, I got to meet Liam. By the way, Liam, are you going to let that last cookie go to waste?"

Liam looked at his mom. "Don't you want it, Dev?" she asked.

"Nope, I had a big breakfast. Did you want it?" Melissa shook her head. "Well, then, Liam, you have to eat it, or it's going to get thrown away."

He grinned, grabbed the cookie, and shoved half of it into his mouth.

"Thanks, Dev, for everything," Melissa said and held out her hand.

"My pleasure. It was great to see you, and Liam, it was very nice to meet you."

Melissa whispered in his ear, and Liam nodded. "Thank you for the cookies. I really liked them," he said.

"Glad you did. Hope to see you again soon," I said. I walked them out to their car and got a wave from both of them as they pulled away. No black Camaro followed. I drove up the block and pulled into my driveway. Morton met me at the door. I went into the kitchen, grabbed his leash, and we went out for a long walk. I grabbed the envelope that I'd written Jeremy Lawrence's license plate number on, and we headed to the office.

Ten

I turned on my computer and called a pal at the Department of Motor Vehicles, the DMV. I'd forgotten it was Saturday and got a recording. I phoned Aaron LaZelle, my pal in homicide down at the police department, and was dumped into his voicemail. I hung up without leaving a message. I went online and logged into the city's Data Practices Center and requested any public records on Jeremy Lawrence. Nothing came up. I tore the license plate number from the envelope and stuck it in my wallet. I decided to swing past Trickle's house just to see if anything was happening. Morton hopped in the backseat, and we drove up the street.

We drove over to Summit Avenue and Trickle's red stone mansion. Nothing appeared to be happening in front of the house, although I found it interesting that there was a black Cadillac Escalade parked in the driveway. A large individual was leaning against the driver's door of the Escalade, scratching himself. None other than Austin, Tubby Gustafson's muscle-bound thug. The same thug who hit me in the stomach the other day.

A part of me wanted to turn into the driveway and run over Austin's toes. Knowing Tubby's need to control and be in charge, I was pretty sure Austin wasn't there on his own. That meant possibly Tubby, but more likely Fat Freddy, was there. Why? was the question I had. Tubby was apparently looking at some form of business arrangement with Casper Trickle. I made a mental note and drove past.

I was thinking it might be the perfect time to drive over to one of the walking paths along the river and take Morton for a walk when my phone rang. Melissa.

"Hi Melissa, what's up?"

"Sorry to bother you, Dev. It's just that, well, Jeremy keeps driving past and leaning on his horn. I'm wondering if you think I should call the police."

"Call the cops? No, even if they respond, it's going to be hours from now. How many times has he done this?"

"At least five or six times that I'm aware of. He doesn't stop. He just slows down and leans on the horn. He drives off, and then he's back and does it again ten or fifteen minutes later." Suddenly, I heard a car horn in the background. "Oh, can you hear that? There he is again. God, the neighbors are going to hate me."

"What's your address?"

"No, you don't have to come over. He's just being such an ass, again."

"Probably because he wasn't able to give you a hard time this morning at the game. Give me your address."

"That's really nice of you, Dev, but you don't have to—"

"Melissa, let's get him to stop. Where's Liam right now?"

"He's hiding in his bedroom. Jeremy scares him. I was thinking of taking him somewhere, you know to the mall or something, but if Jeremy sees us leaving, he'll just follow us, which will be even worse. He drives really close, right behind us, and I'm afraid he's going to cause an accident or something."

"Yeah, you're probably right. So what's your address?"

"Are you sure?"

"Yes, very sure. I've dealt with this type before. I've got Morton with me. Liam can play with him, and I've got another idea for Liam. So where do I go?"

"Well, okay. You sure you're not working? I don't want to interrupt whatever you're involved in and—"

"Address, please."

"Okay," she said and finally gave me her address.

"Good. I'm about fifteen minutes away. I'll see you shortly."

"Thank you, Dev."

I sped a little over the speed limit. I stopped at a red light, looked both ways, and since no traffic was coming, I ran through the light. I was there in just over ten minutes. I pulled to the curb in front of the white stucco

craftsman-style house. Melissa's car was in the driveway. A red brick path and three steps led up to the front
porch.

I was just about to get out of my car when a horn
behind me began blaring and then suddenly stopped. A
moment later, a black Chevy Camaro rolled past. Jeremy
Lawrence looked over with a surprised look on his fat
face. He began to accelerate a second after our eyes met.

I glanced in the side-view mirror. No one was behind him, so I pulled onto the street and followed. We
were going over fifty on a residential street a block later.
Lard Ass Lawrence was increasing his speed. I debated
for a half-second about following and slowed down.
Someone was liable to get hurt, and I didn't want it to be
me.

I drove back to Melissa's and rang her doorbell.

Eleven

She opened the door a moment later. "Oh, Dev, this is so sweet of you. I don't know. Maybe he got tired of being a complete butthead. I thought I heard his horn a couple of minutes ago, but it must not have been him. Oh, where are my manners? Come on in. Would you like a coffee or something? God, I've been hiding back in the kitchen, hoping he would just go the hell away."

"Thanks, but no coffee for me. Is Liam still in his room?"

"Yeah, poor little thing. He's afraid to come out. We've been through this before, dozens of times. He'll be okay in an hour or two."

"That's not right. A kid being afraid like that."

"I know, but he gets so upset, Dev. If stupid Jeremy is done harassing us, Liam will eventually come out."

"Well, I've got Morton out in the car. Would it be okay if I brought him in to meet Liam?"

"Morton, your dog? You mean he's not down at The Spot," she said and laughed.

"No, but it's still early. Would it be okay?"

"Oh, he'd love it. It might be just the thing."

"I'll be back in a moment." I hurried out to the car, looked up and down the street, grabbed Morton, and went back inside.

"Let me see if I can coax him out of his room," she said.

"Maybe let us try. Hey, before I do that, I wanted to run something by you." I told her my idea, and after a little persuading, she agreed. Morton and I headed up the stairs. Liam's room was at the end of the hall, just across from the bathroom. An image of a football and baseball was taped to the oak door. I knocked on the door.

"I don't want to come out, Mom. Just leave me alone, please."

"Hi Liam, it's Dev Haskell. Hey, I've got a friend here I think you should meet. His name is Morton. Would it be okay if we came in?"

There was a long pause, and I was about to call his name again when the door suddenly opened. Liam was still wearing his red jersey with the grass stains, but the shoulder pads and the padded pants were gone. His eyes were red and puffy, and there were tear trails on his cheeks.

"Hey, buddy, good to see you. This is my friend, Morton. Morton, this is the football player I was telling you about, Liam." Morton's tail was wagging. Liam knelt down and petted him. Morton licked the tears from Liam's cheeks, and Liam gave him a hug. The bedroom had all sorts of baseball, football, and hockey pictures taped to the walls. Based on the appearance of the bed, Liam had been there with his head buried beneath the pillow. A baseball mitt and a football were on the far side of the bed.

"Hey, Morton and I were going for a walk, and we were wondering if you wanted to come with us."

"Where are you going to go?"

"Oh, just around the neighborhood. Come on with us. We could use the company, and you can give us directions."

He seemed to think about that for a brief moment, then nodded and said, "Yeah, okay."

"Come on, let's go. Check this out. You tell him what we're going to do and then watch his tail. Okay?"

Liam nodded and then said, "Hey Morton, we're gonna go for a walk."

Morton's tail started wagging back and forth, bouncing against Liam's thigh.

"Oh, now he's really excited. I think you just made a good friend, Liam. Let's go, and you can show us around the neighborhood." I handed the leash to Liam, and he took Morton downstairs.

"Hey, Mom, we're going for a walk," Liam called. Melissa stepped out of the kitchen through a swinging door. "Mom, this is Morton. We're gonna take him for a walk."

Melissa's eyes watered, and she bit her lower lip.

"We'll be back when we're back," I said.

"Thank," she cleared her throat and said, "Thank you, Dev. Have a nice walk, guys."

"See ya," Liam said as he and Morton headed out the door.

"Oh, I better catch up," I said and hurried out before Melissa could say anything.

Liam led us up and down the neighborhood streets. Other than an interest in a few squirrels, Morton behaved. We walked for the better part of a half-hour. We talked about Morton, and Liam would occasionally point out a friend's house.

Three girls playing on a front porch called to him and said, "Hi, Liam," but he just nodded and kept moving.

"Are they in your class at school?" I asked.

"Yeah," was his one-word response. Apparently, the discussion was over.

When we made it back to Melissa's, she was sitting on the front porch with a pitcher of lemonade and a bowl of salted peanuts. "How was the walk, guys?"

"Morton tried to catch three squirrels, but they were all too fast and made it up the tree before he could catch them. Then they just sat on a branch and made noises."

"How about some lemonade?"

"Yeah, great, Mom," Liam said and settled into the chair next to his mother. She poured a glass of lemonade, gave him a kiss, and handed him the glass. She looked at me and mouthed the words 'thank you.'

"I'd love to stay, but we should be on our way. Liam, thanks for your help with Morton. He's going to be thinking about you. You up for another walk later this week?"

He nodded excitedly and said, "Yeah, sure."

"Okay, we'll catch you later. I'll check on that other issue tonight," I said to Melissa. Morton and I climbed into the car. I gave a wave, Morton barked, and we headed home.

Twelve

Morton was asleep on the floor of the den. I was sacked out on the couch. The movie I'd been watching was long over, and the screen on the TV was black. I suddenly opened my eyes and listened. There it was again, a definite noise coming from the front room. I left the light off and stepped into the hallway. The front door was closed and locked. I was in my stocking feet and moved toward the front room. There was the noise again, a bump or a thud, not loud, but something was up.

I moved toward the entry. I heard the noise again. It was actually coming from outside on my front porch. I stepped into the front room and looked out the window. A large figure dressed in black and wearing a balaclava was on my porch.

I had a pretty good idea of who the three hundred pound idiot was. I keep a baseball bat next to my front door, just because. I picked up the bat, quietly turned the lock, took a deep breath, and tore the door open.

"What in the hell do you think you're doing?" I shouted as the large figure jumped and pointed the can of spray paint at me. I took a step and swung the baseball bat as hard as I could. The guy screamed as the bat slammed into his hand, and the can sailed across the front yard and landed in the street.

In one swift motion, he stumbled backward three steps, fell over the porch railing, and landed on top of my hedge. I heard the branches crack as he rolled off the hedge and into the neighbor's driveway. He crawled on all fours for a few feet, groaned as he got to his feet, and took off waddling across the street. He held his right hand with his left, and I could hear him gasping.

"Yeah, you better get your fat ass out of here. I catch you, and you're dead. You hear me? Dead!" I shouted

I watched him disappear between two buildings across the street. I thought about chasing him, but I was in my stocking feet, so that wasn't going to work. I turned and looked at the front of my house. Black spray paint read 'DEB HASLE SUC.' I presumed the last word was supposed to be 'sucks.' So much for getting my name right. Tomorrow was Sunday. Apparently, I would be painting.

The list of people who might have done this was long, but I was focused on one person. Fat, stupid, and apparently a lousy speller, none other than Lard Ass Jeremy Lawrence. It had to be. I picked up the spray paint can from the street, tossed the can in my trash bin, and went back inside. I locked the front door and wedged a chair beneath the doorknob.

Morton popped his head out of the den and then made his way upstairs. I wedged a chair beneath the kitchen door, turned off the lights, then looked out through all my first-floor windows in the dark but didn't see Lard Ass. It took a good half-hour before I fell asleep. I was up at 6:00 the following morning.

I grabbed two cans of paint from the shelf in the basement, one for the siding and the other for the trim. I painted the trim first, which only took about ten minutes. As I opened the can for the siding, bits of rust fell into the paint. I stirred the paint for five minutes or so, then started painting. I was back in the kitchen by 7:15, washing my hands and sipping coffee.

I considered telling Melissa about last night's little run-in with her ex and decided against it. It would just make her worry, and that was the last thing she needed. Morton wandered into the kitchen a half-hour later. I let him out into the backyard and filled his food and water dishes. He was back inside after ten minutes.

I did some more searching online for Jeremy Lawrence and came up empty-handed. I checked my paint job an hour later. The paint I applied was dry to the touch and appeared slightly darker than the existing color, but that made sense given everything had been painted five years ago. Just before 10:00, I called an old hockey buddy, Jimmy Fallon.

"Yeah," was how he answered.

"Jimmy, it's Dev Haskell. Long time no talk. How are things?"

"Things are fine, and no, you can't move in here. We've got two of the boys moved out. One's in college, and the other joined the Air Force. Two down and three to go."

"How old is your youngest?"

"Timmy, he'll be thirteen at the end of the month. Please tell me you want to hire him."

"Actually, that's not why I'm calling." I went on to explain why I'd called.

"That would be great, Dev. We're running to church in a bit, but we'll be home by noon. How about 1:00? You guys stop over then, and we'll get you taken care of."

"See you at 1:00, Jimmy. Looking forward to catching up."

"See you later," he said and hung up.

I phoned Melissa. She answered on the third ring. "Good morning. What's up?"

I decided not to mention the spray paint incident. "I called my pal, Jimmy. We're set to be at his place at 1:00 this afternoon if that works for you."

"Oh, Dev, you have been, well, I don't know what to say. I'm speechless."

"Speechless? It doesn't get any better than that. Hey, I'll see you in a bit. I'll be over around 12:30."

"See you then," she said and disconnected.

I took Morton for a walk, then came back and stretched out on the couch. I grabbed a twenty-minute nap, had some lunch, and headed over to Melissa's. I checked my rearview mirror as I drove down her street. Fortunately, I didn't see anything that suggested her ex was around. I could only hope he was nursing a broken hand.

I pulled in front of her house and hurried up the front steps. Melissa answered the door about ten seconds after I rang the doorbell. "Come on in. We're just finishing lunch. Can I get you something?"

"Thanks, but I just pushed away from the table myself. How's Liam doing?"

"Well, I haven't told him. I thought I'd leave that up to you."

I followed her into the kitchen. "Hi, Dev. Did you bring Morton?" was Liam's greeting. He was still wearing his football jersey with the grass stains.

"Oh, I would have liked to, but I've got to stop at a pal's house and talk to him for a while. Hey, I was thinking, do you want to come along? He's got a bunch of boys, and it turns out they've got all this hockey equipment they're trying to get rid of because the boys have outgrown it. We could see if maybe they had some stuff you could use."

His eyes grew wide, and he looked at Melissa. "Can I go, Mom? Please?"

"I guess that would be okay. Maybe change into a nice shirt and-"

"Actually, the jersey might be better just because we might be trying on some pads and a helmet and things."

Liam nodded.

"Okay, finish that milk and then upstairs to brush your teeth."

Liam downed the half glass of milk. "Back in just a second," he said as he slid out of the chair and ran upstairs.

"Oh, Dev, I can't thank you enough. After yesterday and that damn Jeremy."

"You should file a report. He won't be arrested or anything, but you can begin to document a history of harassment. If he does that again, sit out on the porch and take pictures or, better yet, a video of him driving past and leaning on the horn. He sees you doing that, he just might start to get the message."

"I know that sounds like the thing to do. I mean, I get it. But he scares the hell out of me."

"Was he abusive when you were together?"

She turned away and didn't say anything which answered my question. I heard footsteps charging down the steps and then what sounded like Liam jumping off the last few steps. A moment later, he hurried into the kitchen, smiling and showing bright white teeth to his mother.

"Okay, I guess we're all set. Not sure how long this is going to take."

"We've got nothing planned this afternoon so take as much time as you need," Melissa said.

"Let's go, buddy," I said. Liam ran ahead of me and held the front door. He jumped off the porch onto the brick path and ran to my car.

Thirteen

The Fallon family lived in the Como Park area. Jimmy was a plumber. He'd been with the same company for over fifteen years, working on new buildings, apartments, a couple of sports stadiums, a few schools. His home was a two-story affair in a neighborhood of similar structures. As we pulled up, there were two different groups of kids on the street. One group looked like nine and ten-year-olds, three boys and two girls. The group at the opposite end of the block was four boys, maybe thirteen or fourteen.

As we climbed out of the car, the front door flew open, and a kid carrying a baseball glove jumped off the front porch, gave us a nod, and ran toward the four boys at the end of the block. A moment later, Jimmy stepped into the doorway.

"Hi, Dev, it's been too long."

"You're telling me, Jimmy. Good to see you. Hey, this is my pal, Liam. He's eight, and he's interested in some hockey equipment if you have any."

"You kidding? We could open a store. Nice to meet you, Liam. Come on in, guys. Everything is down in the basement. Donna said to say hi. She had to run to her folks'. It's her sister's birthday, and we're getting together tonight."

We followed Jimmy through the kitchen and down the basement stairs. There had to be a dozen pairs of shoes and flip-flops scattered around the back door. The basement was paneled in knotty pine. A large flat screen hung on the wall opposite a couch and two chairs. Two sleeping bags were laid out on the floor next to the couch.

We walked through the room and into a smaller, unfinished room. Two benches were positioned against the wall. A board with brass hooks was attached to the wall, and hockey jerseys and pants, called breezers hung from the hooks. A chest of drawers painted black and two footlockers were next to the furnace. An empty five-gallon pail filled with hockey sticks stood in the corner. A length of tar paper was rolled out on the floor in front of the benches.

"Grab a seat, fellas," Jimmy said.

"This place looks like a locker room," I said.

"You aren't kidding. I lost count of how many years I've been driving the boys to practice and games. It was a lot crazier than when we were kids. Liam, how old are you?"

"Umm, I'm eight."

"Eight, okay," Jimmy said and pulled the top drawer in the dresser open. He took out a pair of heavy wool socks and tossed them to Liam. "Slip those on. Have you been skating much?"

"Well, no, I never have. I, umm, don't know how, but I want to learn."

"Okay, good. Get those socks on, and let's see what we have for skates." He lifted the lid on one of the footlockers, rummaged around, and pulled out two pairs of CCM jet speed skates. They were black with white laces and the CCM logo on the sides. "See if these fit," Jimmy said, and he handed a pair to Liam.

With the wool socks on, Liam worked at forcing his foot into one of the skates.

"How's that feel?" Jimmy asked.

"Pretty tight."

"Can you wiggle your toes?"

Liam shook his head and said, "No, not really."

"Okay, pull that one off and try one of these," he said and handed a skate from the second pair to Liam. It seemed to fit a lot better.

Once he had it on his foot, Jimmy said, "Lace that one up and put that other one on. Do you know how to tie your shoes?"

Liam nodded.

"Good, get both of those on while I look for a pair of breezers and a helmet." He rummaged around in the footlocker, pulled out a white helmet and a pair of red breezers.

As soon as Liam had the skates laced up, Jimmy told him to stand. Liam started to stand, wobbled back and forth, and fell back onto the bench. "You gonna give the kid a hand, Dev?"

"Oh, yeah, sure thing," I said and helped Liam to his feet. He wobbled back and forth as I helped him stand. "Okay, now straighten those ankles. You don't want them leaning to the sides like that. Yeah, that's it, much better."

The breezers and the helmet fit, and we had Liam walking back and forth on the tar paper. He was wobbly and steadied himself with a hand against the wall a couple of times, but that was normal for his first time. It took a good half-hour, but by the end, Liam had enough equipment, including two hockey sticks, to practice. He untied the skates, and we carried everything upstairs. I carried the hockey sticks. Jimmy gave me a hockey league schedule that listed practices times and places. When I was a kid, we would play in park rinks outside. That was still the case from time to time, but now all of the practices and most of the games were on indoor rinks, all year long.

Jimmy and I chatted for another half-hour while Liam kept examining his skates and grinning. "You sure I can't pay you something for all this, Jimmy?"

"No, I appreciate you guys coming over. Helps me out to get rid of it. Like I told you before, two down and three to go. I love 'em all dearly, but both Donna and I can see a distant horizon with vacations, trips, new furniture, and lower grocery bills. Five, maybe six, more years."

"Hopefully, your boys aren't as crazy as we were."

"Let's just say there are things I don't need to know about, and Donna certainly doesn't."

We thanked Jimmy another half-dozen times. Liam placed the helmet, breezers, and hockey sticks in the back seat. He climbed in front, holding the skates, and we buckled up. I was just about ready to turn the car on when my phone rang. Melissa.

"Hey, mission accomplished. We're just about to head back home. It was a complete success, and you're going to have a hockey player at your house," I said.

"Maybe don't come for a bit."

"What's up?" I asked. Lard Ass Jeremy immediately flashed in my mind.

"Jeremy is parked out front."

"What does he want?"

"I don't know. I'm afraid to go out and ask him."

"How long has he been there?"

"Fifteen or twenty minutes. He's just sitting out there in his car."

"Okay. Just stay there. Don't go out. I've got a pal I can call."

"Are you sure? I don't want to—"

"I'm just going to have him make sure everything is okay. Don't worry. Let me make that call, and I'll get back to you." I disconnected and said, "Hang on a second, Liam. I'm getting bad reception in the car, so I'm just going to make a call outside."

"Who were you talking to on the phone?"

"Just a client of mine. Back in a second."

He gave me a look like he didn't believe me as I stepped out of the car. I thought for a moment, then speed-dialed Junior Swindell. He was a once-in-a-great-while assistant and a P.I. wanna-be. He answered on the second ring.

"Yeah, Dev. Man, talk about karma. I was just thinking about you." I could hear what sounded like a jukebox playing in the background and some glasses clinking.

"And I'm thinking about you, Junior. Hey, is your car running?"

"Yeah, at least I think so."

"Great, I'd like you to check something out for me if you have the time."

"Okay, yeah, I'm good to go. I've got a Glock, an AR15, a twenty-two with a silencer, which one? Or should I just bring them all?"

"Actually, Junior, it would probably be better if you left them all at home."

"Mmm, undercover?"

"Kind of. Here's the deal. A guy is parked in front of a place in a 2017 black Chevy Camaro. He's not doing anything, but I'd like you to check him out. Just pull in front of him and watch him. Don't get out of your car. I think he'll probably get nervous and leave. If he drives away, don't follow him. See if you can check out his right hand. I think it will be bandaged up. I'll be there in about a half-hour. You in?" I asked.

"You bet I am. You just need to tell me where to go."

"Oh yeah, I suppose that would help." I gave him Melissa's address, he disconnected, and I got back in the car.

Liam gave me a worried look.

"You know what I'm thinking?" He shook his head. "I'm thinking an ice cream cone might be just the thing. What do you think?"

"Yeah, me too," he said and nodded.

"I know just the place. Have you been to the Grand Old Creamery before?"

"Yeah, I've been there a few times. They make their own ice cream right there."

"That's the place."

It was a ten-minute drive to the Creamery. The place is always busy, and a sunny Sunday afternoon was no exception. We had to park a block away and across the street. Liam seemed to walk a little faster the closer we got to the place. There was a line coming out the door, but that wasn't unusual. We eventually ordered ice cream cones and sat outside on a bench, eating. I checked the time more than once.

When I finished my cone, I said, "Let's head home. I'm sure your mom will want to see those skates. You can finish that ice cream in the car."

Fourteen

When we turned the corner onto Melissa's street, the only car in front of her place was a rusty red Buick Enclave. Junior Swindell's car. I recognized it immediately. Who else but Junior would have such a vehicle? The rear panel on the driver's side had been replaced and was spray painted flat black. When we pulled to a stop behind Junior, the rusted areas became even more apparent. Both lower corners of the rear door had strips of silver duct tape apparently covering holes. Rusted areas seeped out around the duct tape.

"Why don't you bring those skates in to show your mom? You run ahead, and I'll carry the rest of your stuff."

Liam nodded, said, "Thanks, Dev. This is really cool." He jumped out of the front seat and took off across the front lawn toward the porch.

I pulled the breezers, the helmet, skating socks, and hockey sticks from the back seat and walked to the driver's door on Junior's car.

He lowered the window as I approached. Music blared out of the car, and I could feel the vibration from the bass notes. Junior leaned out of the window. I knew he said something because his lips were moving, but I had no idea what it was. I leaned the two hockey sticks against his car and rolled my right hand, signaling to turn down the noise. Thankfully, he turned off the music.

"Thanks for being here, Junior. Was the guy in the Camaro here when you arrived?"

"Yeah, just like you said. Nice looking set of wheels, by the way. I pulled ahead about three car lengths and then backed up and screeched to a stop just to get his attention," he chuckled. "I could tell he was swearing at me, but I couldn't hear what he was saying. He drove past, and I think he tried to give me the finger, but the car started to swerve, and he had to grab the wheel. You were right. His right arm was in a sling. I can't be sure, but I think he had a cast on. He was a pretty big dude."

"You mean he was fat?"

"Yeah, real fat."

"How long did he stay here?"

"Not even a minute. As soon as I backed up and stopped, he fired up that Camaro and took off down the street. I'm pretty sure it was less than a minute."

"Really appreciate the help. I wanna get you paid. I've got to drop this stuff in the house and talk with my client for a couple of minutes. You want to wait for me down at The Spot? Shouldn't be more than a half-hour."

Junior seemed to think about that for a moment and then nodded. "Yeah, okay. I'll wait for you down there."

"Start a tab, my treat."

That brought a smile to his face, and he said, "I think I can do that. I'll see you down there." I stepped back as he turned on his car. It took a couple of tries, but eventually, the rusty Buick fired up. There was an explosion of sorts. A large cloud of black exhaust fumes settled onto my car parked just behind. Junior gave a wave and headed down the street. Some banging and clanging came from the engine and then gradually faded as he traveled down the street and turned at the corner.

I headed up onto the front porch. I knocked on the front door and stepped inside.

Melissa called, "We're in the kitchen."

I set the helmet, breezers, and both hockey sticks in the front entry and walked through the swinging door. Liam was seated at the counter. A ring of chocolate ice cream surrounded his mouth. There was a delicious smell of something cooking.

"Looks like the two of you had a pretty successful afternoon," Melissa said.

"Oh yeah. There's more out in the entry. A couple of hockey sticks, a helmet, and a pair of breezers."

"Well, I think you better take these skates and all that equipment up to your room. Did you tell Dev thank you?"

"Yes, he did, a couple of times."

Liam slid off the kitchen stool. He picked up his skates, gave me a hug, and hurried out to the front entry. A moment later, we could hear him charging up the stairs.

"Thank you, Dev. He's thrilled. What do I owe you?"

"Nothing, it's free, and my pal was glad to get rid of it. His kids have outgrown all that stuff, and he was glad to get it off his hands."

"Are you sure? I mean, I've checked the prices on some of this and even used it's almost cost-prohibitive."

"Yeah, I'm sure. Honest, he was glad we could use it. What about Jeremy out front?"

"Oh, what a pain in the ass. I just happened to glance out the window, and there he was. It couldn't have been more than ten minutes after you left. He just sat there. As far as I know, he never got his big fat butt out of his car. Then some character pulled up and parked in front of him. I don't know if they were together or what the deal was."

"Actually, that was a friend of mine. I sent him over. He told me Jeremy left about thirty seconds after he pulled in. As a matter of fact, I'm going to meet him in just a bit."

"Well, you're welcome to join us for dinner. I think it's the least I can do after all you've done for Liam and for me."

"Thanks. Would it be all right if I met with this guy and then came back?"

"Not a problem. Dinner won't be ready until 6:00. Plan on eating a lot. I've got chili going in the crockpot."

"Okay, I'll be back before dinner. Would you mind if I showed up with a bottle of wine?"

"That would be perfect," she said,

"Say, do you know where Jeremy lives now?"

"Actually, no, I don't. When we first split up, he sub-let an apartment at the corner of Snelling and Selby. I don't know what happened, but that didn't seem to work out. No idea where he's living now. Could be sleeping in his car for all I know, not that there'd be enough room."

Fifteen

I stopped at the ATM on my way. When I arrived at The Spot, Ollie was tending bar. At the moment, he was sitting behind the bar reading the paper. He looked up as I entered and said, "Hey, Dev, you're in here early. Everything okay?"

"Yeah, just meeting up with someone."

Junior was one of four people in the place. Two guys were seated at the bar with four or five empty stools between them. They both stared at their half-empty glasses. I'd seen it before. They had probably been in here for the better part of the afternoon and were only going to have the one beer. I guess that was better than pounding down six or eight on a nice sunny day.

Junior was seated in a booth. Next to him was a nice-looking red-headed girl named Mollie. She had her arm wrapped around his, probably so he wouldn't escape. I'd run into her before. She was a working girl, but I never had the urge to pay for the service.

"Over here, Dev," Junior called as I looked around.

Ollie set the newspaper down and stood. "Just a Coke for me and probably another round of whatever those two are drinking," I said.

"I'll bring it over to you," Ollie said.

I slid into the booth across from Junior and Mollie. An empty beer bottle and a stem glass with lipstick sat on the table. "Everything work out okay for your client?" Junior asked.

"Yeah, thanks to you. Appreciate you running over there on such short notice. Hi Mollie, my name is Dev. I've seen you in here before," I said and reached into my pocket. I slid five twenties across the table to Junior.

"Mmm, perfect," Mollie giggled and wrapped her arm even tighter around Juniors.

"What's the deal with that fat dude in the Camaro," Junior asked as he stuffed the cash in his pocket.

"He's hassling my client and just being a general pain in the ass. As far as I know, he's following her places and parking in front of her house. The other day, he was driving past every fifteen minutes or so and leaning on the horn. To my knowledge, he hasn't threatened her, but he's got her attention, and she's not too happy with him."

"Sounds like a real creep," Mollie said.

"Yeah, that's probably a pretty accurate description."

"A real fat creep," Junior said, and Mollie rubbed her nose against his ear.

Ollie suddenly appeared with my Coke, a bottle of beer, and a red drink in a chilled stem glass, no doubt a Cosmopolitan.

"What do I owe you, Ollie?"

"Call it even at thirty-four bucks."

That sounded about right. Mollie's Cosmos probably ran eight bucks each. I had the feeling I was going to be needing Junior's help in the near future, so a couple of Cosmos wasn't a problem. I handed Ollie two twenties and said, "Thanks, keep the change." We all took a sip, and I said, "You know, Junior, I have a feeling this Lard Ass guy isn't finished hassling my client. Would you be available to help out?"

"Yeah, sure, Dev. You can call me anytime. You know I'm good."

"Yeah, I do. Okay, I'll be in touch." I took a sip of my Coke. Junior took a sip of his beer. Mollie downed half of her Cosmopolitan and didn't so much as blink.

We chatted for the next twenty minutes or so, and then I said I had to leave. "I'll probably be talking to you in the next day or two, Junior, so don't leave town."

"I don't think I'm gonna be going anywhere," he said, looking over at Mollie. She giggled and nibbled on his ear.

"Mollie, you take care of this guy. Enjoy your evening, you two," I said and slid out of the booth. I stopped at the bar and paid Ollie to bring another round over to the happy couple. I could only hope Mollie took it easy on Junior.

I drove home, took Morton for a walk, then put on a reasonably clean shirt. I purchased a bottle of Pinot Noir wine from Chuck at SoloVino and drove back to Melissa's. I half expected to see Lard Ass parked out front or spray painting her porch, but thankfully there was no sign of him.

I rang the doorbell, and Liam opened the door a moment later. "Hey, Dev. Great! Are you going to stay for dinner?"

"I will if it's okay with your mom."

"Oh, yeah, she was just telling me what a nice guy you are."

"Well, of course. Doesn't everyone think that about me?"

He laughed at that as I stepped inside, and we headed into the kitchen. The counter was set for three, and two of the places had wine glasses.

"Oh, perfect timing. Everything go okay?" Melissa asked.

"Yeah, fine. Just wanted to touch base with a guy and make sure he wasn't going to be too busy this coming week. I may need his help. Say, with all of us here, we should talk about skating lessons if that's okay. It's one thing to have the skates, but it's another to learn how to skate."

"Mmm, yeah. Any idea what this is going to run?" Melissa asked.

"Yeah, nothing. I'm calling in a favor," I lied.

Liam grinned, and Melissa shook her head no. "I don't want you doing that, Dev."

I twisted the cap off the bottle of Pinot Noir and filled the glass closest to her, then filled a glass for me. I raised my glass, and after a brief moment, she raised hers, and we clinked glasses.

"Here's the deal. If Liam is going to play, he's going to have to skate. Which means he's going to have to learn *how* to skate. I can teach him. I can teach him how to use his stick, how to fall and get up, and—"

"Fall?" Liam asked.

"Oh, yeah. Everyone falls, Liam. The best guys get right back up. Part of skating is falling, getting back up, being able to stop, knowing how to turn fast. There are tons of things you'll have to learn, and after watching you on the football field, I'm pretty sure you're not going to have any problems. As long as we practice."

"Mmm, okay," he said and looked at his mother.

"Why don't we have dinner, and we can talk about this later," Melissa said.

"I think that's a good idea," I said.

Liam excused himself after dinner, and Melissa began to take the dishes over to the sink. I refilled her wine glass. "Hey, you want to grab a seat for a minute. I want to explain this skating lesson thing to you."

She stood facing me, holding two dinner plates, one in each hand. "Look, Dev, I get he has to learn how to skate. But, what's that going to cost? And no, I don't want you paying for it."

"I didn't offer—"

"Just let me finish, please. You have been beyond kind and gracious and protective of both Liam and me. I really appreciate that. It's been a long time for me, and I'm not used to it. But Dev, we just met the other day. I'm not complaining, but I feel like you're inserting yourself, and I just need more time. Okay? Do you get where I'm coming from?"

I took a sip of wine. Melissa set the plates on the opposite counter and turned to face me again. "Yeah, I get it, Melissa. Here are the facts on Liam playing hockey. Football will be over in four weeks. The fall hockey season is going to begin in three and a half weeks. Those are just the facts. We can't change them. I can give him lessons every day for thirty or forty-five minutes. That's all he'll be able to do, but he'll be able to skate by the time the season begins. This is Minnesota, Melissa. All the other eight-year-olds have been skating for three or four years already."

"Dev, I'm working. School ends at 2:30. I'm there for at least another two hours after that."

"You don't have to come to the practice. In fact, it would be better if you stayed away. It's just going to be the two of us. I could pick him up after school. Right now, the rinks are empty at that time. It's the difference between him succeeding or failing. It's as simple as that. I can drop him off with you after we practice. You don't have to cook me dinner. I won't insert myself in your life. Look, even if we didn't meet, I would want to do this to help Liam. He's a good kid. He's got a lot to deal with, and you need to hear this, his father is not going to go away. He's going to continue to make life difficult for both of you. Learning to skate will serve as another win for Liam, and that will serve as yet another strength to help him survive whatever his father is going to put him through in the future."

She took a sip of wine and seemed to think about that. "You'd pick him up at school?"

"Yes, and based on your schedule, I could drop him off maybe ninety minutes later. What's he doing after class now?"

"He sits in the school library until 4:15 and then comes down to my classroom."

"If nothing else, he'd get some physical exercise. You could call me and check to see how he's doing if you're worried. He'll be fine."

"You're sure?"

"Scout's honor," I said, holding up my hand.

She took a healthy sip of wine and said, "Let's try it for a week and see how it goes. I'll need more wine," she said pushing her half-empty glass across the counter.

I left that night with Liam's hockey equipment in my car.

Sixteen

I phoned my cop pal, Aaron LaZelle in homicide, at 7:30 the following morning. He answered on the second ring. "No."

"What do you mean, no? I haven't even asked you anything yet."

"I don't care. Whatever it is, my answer is going to be no. There, I just saved you ten minutes of groveling."

"Aren't you just the least bit curious?"

"Yet another question with the same answer, no."

"Hockey?" I said.

"Hockey? Wait a minute. You've got tickets?"

My turn. "No. There, how'd that feel? Actually, I'm going to be helping an eight-year-old learn how to skate. Don't we know someone who runs the indoor rinks?"

"Oh, yeah, played for Washington High. Give me a minute. He was the guy who checked you into the boards and cracked your helmet senior year, wasn't he?"

"Yeah, but I can't remember—"

"Ozzie Brady," Aaron said. "He's with the city. He heads up the Mite Hockey and Vintage Minnesota Hockey leagues."

"Yeah, writing that down as we speak. Also, who can you direct me to for information on a crooked financial guy? He runs a business that's always screwing folks."

"Gee, a biz that screws people, who knew? I think you'd have better luck contacting the state."

I thought about that for a moment. "Yeah, you're probably right."

"So, who are you giving hockey lessons to? You doing something with park services?"

"No." I went on to give him the short version of teaching Liam to skate.

"What the hell is that about? When did you start being a nice guy?"

"Only recently."

"Well, good luck. Check with the state. Try the Attorney General's office or even the Federal Trade Commission on the guy screwing folks."

"Before you go, does the name Jeremy Lawrence ring a bell?"

"Jeremy Lawrence? No, can't say that it does. Why? What did he do?"

"Just being a dumb ass. He's the ex-husband of a woman I know. Right on the edge of violating a restraining order, making life tough for her and her little boy."

"Yeah, dumb ass sounds like the perfect name."

"What about this guy, Casper Trickle? I heard he's thinking of—"

"Enough with the names, Dev. Enjoy your hockey practice. Let's grab dinner one of these next weeks."

"You got it, and it's your turn to buy," I said, which caused Aaron to hang up immediately.

Morton wandered into the kitchen. After his head scratch, I let him out into the backyard and fired up my computer. Rather than call the Attorney General's office or the Federal Trade Commission, I went online and found the address for Casper Analytics. It was located in a structure named the Capitol Building, which had nothing to do with the state capitol other than location. Not that you'd know that based on the website photo.

The photo on the website featured an image of the state capitol. Off to the side, at the corner of University Avenue and Capitol Street, was the Capitol Building. A two-story brick and gray stucco structure that, over the years, had served as a corner store, a bar, a massage parlor, another bar, and for the past couple of years, the office of Casper Analytics.

I decided to pay them a visit and maybe, in the process, get to meet Casper Trickle. After breakfast, I changed into my suit and tie. The tie was one of three I owned. Each one played a Christmas carol if you squeezed it. The one I had on played Jingle Bells. Given the lapels on the suit coat, it had either been out of style for ten years, or it was back and trendy. We headed down to the office. Louie wasn't in yet, so I made a pot of fresh coffee, settled into my desk chair, and scanned the apartment building across the street with my binoculars. Unfortunately, there wasn't any activity.

Louie arrived fifteen minutes later. I filled his coffee mug and set it on his picnic table desk. He settled into his desk chair, and after a few minutes and a half-dozen sips of coffee, he asked, "You going to a costume party?"

"Very funny, not. I'm going to head over to the Casper Analytics office this morning and hopefully get to meet Casper Trickle. Thought I'd have a better chance of suggesting I was a potential investor if I looked the part."

"With that suit, it might be a good idea to make them think you're some kind of wealthy eccentric."

"What? You don't like this outfit?"

"Just a little out of date is all. It'll be interesting to see if he's even in the office. Given his current reputation, it wouldn't surprise me if he was hiding somewhere."

"Well, there's only one way to find out. You going to be here for a while?"

"Yeah, not a problem. I've got a 2:00 that shouldn't take more than an hour. My new client has his first appearance, which schedules his future appearance, actually. I just want to review the basics with him, namely, shut up and answer with either yes sir or yes ma'am."

"You think that's going to be a problem?"

"Shouldn't be, but I just like to be sure. I'll encourage him to meet daily with AA groups, and then we'll hold our breath for six weeks until we go to court."

"I'll be back before the noon hour. Are you up for lunch if I grab some take-out?"

"I could go for something from Roosters."

"Exactly my thought." I checked the apartment building through my binoculars one more time, with no luck. "Nothing left to do but go to work. Wish me luck," I said as I tossed the binoculars back in a desk drawer and headed out of the office.

It was a ten-minute drive over to the Capitol Building. I parked right in front of the place. Nothing on the building suggested Casper Analytics was located inside. I pulled on the front door, half-expecting it to be locked, but it opened, and I stepped into a room with three walls painted white. The fourth wall, behind the reception counter, was painted fire-engine red. A large mirror was mounted on the wall.

A nice-looking Asian woman with long black hair sat behind the counter. She wore a white blouse, revealing a hint of cleavage, and smiled as I stepped inside. In the reflection of the mirror, I could see two black leather couches on the back wall behind me. They were positioned at a right angle. There was a coffee table in front of the couches with a stack of brochures apparently touting Casper Analytics. Seated on the couches were the two muscle-bound guys I'd seen lifting weights the other day on the back patio of Casper Trickle's place.

"Good morning, and welcome to Casper Analytics. How may I help you?" the woman said as she smiled and stared at my suit. I approached the counter. I noticed there didn't appear to be a computer or a keyboard anywhere. As I placed my arms on top of the counter and leaned forward, I spotted what looked like a Kindle. Apparently, she could read.

"Hi, my name is Devlin Haskell. I'm interested in a business opportunity, and a few of my acquaintances suggested meeting with your firm. I'd like to talk with someone. Would Mr. Trickle happen to be available?"

I watched in the mirror. The blonde muscle-bound guy with the crewcut stood, stretched, and nodded at his partner. He walked to the door and stepped outside.

"Oh, I'm afraid Mr. Trickle is unavailable at the moment. He's in a meeting with our board of directors. The meetings usually last a number of hours. Let me give you one of our brochures," she said. She reached up, took a brochure from the pile next to me, and handed it to me.

"This will have some general information, and if you'd like to leave your phone number, I could have someone call you. I can tell you that he is very busy, so naturally, there is an hourly rate charged for a meeting, but depending on what you're looking at, that could be minimized or possibly even waived. In fact, I happen to know that's one of the many subjects being discussed at this morning's board meeting."

'Bullshit,' I thought and said, "Well, it sounds like I've come to the right place. If you would please have

someone contact me, let me give you my cellphone number. That's more private."

As I gave her my number, the guy who had stepped out a moment ago came back inside. I watched him in the mirror behind the receptionist. He returned to his place on the black leather couch, then leaned over and seemed to whisper to his colleague.

"I'll have someone call you just as soon as they're available. Just a word of warning," she said, leaning forward. She looked from side to side as if we were in a crowded room then lowered her voice. "If I could give you some advice. The sooner you're able to act, the less it's going to cost. I can't tell you how many people either call or stop in, begging to speak with Mr. Trickle."

"Thank you for the warning. I look forward to the call."

"Wonderful to meet you, sir," she said, then stood and extended her hand. As we shook hands, I studied her reflection in the mirror. She wore a short gray skirt and sheer stockings with a black back seam.

"A pleasure meeting you. Thank you for your help." I turned and nodded at the two guys seated on the couches. "Enjoy your day, gentlemen," I said and got no response. I stepped outside, climbed in my car, and drove up University Avenue. It wasn't lost on me that only one other car was parked next to the Capitol Building, and that was a faded red Kia. Either the board meeting was off-site, or it wasn't really happening. My money was on the second option.

Just for the hell of it, I drove past Trickle's house. Two women were just stepping out of the front door. One carried a vacuum cleaner and a mop, and the other carried a bucket and a white five-gallon pail with a number of plastic spray bottles. A cleaning crew. I pulled to the curb and climbed out of my car as they opened the rear hatch on a car.

"Excuse me, were you cleaning in that house?" I asked.

They both turned around and watched as I approached. The dark-haired woman, the older of the two, said something to the other woman I couldn't hear.

I stopped a few feet from them and said, "I'm looking for a cleaning crew. Would you happen to be available?"

"We're pretty busy, but we could maybe fit you in."

"You clean this whole place?" I asked and indicated Trickle's mansion. "That's gotta take a couple of days."

"Not really. It's big, but it's just one man, and he only uses a couple of rooms and the kitchen," the other woman said.

"Quiet, Carol. What'd you have in mind? And we don't do anywhere with cats. We both have allergies," the older woman said.

"Oh, well, my tough luck. I've got three cats. Cat hair all over the place."

"Sorry, would like to help ya, but we'd last about fifteen minutes in a place like that," the older woman said.

"You could probably look online. A bunch of folks is looking for work," Carol added.

"Thanks, I'll do that. Is this a nice place inside?"

The woman named Carol looked about to say something, but the older woman cut her off and said, "Sorry we can't help, but if you'll excuse us, we better get going, or we'll be late. Let's go, Carol." She slammed the hatch closed. They climbed in the car and drove off. Interesting, they had just confirmed that Trickle lived alone. Although, there were the two muscle-bound guys in the unit over the garage.

Seventeen

I would have loved to get inside Trickle's mansion, but that wasn't going to happen with all the security cameras around the place. It was approaching 11:00, and I figured, as long as I had a little time, I'd do a quick run past Melissa's place. Good thing. As I came around the corner, a shiny black Chevy Camaro had just pulled to the curb. I stopped and watched from the far end of the block as the driver's door opened and the vehicle shook from side to side. Two legs slowly appeared. A moment later, the large fat figure of Jeremy Lawrence oozed out of the car. He held onto the doorframe for support as he stood. His right arm was in a sling. He casually turned, looked in my direction, and apparently recognized my car because he scrambled back behind the wheel. A moment later, he took off down the street, closing the driver's door as he accelerated.

Not this time, I thought and floored it. I was doing close to sixty as I raced past Melissa's house. Lard Ass Jeremy was increasing the distance between us. We were on a residential street, and I decided I'd better slow down. Lard Ass certainly wasn't worth the risk.

He was a block and a half ahead of me when he sailed across St. Clair Avenue. No sign of any brake lights on the Camaro. A white SUV clipped the back end of the Camaro, which spun sideways, slamming into the side of the SUV and sending it into a parked car on the opposite side of the street. The Camaro seemed to stop for a long moment and then sped off down St. Clair Avenue.

I hurried to the intersection and pulled to the curb. Two cars had already stopped, and the drivers were out of their cars running toward the SUV. I climbed out and ran over.

There was an older woman behind the wheel of the SUV. She appeared to be shaken but thankfully not injured. Another woman was helping her out of the SUV, telling her that she was all right. The SUV wasn't all right, nor was the parked car she'd smashed into.

A guy was on his cellphone reporting the accident.

"Tell them the driver may be injured," I said to him.

He shook his head and said, "She's okay. Just a little shook up."

"If you tell them she's injured, the response will be faster. I've got the hit and run guy's license number, and I know his name."

An ambulance was at the scene in less than ten minutes. A squad car arrived five minutes after that. I recognized one of the cops but couldn't remember his name. Fortunately, his name was on his shirt.

"Hey, Officer Rogers, Dev Haskell, good to see you. Sorry, it's under these circumstances."

When he gave me a look, I remembered why I'd tried to forget his name. It was a long time ago, high school, but apparently, having your clothes stolen from the visitor's locker room can leave an impression. I was suspended for a week, did a month of community service after school, and my folks were ready to kill me.

"Did you place the call, Haskell?"

"No, sir. I did," the guy who made the call said.

"Oh, so you were driving the hit-and-run vehicle?" Rogers said, glaring at me and sounding hopeful.

"No, I wasn't, but I have the license number of the guy who was driving, and I got his name."

"How'd you get his name? Is he a friend of yours?"

I shook my head. "Never really met him. He's just been pointed out to me. He's a troublemaker. He's been hassling his ex-wife. She's got a restraining order on him and everything. I took down his license number the other day. It's a black Chevy Camaro." I pulled out my wallet and handed Rogers the note with the license plate number.

"You said you know the guy's name?"

"Yeah, it's Jeremy Lawrence. I don't know where he lives, but there's a pretty good chance it's somewhere in town."

Rogers looked at my note with the license number and then stepped off to the side. He clicked on the microphone attached to his shoulder and began talking. He gave them the license number and Jeremy Lawrence's name. With any luck, Lard Ass Jeremy would be behind bars shortly and facing some serious charges.

The woman involved in the accident called a friend to give her a ride. Two tow trucks appeared and prepared to haul the damaged vehicles away. Rogers copied the license number and gave the note back to me. I gave him my business card in case he needed to get in touch with me.

He gave an evil smile as he read the business card and then said, "Don't think for a minute that I've forgotten, Haskell. I still owe you."

"You know, I think I've apologized on at least two different occasions. Let me tell you again. I'm sorry for my actions all those years ago. It was very stupid of me, and I'm very sorry."

"Not good enough," he said and walked over to one of the tow truck drivers.

I waited for another half hour, finally gave a statement and decided it might be a good idea if I left. I headed down to Roosters and waited in line. Eventually, I ordered two BBQ pork sandwiches with coleslaw, along with a pork bone for Morton, and headed back to the office.

Eighteen

Between the accident and Officer Rogers making me the last person to give a statement, it was almost 1:00 before I made it back to the office. I was two steps in the office when Morton caught the scent of the BBQ pork and was off his pillow. I set the bag on my desk, pulled out the pork bone, and gave it to Morton. He hurried back to his pillow and faced the wall so he wouldn't have to share.

I set a Styrofoam carton on Louie's picnic table and another on my desk and settled in. Louie typed on his computer for another minute or two and then directed his attention to the BBQ.

"Any luck meeting up with Casper Trickle?" he asked, dropping BBQ pork down the front of his shirt and tie in the process.

I gave him the short version of the event and went on to tell him about the hit and run that Lard Ass caused and how he fled the scene.

"That is going to cost him big time. Good thing you had his name and license number. The cops called it in?"

"Oh yeah, right away. If all goes well, he'll be eating dinner tonight compliments of Ramsey county."

"Sounds like that guy has some serious problems."

"Oh, my God, let me count them. He's fat, probably unemployed, and apparently has anger issues. There's a restraining order against him, his son is afraid of him, and now the police will be on the lookout for him. Yeah, I'd say he's got some problems."

"You know one of the ways this could go is that he gets even crazier. Up until now, he's been an idiot and a pain in the ass, but based on what you say, he could really snap and do something very stupid. You might want to warn your friend Melissa."

"Yeah, and she's already wound tighter than a drum when it comes to this moron. Who can blame her? I don't know. You think I should tell her about this latest incident, him being at her house and then the accident?"

"You have to. She probably doesn't want to hear about it, but she has to know."

"Yeah, I suppose you're right." I checked the time. "I'm going to pick up her son in an hour. I guess I can tell her then." We finished lunch. Louie attempted to wash the BBQ stains from his shirt and tie, which only made them worse. Once he headed over to the courthouse, I put Morton and his pork bone into the car, and we drove home.

I changed into jeans and an ancient hockey jersey and headed to Melissa's school. I arrived about five minutes before classes were finished. I parked a half-dozen spaces away from her car, headed into the school, and reported to the front office.

"May I help you?" a woman asked as I entered the office. She was seated at a desk with two stacks of files. Behind her was an office with the door closed. The name on the office door simply read 'PRINCIPAL' in capital letters, which brought back all sorts of bad memories from my school days.

"Hello, I'm here to see Melissa Donnelly."

"Is Miss Donnelly expecting you?"

"Yes, she is. I'm actually taking her son Liam to hockey practice, and I'll be doing that every day for the next few weeks. She wanted me to touch base with her today before we left."

"Oh, you must be the individual she was talking about, Devlin," she said.

"Yes, I am. Dev Haskell is my name. Very nice to meet you."

She smiled but didn't offer her name. "Classes will be over in just a minute or two. If you'd like to take a seat, I'll take you down to the classroom in a few minutes. Once the bell rings, the teachers escort the students' to their lockers. That usually takes about five minutes." The bell suddenly rang, and she said, "There it is now. Please have a seat."

As I settled into a chair against the wall, the volume of noise out in the hall began to rise. A few minutes later, doors on lockers were slamming shut, and kids began to run out the front door of the school.

"I think we can head down to the first-grade classroom now if you'd like to follow me," she said. She placed a sign on the office door that read, 'Back in 5 Minutes,' and we headed to Mellissa's classroom. There were a few hundred kids heading out the door, but they all gave her a wide berth. We made it down to Melissa's room in just a few minutes. The woman knocked and then opened the door. Melissa was seated at her desk and appeared to be going over a stack of papers. She looked up as I stepped into the room.

"Mr. Hassle to see you," the woman said and closed the door behind me.

I waited a second or two until she was down the hall and then said, "Charming."

"Audrey has a lot to deal with on any particular day. She runs a tight ship."

"If I was a kid, I wouldn't want to cross her."

"As I said, she runs a tight ship. Any problems?"

"No, at least not here. Is Liam around?"

"He'll be here in a few minutes."

"I do have some news."

"Oh?"

I went on to tell her about seeing Lard Ass stop in front of her house and the car accident.

"He was at the house? He knows I'm not there until almost 5:00."

"Well, he was there, climbed out of the car, recognized my car at the end of the block, and took off."

"Good lord. You said the woman was all right?"

"Seemed to be, other than obviously upset. But she didn't appear to be injured. I can only hope the cops pick him up." I debated telling her about the spray painting incident and decided against it. Good thing, because a moment later, the door opened, and Liam rushed in.

"Can we still go to the hockey rink?"

"As long as it's okay with your mom," I said.

He turned toward Melissa. "Yes, you can go. I want you to follow instructions and do whatever Dev tells you to do. Got it?" Liam nodded.

"Okay, let's get going, Liam. We'll be back before 4:30," I said as Liam hurried out the door.

"Thanks for doing this, Dev."

"Hey, it's my pleasure."

"Is Morton in the car?" Liam asked as we stepped out of the school.

"No, he's not very good on ice, and we're going to be doing a lot of work, so I figured it would be best if I left him at home. Hey, part of what we're gonna be doing is having fun. So we'll work, but let's make sure we have fun too. Okay?"

Liam nodded, and we climbed into my car. As I drove, I checked the rearview mirror more often than normal. I was looking for a black Camaro, but fortunately, I never saw one. We pulled into the parking lot at the Pleasant Arena. It was named that because it's located on Pleasant Avenue. I scanned the small parking lot for a black Camaro before we got out of the car.

I opened the rear door of the car and said, "Liam, why don't you grab one of those hockey sticks. I'll grab the equipment bag," I said.

We headed into the arena and toward the office. There were five kids on the ice, all girls, in what looked like a figure skating class. I guessed their ages at maybe eleven or twelve.

"You want to watch those skaters for a second? I need to check on something with the manager," I said.

Liam hurried over to the hockey boards surrounding the rink and watched the girls through the glass. I headed into the office labeled 'MANAGER.' A guy was seated behind a desk, talking on the phone. He gave me a quick wave and said, "Okay, Bertie, hey, I gotta get back to work. A guy just came in." He hung up the phone and said, "You must be Haskell?"

"Yeah, Dev Haskell," I said and held out my hand.

"Terry Hogan," he said as we shook. "Yeah, Aaron LaZelle gave me a call and said you'd be coming in. You're giving lessons to a kid?"

"Yeah, an eight-year-old, just teaching the basics for hockey. I would like to do it for the next few weeks. Hopefully, get him to the point where he could make it on one of the league teams. How do you know LaZelle?"

"One of our employees had a problem he was involved in."

"Was this that random shooting last February? Happened at a bar downtown?"

The guy nodded. "Yeah, when he called, he told me you were involved. You got the shooter's name and passed it on."

I nodded and said, "Lucky guess on my part. Did your guy recover?"

"Yeah, he was a good employee. Unfortunately, he left town. I get it, but I was sorry to see him go."

"I got the kid out there watching that group of figure skaters. Will it be okay if we're down at the far end of the rink? We're going to be working on taking four or five strides, falling, and getting back up. He's never been on the ice before."

"That shouldn't be a problem."

"Thanks, Terry, much appreciated."

"Just call if you need anything," Terry said as I headed out of the office.

Liam was standing at the hockey boards, watching the figure skaters.

"You ready to get started?" I asked.

"Yeah, wow, those girls are really good."

"Well, you know, practice makes perfect. Come on, let's get those pads on and get started." Rather than change in the locker room, we sat down on a bench. I strapped the pads over Liam's jeans, pulled the elbow pads over his sweatshirt, and tied his skates. I pulled on my skates, snapped Liam's helmet in place, and we headed onto the ice. Liam went down in three strides.

Nineteen

We practiced taking four or five strides, going down, and getting up. Quite often, it was only two or three strides before Liam went down, but to his credit, he kept at it, and at least he was laughing. At 3:45, I called it quits, and he didn't argue.

On our way out the door, I popped my head in the office, thanked Terry, and told him we'd be back tomorrow. I drove Liam back to the school. When I dropped him off, I told Melissa he did very well.

"Give me a call tonight, after dinner," I said, and she nodded.

I headed home and took Morton for a walk. It had been a long time since I'd been on skates, and I could feel my leg muscles reacting while we walked. I dined on a dinner of tortilla chips and a cheeseburger. Melissa phoned me just after 8:00.

"Hey, how's it going?" was how I answered.

"Great, I don't know what you did with Liam this afternoon, but he talked about how much he enjoyed it the whole way home. I checked on him a moment ago. He's sound asleep already."

"Good, that's just what he should be doing. If he continues the way he did today, he won't have any problems. Any sign of your ex?"

"No, thankfully. It really worries me that he was actually here today."

"Well, he didn't do anything except get out of his car, and that couldn't have been for more than ten seconds."

"That's the good news," she said. "The bad news is, he no doubt intended to damage something or go through the house, maybe steal the TV or all our food. Who knows? Thank God you just happened by and chased him off."

"Well, I'm going to drive past a number of times tomorrow, and I know a guy who will do the same thing. Hopefully, between the two of us, he'll catch on that doing something to your house is not in his best interests. Did you get the locks changed when he moved out?"

Her long pause answered my question.

"Okay. I'll take care of that tomorrow morning. Do you have a spare key to the front door?"

"Yes, I do."

"Good, leave it in your mailbox. Or, better yet, what time do you leave in the morning?"

"We have to leave at 7:15."

"I'll be there tomorrow before you leave. I'll get a locksmith over there to change your locks. I'm sure that's what Jeremy was going to do, get in the house and screw something up."

"Oh, are you sure you want to come over? Maybe if we waited until the weekend we—"

"Melissa, he's not going to wait until the weekend. The sooner we make the house safe for you and Liam, the better it will be. As of this morning, he has the police looking for him, and they have his license plate number. That has to put additional pressure on him."

"I suppose you're right."

"Thank you. I'll bring the new keys over to you tomorrow afternoon when I take Liam skating. I'll see you bright and early tomorrow morning."

"Yeah, okay, and thanks, Dev," she said and hung up.

I called a pal at Kat Key Locksmiths and left a message. I took Morton on a quick walk. As we wound our way through the neighborhood, I watched the traffic more than usual, checking for a black Camaro. Unfortunately, thinking of Lard Ass had me expecting the worst. Just after 11:00, I turned all the lights off on the first floor and then looked out windows on each side of the house. I didn't see anyone and went upstairs to bed.

My alarm went off at 6:00 the following morning. I shook a reluctant Morton awake and let him out the kitchen door. I shaved, took a shower, and had two pieces of toast for breakfast. Morton devoured his food and settled onto his pillow in the kitchen. We were at Melissa's just after 7:00. Morton was sleeping soundly in the back seat, so I left him there.

Liam answered the door nibbling on a piece of toast with peanut butter. "Oh, great, are we going skating this morning?" he asked and took a bite.

"Sorry, pal. I'm going to change the locks on the doors, but I'll see you right after school this afternoon. You do your best in class today, and we'll hit the ice this afternoon."

"Down in just a minute," Melissa called from up-stairs.

I followed Liam into the kitchen and poured a coffee for Melissa. She was down ten minutes later and said, "Hi Dev. Okay, Liam, we better get going. I'm running late."

"I poured a coffee for you," I said.

She glanced at the mug, took a quick sip, and said, "Sorry, but we have to run. Thanks, Dev. I really appreciate this."

"Not a problem. Liam, I'll see you after school."

He grinned and nodded as his mother pushed him out the door.

My phone rang a half-hour later. "Was that you leaving a harassing message on my phone last night?"

Francis Stillman, an ex-con and now working at Kat Keys. Amazingly, after burglarizing homes and businesses for the better part of twenty years, he was now gainfully employed in the legal side of the trade.

"Hi, Francis, thanks for calling. Yeah, I've got someone who should have changed her locks a year ago. She's dealing with ex-husband problems at the moment.

I caught the guy about to get into the place yesterday. Are you available to do a quick lock change?"

"Yeah, you happen to know what brand the locks are in the place?"

"I'm here now. Hang on." I hurried out to the front door and opened it. The manufacturer's name was written just above the keyhole. "Yeah, Francis, they're Schlage. You want me to check the back door?"

"They'll be the same. This the right address?" he said and read off the address I'd left last night in my voicemail message.

"That's it."

"See you in fifteen minutes," he said and hung up.

He lied. It only took twelve minutes. I glanced out the window as he pulled up in front. Once he lifted his toolbox out of the truck, I opened the front door and watched as he headed up to the porch. "Nice, digs," he said, climbing the front steps. "You're not living here, are you?"

"Good to see you, Francis. Thanks for coming on such short notice, and no, this place isn't mine. I'm still living over on Selby. A client of mine lives here. Her ex is giving her a hard time." I went on to tell him about Lard Ass Jeremy Lawrence and yesterday's hit and run as Francis opened up his toolbox. He studied the lock for a moment, nodded, and pulled out a new latch. Including unscrewing things and putting everything back together, it took him maybe six minutes. The back door went even faster.

"That's it? You're already done?" I asked.

He reached into his pocket and handed me the bill. "I can do it again if you'd like. Of course, I'd have to charge you for my time."

"You want to email me this bill? I'm guessing you don't take credit cards, do you, Francis?"

"As a matter of fact, I do take credit cards."

Damn it.

TWENTY

Once Francis left, I phoned Junior Swindell. "Hi, Dev."

"Good morning, Junior. What's your schedule look like for the rest of the week?"

"My schedule? Oh, it's pretty open. I think I can adjust anything to fit your needs. What's up?"

I gave him an update on Lard Ass, then said, "I'm thinking if you could drive past the house, maybe on an hourly basis. The only way I can see him getting in is by breaking a window, but he's so fat I'm not sure he'd be able to climb in. I'm more worried about him just sitting out front in his car waiting to hassle his ex when she comes home or leaving some nasty note in the mailbox."

"I can certainly do that. You want me to start today?"

"Yeah, if that works for you. I'm at the house now, but I'll be out of here in about a half-hour. Then I'm tied up every day, until 4:30."

"Happy to help you out, Dev. Now, if I get this guy at the house, do you want me to cuff him and call the cops?"

"I think the best plan would be to avoid any contact with him unless he's doing damage to the house. If you see him just sitting in his car in front of the place, drive past, and call the cops. They'll no doubt have a warrant out on him after that hit and run."

"Well, okay, I won't hassle the guy if that's what you want. He sounds like a real jerk."

"Yeah, I'd say that's pretty accurate." I was curious how things went with Mollie the other night but didn't ask. I was sure he was short the hundred bucks by the time morning rolled around. "Thanks in advance. If you see him, give me a call."

"Will do, and thanks, Dev."

Once he hung up, I called Heidi. "Dev, I was just thinking about you. You learn anything new on your friend Casper Trickle?"

"Nothing other than he apparently has what would be called a high profile social existence."

"No surprise. I would say the list of people who would just love to cause him a good deal of harm is pretty long," she said.

"I was at his office. He wasn't there, but his receptionist told me I should invest right away before the price went up. Are you aware of any other locations he might be at? Does he have a lake place? Or a condo on the coast or in the mountains?"

"Nothing like that, that I'm aware of. Say, while I have you on the phone. I'm guessing your wardrobe is just as awful as ever. I mentioned I've put all of Cletus's clothes out in my garage. Despite belonging to Cletus, there are some very nice items out there. Feel free to stop over, go through them, and take whatever you want."

"Oh, I might just take you up on that."

"Please do. In fact, whatever you don't take, if you want to run the rest to Goodwill or some other donation site, that would be fine with me."

"Yeah, I can do that."

"I'd be forever in your debt," she said, which started a number of images percolating in my mind.

After I hung up, I did a walk-through on Melissa's first floor, checking to make sure all her windows were locked. I walked around the exterior just to make sure Lard Ass hadn't done something earlier. Everything appeared to be okay, so I climbed in the car, drove around the block, did another drive-by, and headed to the office.

The office was empty. As we stepped inside, Morton wandered over to his pillow and went back to work on his pork bone. I picked up the scent of burning coffee. It looked like Louie hadn't been in yet this morning which meant the coffee pot had been on since yesterday. There was barely enough coffee in the pot to cover the bottom. I turned off the burner, dumped the remnants down the drain, and then set the pot off to the side to let it cool.

Twenty minutes later, I heard the stairs begin to creak. I glanced out the window, thinking it was Louie, but I didn't see his car anywhere. There was a black Mercedes parked behind my car. I figured it must be a large woman heading into the hairdressers across from our office.

The office door opened a moment later, proving once again, I'd been wrong. Two men stepped in. I recognized them as the guys who had been lifting weights out on the patio at Casper Trickle's house. The same two guys who were sitting on the couches in the corner of the Casper Analytics office. Morton curled protectively around his bone.

"Mr. Hassle," the blonde guy with the crewcut said, and they both grinned.

"Gentlemen, great to see you. Listen, I would love to sit and chat, but I'm working a pretty tight schedule this morning. If you'd like to make an appointment, we could—"

"Let's go, Hassle. Mr. Trickle would like to meet you."

"Trickle? Let me check, but I don't think he's made an appointment."

"You going to walk, or would you prefer to be carried out on a stretcher?"

"The walk sounds like just the thing. I'm coming. I'm coming," I said as I got up from behind my desk.

The dark-haired guy raised his hand to get me to stop and said, "Just a quick check. You carrying?"

"No, honest."

He smiled and said, "Okay, maybe assume the position anyway."

I leaned against the wall next to the door, and he patted me down. Once he was finished, we headed out the door and down the stairs. I was sandwiched between the two of them as we went.

They were both nice enough. One of them held the door for me, and I climbed into the back of the Mercedes. It wasn't until they closed the door that I noticed there were no door handles on the inside of either rear door. I was essentially locked in.

The dark-haired guy slid in behind the wheel, they both buckled up, and he started the car.

"Where, exactly, are we headed?" I asked.

"Might be a good idea if you just sat there quietly and enjoyed the scenery," Crewcut said. He turned around and gave me a look. The dark-haired guy just shook his head.

"Yeah, sure, no problem."

Twenty-one

No one said anything until we pulled in front of Trickle's red stone mansion on Summit Avenue. Crewcut opened the rear door on the passenger side, and I slid out.

Once again, I was sandwiched between the two of them as we walked to the wrought iron gate and the sidewalk leading to the front porch. They suddenly stopped, and the dark-haired guy, who was in front of me, turned around and smiled. As he did so, Crewcut placed a hand on my right shoulder from behind and squeezed very hard.

"Ouch, God, will you knock it off? That really hurts, man. Hey, come on."

"Just a little word of advice. We expect you to be on your very best behavior when talking to Mr. Trickle. He does not suffer fools very well. Any problems and you'll be given to us, and we'll have to fix the problem. Clear?"

I nodded.

"I'm sorry. I didn't hear that," he said as Crewcut applied another steel grip on my shoulder.

"Ahh, ouch, God, you're killing me. Okay, okay. Yeah, I'll be the perfect gentleman. You happy now?"

"Yes," he said and gave a nod to Crewcut, who released his grip.

We walked up to the front porch and climbed the four steps. The steps were of the same red stone as the house, but after a hundred and twenty years of people going up and down, they were worn. The front door was a massive oak thing with a round window of beveled glass a little bigger than a dinner plate. A star-shaped brass frame was over the glass window to prevent someone from breaking the glass and reaching in.

There was a brass door knocker below the window. They ignored the door knocker, opened the door, and stepped inside. The entryway was about twelve feet wide, paneled on both sides, and led to a massive staircase at the far end. We took an immediate right and entered a small library through a set of double doors. Trickle was seated behind an ornately carved desk. He lowered his head, looked over the top of his glasses, and studied me.

"Thank you. I'll take it from here. Sit down, Mr. Haskell," he said and nodded toward one of the leather chairs in front of his desk.

The two weightlifters backed out of the room, closing the double doors behind them as they left.

I glanced around the room. Two landscape paintings hung on the walls. Ancient leather-bound books filled two bookcases. A small cabinet with a crystal carafe that looked to be filled with whiskey and four crystal glasses rested between the bookcases.

"Please, take a seat, Haskell." As I sat down, he said, "I understand you expressed an interest in the organization."

"Yes, I did. You were recommended to me by two individuals, and it sounded interesting."

"And who was it that recommended me?"

"I'm really not at liberty to say."

He flashed a quick smile. "You're aware I charge by the hour?"

"Yes, the woman at the front desk informed me of that. My friend suggested it may be money well spent."

"What makes you interested in this opportunity?"

"I've been watching you for the past two years," I lied. "You have your ups and downs, but you, unlike many in today's economy, always seem to come out on top. I'm interested in getting involved with something, somewhere, and staying in for the long haul. I believe riding out the ups and downs may well lead to a very profitable, mmm, relationship."

Trickle nodded. "I've studied you a bit. My sense is you live from paycheck to paycheck. How do you intend to come up with the funds for any sort of investment?"

"First of all, I don't intend to make a minimum investment. That said, I'm glad you've studied me, and that's your perception. That means my efforts have paid off. Why in God's name would I want to admit to the funds I've acquired over the years and then pay taxes on them? That's not how I work. If you've studied me, you must be aware that I work in what might be referred to as a gray area. People disappear. People are incarcerated. People are caught up in questionable circumstances that they would prefer to remain private. There's always an opportunity to look at a profitable outcome in situations like that."

Trickle leaned back and seemed to think. "You're familiar with the Gustafson organization?"

"To a point. I have a bit of a working relationship with Mr. Gustafson. I'm sure there are business activities regarding him that I have absolutely no knowledge of, and the same could be said of him with regard to me. On the surface, we have what might be called an adversarial relationship. Privately, we deal very well together," I lied.

"Interesting, and would you consider sharing the information you have?"

"Regarding Mr. Gustafson?" I shook my head and said, "No. Nothing against you, but that's a private interaction that has served both of us very well, and I wouldn't want to jeopardize it. With Mr. Gustafson, need I mention the price to pay would be, mmm, extraordinary."

He leaned back and appeared to think for a long moment. I was hoping he bought my line.

"Very well, Haskell. Give me a day or two to consider this, and I'll let you know." He reached over to the far side of his desk, picked up a small brass bell, and shook it back and forth, ringing the thing.

A moment later, the double doors were opened, and the weightlifters walked in.

"Where can they take you, Haskell?"

"Oh, umm, just back to my office would be great."

"Very well, see to it, gentlemen."

Twenty-two

I followed them out of the office toward the front door. Just before we got to the front door, the guy in front turned and said, "I hope you'll forgive our initial attitude. We have to be so careful with people who want to be involved with Casper Analytics. Mr. Trickle is constantly being sued by disgruntled clients."

"Don't worry about it. Believe me. I'm familiar with the problem."

"Thank you for understanding. By the way, my name is Jacob. We'll get you back to your office," he said.

"My name is Arthur, but everyone calls me Arty," Crewcut said behind me. Jacob held the front door open, and I stepped out onto the porch as Arty said, "I think you'll find that, long term, the profitability of—Hey! What the hell do you think you're doing?"

Jacob suddenly rushed past me and jumped off the front porch, landing on the sidewalk. He intentionally somersaulted and was on his feet running toward the front gate. As he opened the gate, there was a screech out on the street. A black Camaro suddenly appeared from alongside the Mercedes and raced down the street, picking up speed. I recognized the jiggling fat chins on the driver.

Jacob was out in the street swearing and shaking a fist as we hurried down the porch steps toward the front gate. "Oh, who in the hell was that? What in the hell was he thinking?" Jacob shouted and punched the rear of the Mercedes, denting the trunk.

As I stepped out of the front yard and looked at the Mercedes, I noticed it was leaning decidedly to the left. Stepping into the street around the back of the car, I couldn't help but notice that both tires on the driver's side had been slit and were now flat.

I could think of only one fat person in a black Camaro, Lard Ass. I thought about mentioning his name and decided I had better not. "Who would do that? That bastard have something against Mercedes?"

"This is exactly why we don't park out on the street. Damn it," Arty said. "Probably another pissed-off investor having a hissy fit."

"That's really crazy."

"You're telling me," Jacob said. "Look, Mr. Hassle, I'm sorry, but we're still going to be one tire short after we change one of these. God, we're going to have to get the car towed and buy two new tires. It'll take the better part of the afternoon."

"You guys don't need me in the way. Let me make a phone call and get someone to pick me up." I thought about calling Louie and then remembered he was probably in court. I called Junior Swindell instead.

"Hi, Dev. I just went past the place about twenty minutes ago. Everything looked quiet."

"That's great, Junior. Hey, I'm in a bit of a bind at the moment. Do you have time to pick me up? I'm down on Summit Avenue."

"Yeah, sure, I can do that. You gonna need some firepower?"

"No, nothing like that. Listen, here's the address where I am," I said and read the house number off one of Trickle's porch columns.

"I can be there in just a few minutes."

"Thanks, much appreciated. I'll be waiting out front."

"You're going to be okay?" Jacob asked. Arty was on his phone lining up a tow truck.

"Yeah, I'll be fine. Hey, look at it this way. At least this happened here in front of where you live. What if you were out of town or even just on the other side of town? Thankfully, you don't have to pay a hundred bucks for a taxi ride on top of the tow truck."

"God help that guy if we ever find out who in the hell he is."

"Let me get in touch with my friends down at the police station. They just might have a line on that car. You know what it was? It looked kind of sporty."

"That fat ass was driving a Chevy Camaro," Arty said as he hung up the phone.

"Some fat guy driving a car like that," Jacob said and shook his head. "You know, I'm thinking if we hadn't come out here when we did, he would have slit all four tires. What the hell is wrong with that guy?"

"It had to be some pissed-off investor. We get 'em all the time, although usually, they ring the doorbell and just start bitching if the boss answers," Arty said.

"Which is why he never answers the door."

"Does he have family living in there with him?" I asked, remembering the cleaning woman told me he was in there alone.

They both shook their heads. "No, the wife left a few years back. We never met her. I think he's got a couple of kids, but he never mentions them."

"They're in college somewhere outside the US. France, Spain, somewhere in Europe," Jacob said.

"How'd you guys end up here?"

"Someone actually shot at him, maybe a year and a half ago," Jacob said.

Arty nodded. "Another unhappy client. We were both competing in the Upper Midwest weightlifting competition at the time. He offered us room and board, plus a salary if we acted as security."

"Does he have a lot of problems? I mean, if someone was taking shots at him, that's pretty serious."

"Yeah, it's been pretty constant. He disappears for periods of time. He has a place up in northern Minnesota—"

"The north woods," Jacob said, "a place called the Gold Club. We've flown up there a couple of times. It's on a lake, Ash Lake, I think. No roads into the place. You have to fly in and land on the water."

Arty shook his head. "Yeah, well, unless you want to walk about twenty miles and hope the wolves or bears don't get you. When things get crazy down here with investors going nuts, we take off up there for a couple of weeks."

"Clients get that crazy that Mr. Trickle goes up there? It sounds like he's hiding," I said.

Arty nodded. "You wouldn't believe how crazy it gets. You know how the market goes up and down? I mean, every day is different. Everything is fine when folks are making money, and the values are increasing. The moment things change, we're screwed. There are people who come to Mr. Trickle for advice, which he generously provides. They decide not to follow that advice, and then, when things go horribly wrong, somehow Mr. Trickle is to blame. It's absolutely bizarre."

"But they took his advice, right?"

"Yeah, correct, to a point. The problem seems to be that when things go well, they begin to believe it's because they know what they're doing. When, actually, they simply followed directions."

"Mr. Trickle refers to it as the gravity flush, you know, like a toilet flushing. Think about it, you're either going to come out okay if you follow directions and don't plug the toilet, or you're ultimately going to be shit on," Jacob said.

"That's probably enough, dude," Arty said just as a rusty red Buick Enclave pulled in behind the Mercedes. Junior Swindell's car.

"Oh, thanks, guys, here's my ride. Great talking with you. Good luck with the tow truck," I said and climbed into the passenger seat in Junior's car.

I gave a wave as Junior backed up and then drove down the street. "Oh man, you hang with those two muscle-bound guys?" Junior asked.

"Not really. They work for the guy I was meeting with. They're okay, I guess. But I plan on keeping my distance."

"You want to head down to The Spot?" he asked.

"Much as I'd like to, you better just drop me at the office. Thanks for coming so quickly."

"Not a problem. All I got going on today is driving past that house."

"Well, keep an eye out. That fatso in the Camaro is the guy that slit the tires on their Mercedes. We just happened to see him drive off. You meeting up with Mollie at all?"

He glanced over and shook his head. "Can't see her until I come up with some cash."

"Well, if you've got time to drive past my bank, I can stop in and pay you for today."

"Tell me how we get there."

Twenty-three

Junior dropped me off across the street from my office. He was dialing Mollie's phone number before I was out of the car. Louie hadn't made it back from the courthouse yet, and Morton was still involved with the pork bone.

I spent the next hour constantly looking out the window for Lard Ass and his black Camaro. He was no doubt unaware of the trouble he had caused for himself after slitting the tires on the Mercedes. Add to that the hit and run and, if he was lucky, the cops would get to him first. I skipped lunch, took Morton for a walk, and then took him home. I was back at Melissa's school before the final bell rang, so I stepped into the front office. As I entered, Audrey, the woman seated at the desk, looked up and smiled.

"Here to see Melissa, Mr. Hassle?"

"Yes, taking her son to skating lessons. How are you doing, Audrey?"

"Always fine," she said and didn't appear to be joking. "Take a seat."

The bell rang a minute or two later. I waited another five minutes, and then Audrey said, "If you'll follow me, we'll get you to Melissa's classroom."

Just like before, the kids gave her a wide berth walking down the hall. She knocked on the classroom door, opened it, but didn't walk in. "You go on ahead," she said.

"Thanks," I said, and she walked back to her office.

"Liam should be here in just a moment. Everything okay with you?" Melissa asked as a worried look washed over her face.

"Yeah, everything's fine. What are you worried about?"

She frowned and said, "I just got a text from Jeremy. He said to ask you how your day was going."

"My day is fine. Can you show me his text message?"

She reached into her purse and pulled out her cellphone. "He sent this just after lunch, but I only read it a couple of minutes ago. Are you sure everything is okay? I don't want Liam exposed to whatever his idiot father is up to."

"Everything is fine." I went on to tell her about the slit tires on Trickle's Mercedes. "Jeremy doesn't know it, but he's got two rather tough characters that are not going to be very polite if they ever get their hands on him."

She shook her head. "Oh, Dev, I am so sorry. He did this to the two other men I met online. We never really got to the actual dating part. After my initial meetings with them, he spray-painted one man's car and poured sand in the other's gas tank. After that, you can imagine they weren't really interested in getting to know me any better."

"Not to worry. You need a key to open my gas tank. Can you recall what his last address was?"

"His last address?"

"Yeah, where he was living."

"I've got it on my phone, but he hasn't been there for at least a year. I don't know where he is now."

"Let me get that address from you. I've got some contacts I can check with. Don't worry, nothing bad is going to happen. I promise I'll be nice," I said.

She pulled out her phone, and I copied down the address on the back of an envelope. The place was located in the Midway district of town. I wrote Jeremy's phone number after the address. "I promise to keep a close eye on Liam. Okay?"

"You're sure?"

"Scout's honor," I said and held up my hand just as Liam came into the room. "Well, there he is. You ready for some time on the ice?"

"Yeah, let's go. Oh, hi, Mom."

"Hi, Liam. Now you listen to Dev, honey."

"He always does," I said, and we headed out the door.

We did more of the same on the ice. Up and down, up and down. For the final ten minutes, we skated laps around the rink or at least attempted to. I skated back-ward, and Liam did his best. On average, he fell two or three times on each lap. Truth be told, that was a lot better than I'd expected.

We pulled back into the school parking lot, and I walked Liam down to his mother's classroom. We chatted for a couple of minutes, and I left. Once again, I looked around before I climbed into my car but never saw anything that resembled a black Camaro. I drove home, picked up Morton, and headed to the office.

Louie was at his picnic table desk typing away.

"Well, there you are. How's the day going?" he asked without looking up from his computer screen.

"No problem. How'd things go in court?"

He shook his head. "Not surprisingly, my client thought it would be a wise move to ignore my advice, and he opened his big mouth."

"How'd that work?"

"After his stupid comments, he'll have the next six days in the workhouse to consider the wisdom of that particular decision."

"You have to wonder," I said.

"I always do," Louie replied and continued typing.

I settled in at my desk and turned on my computer. I pulled out my note with the last known address for Lard Ass. I brought up the county tax records site and input the address. The building was actually a former single-family structure converted into three rental units. It was owned by a group called Downer Properties. It took five minutes, but I found a website and a phone number for them.

"Downer Properties," was how the woman answered the phone.

"Mr. Downer, please."

"Who may I say is calling?"

I cheated a little and said, "My name is Detective Devlin Haskell."

There was a brief pause, and she said, "One moment, please. I'll connect you immediately."

The phone rang twice before a voice said, "Melvin Downer."

"Hello, Mr. Downer. Thank you for taking my call. My name is Detective Devlin Haskell. I'm looking into an individual who was a tenant in a property you own." I gave him the address and mentioned the name Jeremy Lawrence.

"Lawrence, oh yeah. I don't even have to look him up. Large fellow, left in the middle of the night owing me two months' rent. Can't say I was sorry to see him go. Strange circumstance, I received a voicemail from another property owner looking for a reference on Lawrence two or three days later. I called Lawrence and told him if he expected to rent anywhere in town, he'd better pay me the two months' rent plus a cleaning fee."

"Did you ever hear back from him?"

"That's the interesting part. He was in the office with a cashier's check before the end of the day."

"And you provided a reference?"

"I did. I stated that he was current with his rent and that no other information was available. I'm curious, what's he done now?"

I gave him some general information and asked, "Do you recall the name or address of the new location?"

"Hang on just a moment. I made a note. Part of my concern was the damage Lawrence might consider doing if I didn't provide him with a positive reference."

"You had some experience?" I asked.

"Nothing I could ever prove. My other two tenants at that location are still there, both women. One is in her fifties and has been there for five or six years. The other has been there for three years. Never any problem. They always pay on time. Lawrence was a problem. There was damage to the garage, a broken basement window, spray paint in a common area. It began shortly after he arrived, and we've not had another incident since he left. Okay, here's that address. Ready to write this down?"

"Yes, go ahead."

He gave me an address on Jackson Street then said, "He definitely has some issues. The only reason I didn't evict him was I was worried about what he might do to the unit and my other renters. Mr. Lawrence is not a happy individual." We chatted for another minute or two. Downer had nothing positive to say about Lard Ass and wished me well in my investigation.

As I got out of my desk chair, Louie remained focused on his screen and said, "Are you maybe thinking The Spot?"

"Maybe in a bit. First off, I'm going to take Morton for a walk and then run a quick errand."

"I've got about twenty minutes more on this brief, and then I'm going to wander over," Louie said.

"Hopefully, we'll catch up," I said as Louie continued typing.

Twenty-four

I took Morton on our standard walk, and then loaded him into the backseat of the car, and we drove over to the address Melvin Downer had given me. Jackson Street runs north out of downtown until it butts into Oakland Cemetery. It starts up again one block to the east, which makes absolutely no sense unless you're from St. Paul, in which case, it's par for the course. I was looking for 980 Jackson. I actually drove past the place and had to back up.

Sure enough, 980 Jackson was a wood frame building that was probably about a hundred and fifty years old. The place was white but, based on all the peeled paint, it must have been painted back during the Nixon administration. The sign above the door read 'Greasy's Open till 2:00 AM'.

I got out of my car and walked around to the side. There was an enclosed staircase leading up to the second floor. Five black mailboxes were attached to the door-frame. The mailboxes were numbered one through five, so there was no way to determine if Lard Ass actually still lived there. I lifted the lid on all five mailboxes, but other than a couple of envelopes addressed to 'occupant,' they were empty. The door wasn't locked, so I stepped inside and climbed the stairs. At the top of the stairs was a wooden door that was locked.

Based on the bootprints on the door, it had obviously been kicked in more than once. I climbed down the stairs and checked out the rear of the building. There was a muddy parking area with two older cars, a white Mazda, and an old Ford station wagon with fake wood panels, but no sign of a black Camaro. I walked back to the front of the building and went into the bar. I was pretty sure I'd been in worse places, but it had been a while. The place was dingy and needed an airing out.

A half-dozen bar stools were in front of the ancient bar. Three of them had strips of silver duct tape around the edge of the seat. Some old bald guy was face down on the bar sitting on the end stool. He was still holding an empty shot glass in his hand. It had been against the law to smoke in commercial establishments for a number of years, but there were overflowing ashtrays on all five tables.

"You gonna get something?" the guy behind the bar said. He was wearing a white t-shirt with the sleeves torn off. Just now, he was in the process of pouring himself a shot of bourbon. He set the bottle down on the bar. I read the bottle label, Kentucky Gentleman. He did not seem very happy to see me, and I had the immediate sense I had interrupted whatever plans he had for the day.

"Yeah, hi. I'm actually looking for a guy named Jeremy Lawrence. He's a pretty big guy, and I thought this was his address. I owe him some money and want to pay him."

He tossed the shot back, didn't so much as blink, and said, "He's not just big, he's a fat ass, and he ain't here."

"Yeah, I can see that. You know where I can find him?"

He shook his head and said, "You can leave it with me, and I'll see that he gets it."

"You know if he'll be back soon?"

He shook his head.

"Does he live upstairs?"

"He's got a room up there. Comes and goes. You don't want to leave it with me, there ain't a hell of a lot I can do for you."

I glanced around for a brief moment and said, "Yeah, I'd say you're right. You have a good day." I turned and headed out the door.

"I didn't catch your name," he called after me.

"That's cause I didn't give it to you," I said. I stepped out the door and closed it behind me.

I felt the urge to drive home and take a hot shower. Instead, I climbed back into my car and drove down to The Spot. I parked across the street from the office, just behind Louie's faded Ford Fiesta. As soon as we stepped inside, Morton damn near pulled my arm out of the socket as he hurried to the end of the bar and Louie's stool. "Pour me a Summit, Mike, and better give Louie a refill," I said as Morton rounded the corner to Louie's stool. Louie already had a handful of pork rinds, and he bent down and presented them to Morton. His hand was licked clean in just a second or two.

"Get what you were looking for?" Louie asked.

I shook my head and said, "You ever hear of a bar called Greasy's?"

"It sorta rings a bell, but can't say I'm familiar with the place. You thinking of going there?"

"Just came from there, actually. Trying to find where Jeremy Lawrence lives. A guy gave me the address, which turns out to be that bar. There were five mailboxes on the rear door, and when I told the bartender I owed Lawrence some money, he said he'd take the money and give it to him. The place was a real dump, and I'm still not sure if Lawrence lives there."

"So you didn't give the bartender the money?"

"Louie, the only thing I want to give that Lard Ass is one hell of a beating. I might just pass on that address to a couple of unhappy guys who were getting two new tires, compliments of him."

Mike placed a fresh drink in front of Louie and set a beer in front of me. I pulled out a twenty and handed it to him. He waited a second or two, so I could tell him to keep the change. When that didn't happen, he walked down to the cash register and returned with the change.

"Say," Louie said and took a sip. "You doing anything with your mentor, Tubby Gustafson?"

"I'm supposedly checking on Casper Trickle for him, but that's all. As a matter of fact, I think I mentioned that I met with him earlier. Why do you ask?"

"Just thought I saw Tubby's Cadillac SUV with that fat guy—"

"Fat Freddy Zimmerman?"

"Yeah, that's who it was. I've been thinking about it for the past hour, trying to come up with the guy's name. Anyway, he was in the car sitting behind the wheel. It was parked across the street from the office for at least a half-hour before I came over."

"God, that's all I need at the end of the day, having to spend time with Fat Freddy Zimmerman."

"Bad day?"

"Let's just say there are a number of things going on with no real conclusion in sight on any of them."

Louie filled me in on his client getting six days in the workhouse for opening his big mouth and telling the judge what he thought of him. I told him about Lard Ass and the tires on Trickle's Mercedes. I had just ordered another beer when my phone rang.

I checked the screen and answered, "Yeah, Junior, everything okay?"

"Yeah, I drove past that house a bunch of times today. Walked around it looking for any damage Fat Ass might have done, but everything looked okay."

"Really appreciate the help, Junior. You able to do the same thing tomorrow?"

"You bet I am. Looking forward to it. Hey, I was just wondering if, umm, maybe I could get paid for today. Mollie's fixing to go out, and I was thinking, you know…"

"Yeah, I know. Tell you what. I'm just five minutes from the bank. If you want to meet me there, I'll hit the ATM, and I can give you the cash at the bank."

"I'll see you there," Junior said and hung up.

"Problem?" Louie asked.

"Fortunately, no. Junior just wants to be paid. He's apparently got a thing going with that redheaded Mollie who's in here from time to time. She dates by the hour, if that translates. Can you watch my beer and Morton for the next ten minutes?"

"Consider it done," Louie said.

I hurried out to my car. I glanced up and down the street for Fat Freddy or Lard Ass. Thankfully, I didn't see either one and drove to the bank. I was just pulling out of the ATM lane when Junior pulled up. He walked over to my car as I lowered the window.

"Thanks for doing this, Dev. I'm going to walk around the place every time I drive by tomorrow."

"That would be great, Junior." I handed him the cash and nodded at Mollie sitting in the front seat of his rusty red Buick Enclave. "Your date for the night?"

"Yeah, she is now," he said and fanned the five twenties I'd given him. "She told me it's two for one night."

"Enjoy. I'll talk with you tomorrow," I called as he ran back to his car. He slid behind the wheel, handed the cash to Mollie, and took off.

I drove back to The Spot. My beer was still on the bar. It looked like Louie had a fresh drink. We chatted for thirty minutes, and then I headed home. As I turned into the driveway, a black SUV pulled across the entrance, blocking any opportunity to escape. Braindead Austin was behind the wheel, and Fat Freddy was in the passenger seat.

I got Morton out of my back seat, and we walked over to Fat Freddy's side. He lowered his window, said, "Hi, Morton," and tossed a couple of French fries out the window. Morton snatched them up before I could stop him.

"What can I do for you, Freddy?"

"Mr. Gustafson would like a word."

I glanced in the empty back seat. "Is he coming in a different car?"

"No, we're going to give you a ride."

I took a deep breath and exhaled. "Tonight? Really, I was just going to settle in after a long day. How about I show up first thing in the morning?"

Freddy shook his head.

"Okay. Let me get Morton in the house, and I'll be right back."

"Please don't try anything. It will just give Austin the opportunity to kick in your front door."

"And I'd love to do it," Austin said and laughed.

Freddy gave him a look that suggested he wasn't helping.

"I'll be back out in just a minute," I said and walked Morton up the front steps. We stepped inside, and I undid his leash. He followed me into the kitchen, where I tossed him a biscuit. He finished the biscuit in three quick bites, settled onto his pillow, and closed his eyes. So much for my guard dog. I locked the door behind me and climbed into the back seat of the SUV.

Twenty-five

It was a quiet drive to Tubby's mansion. Other than Austin yelling profanities at a car making a left-hand turn, no one said anything. Austin pulled to a stop opposite the front door to the mansion. Fat Freddy oozed out of the front seat and then said, "Let's go, Haskell. You're keeping the big man waiting."

I climbed out of the back seat just as one of the guards from the front door stepped over and said, "Assume the position."

I leaned forward, placed my hands against the roof of the SUV, and spread my legs. He quickly patted me down. Just as he stood and said, "Okay," idiot Austin floored the SUV. I bounced off the side of the thing and stumbled forward. Fortunately, I didn't fall. Everyone but me laughed.

Fat Freddy led me into the mansion. The guy inside the door stopped watching the porn on his cellphone, gave me another quick pat-down, and said, "He's clean."

Fat Freddy led me down the hall, knocked on Tubby's door as he opened it, and held the door open for me. He followed me inside. Tubby was seated at his desk, dressed in a shirt and tie. A chilled stem glass rested on the desk in front of him. There were two olives in the glass. I guessed he was drinking a martini, probably not his first.

A dark-haired woman wearing a sleeveless black minidress was standing behind him, massaging his shoulders, and whispering in his ear.

Tubby focused on me as we approached and began to shake his head. "I'm in the process of enjoying a wonderful evening. I knew it was too good to be true. What do you want, Haskell?"

"Actually, I'd like to go home, if that's all right with you, Tub—err, Mr. Gustafson."

Fat Freddy cleared his throat and said, "Sir, you mentioned you'd like to see Haskell and get an update on the status of Casper Trickle."

Tubby seemed to twitch for a second and said, "Oh, yes, thank you, Frederick. Tell me what you learned regarding Mr. Trickle, Haskell."

I took a deep breath and said, "I've found your initial observations to be correct, sir. He appears to be a rather private individual who—"

Tubby twitched again, closed his eyes for a long moment. When he opened his eyes, he said, "Stop with the long-winded nonsense, Haskell. What in God's name did you find out?"

"Actually, not much, sir. It would appear that he has twenty-four-hour security. Casper's wife and children left him some time ago, and he lives alone in his home on Summit Avenue. His security, two gentlemen, Jacob Hammen and Arty Wright, reside in a unit above the triple car garage in the back of Casper's home. The place is monitored by security cameras, a number of security cameras, twenty-four hours a day."

Tubby made a couple of audible noises and took hold of the edge of his desk. I looked over at Fat Freddy, who didn't seem to be picking up on Tubby's reaction.

"I have not had the opportunity to get close to him. I did see your Cadillac Escalade parked in his drive the other day, and your man Austin was leaning against it. I presumed that you were inside meeting with Mr. Trickle."

Tubby's eyes grew large, and he continued to hold onto the edge of his desk. He groaned a half-dozen times. After a moment, he took a deep breath and settled back into his chair. I thought he might be experiencing a seizure of some sort. The woman in the black minidress continued to massage his shoulders and neck. She leaned down and gave him a kiss and a nibble on the top of his ear. He closed his eyes and took another deep breath. A blonde head suddenly appeared and crawled out from beneath his desk.

"Did you just—"

"Shut up, Haskell. We'll give you a moment to recover, sir. Follow me, big mouth," Fat Freddy said and tugged on my arm to follow him. We headed out of the room. Freddy pulled the door closed as we stepped into the hallway.

"What in the hell was all that? He's got some blonde woman under his desk giving him a—"

"Enough, Haskell. If you must know, it's Dr.'s orders. A regime to strengthen the cardiac condition Mr. Gustafson has been dealing with."

"Please give me that Dr.'s name. I want to make an appointment just as soon as possible."

"Frederick!" Tubby shouted from inside his office.

"I'm warning you. Do not make a comment," Fat Freddy said and opened the door. We walked up to Tubby's desk. The two women were nowhere to be seen. I figured there wasn't room enough for both of them beneath the desk.

"You were just about to tell me the Escalade was parked in front of the Trickle residence, and Austin was there," Tubby said.

"Yes, sir, I think that was three or four days ago."

"What time of the day was this?"

"It was in the afternoon," I said, remembering it was only ten minutes before Lard Ass had his hit and run incident.

Tubby looked at Fat Freddy, who shrugged and shook his head.

"Interesting. You learn anything else?" Tubby asked.

"Only what I mentioned previously. That the reactions from angry clients seem to be violent enough that Trickle has round-the-clock security. If things get too violent, he flies up to a place in northern Minnesota. I believe it's on Ash Lake. It's remote. In fact, a plane is the only way to reach the place. The plane lands on the water. Apparently, you can't travel there by vehicle. I think I heard it was a twenty-mile walk through the wilderness to get there. They call the place the Gold Club."

"The Gold Club? Interesting, and you said it was on Ash Lake?"

"That's what I heard. Obviously, I've not been to the place, sir. I have spoken to some of Mr. Trickle's former clients, not a happy group. There are a number of pending lawsuits suggesting cheating and fraud. I guess they'll probably be going on for years. If you were considering becoming involved in a Trickle enterprise, sir, I would have to think there were some much safer and more successful opportunities out there."

"Business advice from you, Haskell? I don't think so. Anything else?" Tubby said.

"Only that if you're finished with me, sir, could I get a ride home, please?"

Tubby got a questioning look on his face, shook his head, and said, "Haskell, just get the hell out of my sight."

"Happy to do so, sir," I said and followed Fat Freddy out of the office. Once Freddy closed the door behind him, he said, "What the hell was that last bit?"

"I just need a ride back to my place, that's all."

Freddy shook his head and said, "Let's get your dumb ass out of here."

Austin drove, and Freddy sat in the front passenger seat, munching from a bag of chips. When they dropped me off in front of my place, I thanked Freddy, then said, "Thank you for driving me all the way home."

Austin glared but didn't say anything. Freddy tossed the empty chips bag at me. I picked up the bag, hurried inside the house, and locked the door.

Twenty-six

The following morning, I was up early. Once Morton came downstairs, I let him out. I scrambled a couple of eggs and ate them out of the pan while Morton inhaled his food. As soon as he was finished, I put him in the car, and we drove over to 980 Jackson Avenue. It was ten minutes before 8:00, and amazingly, Greasy's Bar was open. Even more of a surprise, or maybe it made sense, the customer going inside was the same bald guy who had been passed out at the bar when I was there yesterday.

I didn't feel the need to go into the place and introduce myself. Instead, we turned at the corner and then drove down the alley. There were three cars in the muddy parking area. The white Mazda and the old Ford station wagon looked to be in exactly the same place as when I first spotted them late yesterday afternoon.

This morning, parked between them, was a black Chevy Camaro. The passenger side of the vehicle was scraped and dented from the hit and run Lard Ass had caused on St. Clair Avenue. I had to fight with myself not to get out and let the air out of all four tires and smear the windshield with mud after snapping the wipers off. I was pretty sure of one thing. Apparently, Jeremy Lawrence was still living in one of the upstairs units.

I thought about sitting and waiting until he appeared, but then what? I made the wise decision to head down to the office. It was empty when we arrived. Once again, the coffee had been left on overnight. I emptied the pot into the sink, rinsed it out, and made a fresh pot.

I focused on the apartment building across the street and watched while a woman was putting on her makeup at the kitchen counter. Unfortunately, she was covered by a blue terrycloth bathrobe. A few minutes later, Louie pulled in and parked behind my car. I heard the stairs begin to creak as he climbed to the second floor. I filled his coffee mug and was just settling into my desk chair when the office door opened and red-faced Louie waddled in.

He nodded and gave a wave.

I turned on my computer and said, "Fresh coffee in your mug."

He nodded again and settled into his desk chair. After a couple of minutes and a half-dozen sips, he said, "You're in early. What's the latest?"

I gave him an update on Lard Ass.

He took a sip and said, "Did you ever think that instead of involving yourself with that idiot, it might be wiser to mention him to Tubby Gustafson?"

"You're half right. I'm going to mention him, all right, but not to Tubby. I'm going to tell the weightlifters who provide security for Casper Trickle. They saw him racing away after he slit two of their tires. I'm thinking they just might have a clever idea about how to deal with him. I'll make sure I'm doing something like visiting the police station when they decide on whatever it is they have in mind."

"Why don't you just give the cops the address where he lives? He's wanted in a hit and run, isn't he?"

"Yeah, and you know as well as I do that even if they haul him in, he'll be out on the street before the arresting officer has finished writing up the paperwork."

"Yeah, unfortunately, you're probably right," Louie said and shook his head.

"But that gives me another idea." I pulled out my cellphone and called Junior. He answered on the fifth ring. "Hell…," he cleared his throat. "Hello?"

"Mmm, keep it down. I'm trying to sleep." A female voice groaned in the background. Most likely, Mollie, another hundred bucks richer.

"Dev?"

"Hi, Junior, sorry to call you so early."

"Oh, not a problem. I was just, umm, finishing up my morning workout."

Yeah, sure he was. "Listen, after you check out that house today, I want you to drive past a place and see if that black Camaro is parked in back. Can you do that?"

"Yeah, I guess. You got an address on that dude?"

I gave him the Jackson Street address and said, "Don't get out of the car. I just want to know if the car is parked in the back. The place is a bar named Greasy's, and there are rental units up on the second floor. I'm pretty sure Lard Ass is renting one of the units. I just want to know if he leaves the place. Don't interact with the guy. He's liable to do something crazy."

"I can deal with that."

"Yeah, I know you can. But do me a favor and stay in the car. All you have to do is drive past and see if the Camaro is there. If it's gone, give me a call. I want to see if there's a pattern he follows. Maybe he has to be some-where. God forbid he'd have a job."

"Okay, okay, I'll stay in my car. I'll check it out and see if the Camaro is there."

"Good. Oh, give my best to Mollie," I said, but I think he'd already hung up.

"You gonna be here for a while?" I asked Louie.

"I'm in all morning. Feel free to leave Morton if you want."

"Thanks, I'm going to make a quick drive past Melissa's house. With any luck, I'll be back here in twenty minutes," I said and headed for the door.

Morton watched me but made no effort to get up off his pillow. I drove over to Melissa's. I parked in front and then did a quick walk around the house. Everything appeared to be in order. I debated driving over to Trickle's and giving the weightlifters the information on Lard Ass but decided to wait. Instead, I climbed into my car and phoned Aaron LaZelle. I ended up leaving a mes-sage and headed back to the office.

"Oh man, that was quick," Louie said as I stepped into the office. Morton was still on his pillow. He opened one eye, saw it was me, and went back to sleep.

"Yeah, everything seemed fine over at Melissa's. I—" My cellphone rang, Aaron LaZelle returning my call. "Hi, Aaron, thanks for calling back."

"I got about two minutes. What's up? And no, I'm not going to eliminate any of your parking tickets."

"I'm happy to report that I don't have any parking tickets, and I haven't had a speeding ticket in over three years."

"I'll have to see why they're not doing their job. What else can I do for you?" Aaron asked.

"I mentioned this Jeremy Lawrence character to you a few days ago. He was involved in a hit-and-run. Fortunately, no one was injured, but two vehicles were seriously damaged. Anyway, I found out where he's living, saw his car parked out back, and I was hoping you could direct me to whoever I should pass this information on to."

"You said no one was injured?"

"Yeah, thankfully."

"Contact the Ramsey County Sheriff's Department. They handle all those reports. Are you mentioned in the report?"

"Probably, I gave them the license number and the name of the driver who caused the accident and fled the scene."

"Great. They'll take that information and pass it on to whoever is going to act on it."

"Okay, thanks, Aaron. I'm calling you next week for dinner."

"Thanks for the warning," he said and disconnected.

I phoned the Sheriff's Department. After being transferred three different times, I was finally able to give Lard Ass's address to someone who added it to the report and promised to pass it on.

I knew it could well be a month before they sent someone out to get him, but at least my call began the process. I was online for the next hour Googling Ash Lake and the Gold Club. I got more information than I wanted on the lake and found nothing related to Casper Trickle's Gold Club getaway.

Louie had a court appearance that afternoon and left the office just before 1:00.

I filled Morton's water dish a little before 2:00, tossed him a biscuit, and headed over to Melissa's school. I arrived fifteen minutes before the end of class and was sitting in my car when my cellphone rang, Junior Swindell.

"Yeah, Junior, what's up?"

"Hi, Dev, just drove past the address on Jackson Street. The Chevy Camaro has been there all morning, and now it's gone. I didn't see it leave, so it happened sometime in the last sixty minutes."

"Okay, Junior. Stick to your schedule. Let me know if you see anything or if it ends up parked behind that dive bar again. You gonna need to get paid again to-night?"

"No, Mollie's got dinner with her folks, and then she's going back to her place. I got a night off, and not that I haven't enjoyed it, but I could maybe go for a little rest."

"Yeah, well, don't call me in the middle of the night telling me you changed your mind."

"Not to worry, Dev. If I see that Camaro, I'll give you a call," he said and hung up.

I entered the school five minutes before the bell was set to ring and went to the front office. Audrey was on the phone. I gave a wave, and she pointed at a chair. I sat down and waited.

The bell rang, and she continued talking for another ten minutes. Eventually, my phone rang.

"Hi, Melissa, how are you?" I answered.

"Fine, just wondering if you're going to be able to make it over this afternoon."

"I'm already here," I turned away from Audrey, now laughing on the phone, and lowered my voice to almost a whisper. "I'm in the front office, but Audrey's on the phone."

"Oh, okay, no problem, we'll come to you."

"That would be great," I said, and she disconnected. They stepped into the office a minute or two later.

"Oh, thanks for bringing him. You all set to have some fun, Liam?"

"Yeah, can't wait. I've been doing some exercises at night."

"Exercises?" I said,

"Sit-ups," Melissa said and grinned.

"Great idea. Let's get started. We'll be back at the usual time," I said. Liam, with a little prodding on my part, thanked his mother and said goodbye. I waved at Audrey, still on the phone, and we hurried out to the car. I did a quick look around, didn't see anything that resembled a black Chevy Camaro, and we drove to the rink.

Twenty-seven

We did more ups and downs and finished with fifteen minutes of laps around the rink. Liam still fell two or three times per lap, but we had picked up speed. In fact, he could keep up with me skating backward, so I had to turn around and skate alongside him. When he fell, he was immediately back up on his feet and picking up speed. I don't know who was more tired when we finally finished, Liam or me. I'd worked up a sweat just trying to stay ahead of the kid.

There was no sign of the black Camaro. We pulled into the school parking lot, and I delivered Liam to his mother.

"How did it go?" Melissa asked.

"Those sit-ups must have done the trick. Liam was skating so fast I could barely keep up."

Liam grinned at that. "And I can get up really fast when I fall," he said.

"Yes, he can. Okay, I'll see you tomorrow, Liam. Keep going on those sit-ups. They're really helping."

"Thank you, Dev," Melissa said.

"My pleasure."

I walked down the hall and was just about to step outside when Audrey opened the door to the front office and said, "Might I have a moment of your time, Mr. Hassle?"

I followed her into the office. She turned to face me, leaned against the front of her desk, and crossed her arms. "I just wanted to make you aware. A few minutes after you left, a black car pulled into the lot. I just happened to be walking past the door and looked out and saw it."

"A black Chevy Camaro?"

"If you say so. I don't know cars very well, but I recognized the man seated behind the wheel and—"

"Jeremy Lawrence?"

"Yes. He's not allowed on school property and certainly not allowed in this building. I locked the door and called the police."

"Did they come?"

"Oh, yes. They get a call from a school, they're here immediately. I suspect he saw me watching him at the door and left. The police have been past two other times since then that I'm aware of."

"Did you speak with them?"

"Yes, initially, they came into the office."

"Let me leave some information for you," I said. There was a large copy machine off to the left, and I grabbed a blank sheet of paper from the tray. I pulled out my note with the license number, wrote it down along with Lawrence's address and phone number. "I would recommend that you phone this information to the police. They'll have a report filed, and this should be added to it. If it's you calling, they'll pay attention. Have you seen him here in the past?"

"Yes, he would show up at different times on any given day last spring. Haven't seen him at all this fall, but obviously, that just changed."

"Thank you for letting me know. Did you mention this to Melissa?"

"Not yet, but I intend to before she leaves. I don't want this individual anywhere near our school."

"I couldn't agree more. Please let her know today as soon as you can. I'll get in my car now and do a check around the neighborhood. Two of us are keeping an eye on her home throughout the day. He's been a problem of late, more harassment and intimidation rather than anything physical, but his behavior is simply unacceptable, and I won't stand for it," I said.

"Thank you. I can't tell you how happy I am to hear you say that. I've been so worried about her ever since she began this divorce proceeding."

"Yeah, this has been going on for far too long."

I went out to my car, looking around in all directions as I did so. I walked around the car just to double-check my tires then did the same thing to Melissa's car. I couldn't spot anything out of order on either vehicle. I climbed behind the wheel and pulled out onto the street. I did a quick tour of the streets around the school and then drove along the route Melissa would take home. I never saw anything resembling the Camaro.

I waited down the block on Melissa's street. I was just about to call her when she suddenly appeared, drove down the block, and turned into her driveway. I waited another five minutes after she and Liam had entered the house just to be sure they hadn't been followed.

I drove down to the office. Louie wasn't in, and it was too late for court to still be in session, so I figured he was probably over at The Spot since his car was parked on the street. I turned off the coffee and dumped what was left down the sink. I grabbed Morton, and we took a quick walk for a couple of blocks. I put him in the back seat and drove over to Jackson Street. The white Mazda and the station wagon were parked behind Greasy's, but Lard Ass's Camaro was gone.

We drove back down to the office. I parked behind Louie's car, and we walked over to The Spot. It wasn't quite 6:00, and the place was pretty full. Morton immediately had the leash pulled taut as he headed down the bar. Mike was in the process of filling beer glasses at the tap, and I gave him a signal to get a round for Louie and me. He nodded in reply.

As we turned the corner, Louie drained his glass, grabbed a bag of pork rinds from the rack, and poured half the bag into his hand.

Morton's tail began wagging and banging against the side of the bar.

"Oh, Morton, talk about a long day, and you were stuck with Dev for most of it. I think you could use some sustenance," Louie said and leaned down with his hand full of pork rinds.

Morton had Louie's hand licked clean in about two seconds.

"How'd the skating lesson go?" Louie asked.

"Liam's making progress. He's doing really well. He's skating fast enough that I can't lead him skating backward anymore. I have to be alongside him. If he falls, and he does that regularly, he's right back up."

"And he still likes it?"

"Yeah, in fact, his new thing is doing sit-ups to improve his skating."

Louie shook his head and laughed. "That's perfect," he said just as Mike arrived with a fresh drink and a beer. "I got this, Dev. Put it on my tab, Mike, and don't forget to add the bag of pork rinds."

I stayed for two beers. Louie gave Morton the rest of the pork rinds, and we headed out the door. I looked up and down the street but didn't see the Camaro. We took the long way home and drove past Melissa's. All the lights were off on the first floor. They were on upstairs in the bedrooms. I drove around a couple of blocks, but thankfully, I didn't see the Camaro anywhere. As long as we were taking the long way home, I drove over to Jackson Street and turned just before Greasy's. The two cars were still parked in back, but the Camaro was nowhere to be seen.

There was nothing I could do about that, and so we headed home.

Twenty-eight

I'd just pulled into the driveway when the phone rang, Melissa. If she was calling me now, it couldn't be good.

"Melissa, everything okay?"

"It's Jeremy. He keeps driving past the house."

"I'm on my way. If he stops in front or gets out of the car, don't do anything. Just keep the doors locked. I'm there in ten minutes."

I lied. It was closer to six minutes when I pulled in front of her house. The lights were still off on the first floor, but now all the curtains were pulled. On the second floor, the only light on was Melissa's bedroom. I figured if Liam wasn't already asleep, there was a good chance he would spend the night in her bed.

I turned off my car and waited. Maybe fifteen minutes later, a pair of headlights turned onto the street, heading my way. The vehicle stopped, made a U-turn, and disappeared. I was tempted to follow but didn't. Instead, I phoned Junior.

"Hey, Dev," was how he answered over the music blaring in the background.

"Hi, Junior. You doing anything tonight?"

"Sipping a beer and watching the game on TV. We're losing, again, in case you didn't know."

"Interested in working tonight?"

There wasn't even a pause. "Yeah, sure. Are you at Melissa's house?"

"I am," I said and went on to give him a brief update.

Junior pulled in behind my car thirty minutes later. I climbed out of my car and walked to the passenger side of Junior's Buick Enclave. As I opened the passenger door, it screeched loud enough that I was afraid I might wake the neighbors. Junior tossed the pizza box and the six-pack into the back seat.

"Thanks for coming on such short notice," I said as I climbed in. The car smelled of fresh pizza, and my stomach growled. I waited a long moment, but Junior never offered me a piece. "Lard Ass has been going past every so often, driving Melissa crazy. I think he may have been here about a half-hour ago. He saw my car and took off. You up for sitting here for a while?"

"If you're up for paying me, I got nothing better to do."

"Yeah, happy to pay you. Let me know how long you stay. I'm going to head over to Greasy's, see if his car is there and suggest he quit bugging Melissa."

"Two guys would make a better impression. You want me to go with you?"

"Thanks, but I want to keep things calm. Just sit here. Chances are he may not be at Greasy's. I've got

Morton in the back seat, and it's time to get him home. You're good to go?"

"I'm all set, don't worry about me. You go deal with this guy. Hope you can find him."

"Yeah, me too. Thanks, Junior. Give me a call tomorrow, and I'll get you paid," I said and climbed out of his car. We drove over to Greasy's. Surprise, surprise, the Camaro was parked in the muddy parking area in back. I drove down the alley and parked on the next street. I left Morton asleep in the back seat and walked down the alley.

I went in the front door at Greasy's. The place wasn't quite half full. I recognized the bartender from the other day. Tonight he was talking to two women who looked like they couldn't wait to leave. The same bald guy as before was passed out at the end of the bar. There were three guys at a table in the far corner. I recognized all three from a case maybe two years ago. One of them gave me the finger and an evil eye, but he didn't get up. I looked around and couldn't see anyone the size of Lard Ass. I figured this might be a good time to leave. I stepped back outside and walked around to the rear of the building.

There was no point in leaving a note on the windshield of the Camaro. I had a small bottle opener attached to my car keys. I gave a quick look around, then bent down and shoved the bottle opener into the side of the front tire on the driver's side. When I pulled the opener from the tire, I heard a slight hiss. I did the same thing to the rear tire, just like Lard Ass had done to Trickle's Mercedes.

I walked back to my car and drove off. I decided to stop at the bank ATM, grab some cash, pay Junior for his time, and send him home. No point in him having to sit outside Melissa's in his car all night.

When I turned onto Melissa's street, Junior's car was still parked in front of her place. The car appeared to be rocking back and forth. As I drove closer, I noticed all the windows were steamed up, and yes, the car was definitely rocking back and forth. I drove past and gave a quick glance, but with the steamed-up windows, I couldn't see anyone. I headed home, parked in the garage, and we went up to bed.

I was up before my alarm the next morning. Morton was still asleep, so I hopped in my car and drove over to Jackson street to check on the Camaro. I didn't have to hurry. It was still parked behind Greasy's, leaning to the left. I stopped at the bank, got more cash from the ATM, and drove down to Melissa's. I pulled behind Junior's rusty Buick Enclave and tooted my horn a couple of times. A shadow suddenly rose in the back seat, and the door opened a moment later. Junior appeared, buckling his belt and zipping his fly. He gave a wave and hurried into my car.

"Hey, how'd it go last night?" I asked. I didn't bother to comment on the red lipstick smeared on his left cheek.

"Mmm, better than expected."

"Anything happen?"

He gave me a look for a moment and then said, "Oh, yeah. You mean with Lard Ass. No, nothing, never saw him."

"Good, thanks for coming on such short notice," I said and handed him the cash.

"Believe me, my pleasure. Glad I could help," as he stuffed the cash in his pocket.

"Maybe take the day off. Give me a call after you've rested up."

"Thanks, Dev," Junior said and got out of the car.

I watched as he climbed in behind the wheel. He looked into the back seat and seemed to say something. He nodded, started the car, and drove down the street. I waited a minute and drove home to let Morton out.

Twenty-nine

We were down at the office and had the coffee going before Louie arrived. My phone rang around mid-morning. "Heidi?"

"Hi Dev, are you still investigating Casper Trickle?"

"Yeah, investigating might be too strong a term. I'm just checking him out, but I haven't come up with much. I did learn that when things get really bad, he flies up north to a lake that's twenty miles from the nearest road. Oh, and apparently, he has unhappy clients quite often."

"No surprise. I'm meeting with some people who fit your description of 'unhappy' later today. Wondered if you might want to join us."

"What time would that be?" I asked, thinking about Liam's skating lesson.

"We're meeting at 5:00 in a room on the second floor of the Gnome."

The Gnome, a bar and restaurant just a block from my place. "Yeah, I would love to be there. Anything I can do to help? You need someone to set up chairs or tables?"

"They're going to take care of all that. I'm just going to be an attendee. A couple of attorneys will actually run the thing. It's open to the public. They've sent emails to current and past clients of Trickle."

"5:00 at the Gnome. I'll be there. I look forward to seeing you," I said, hoping I might get her thinking about some possibilities after the meeting.

"Yeah, maybe we can get together afterward and catch up," she said.

"I'll be sure to be there."

Louie arrived with lunch just before the noon hour, Big Macs and fries. He'd been at the courthouse all morning, waiting for three hours until his client's name was called and they made their ten-minute appearance. "The good news is she got off with a warning. The bad news is I'm going to bill her for four hours," Louie said through a mouth full of French fries.

I went on to tell him about my phone call from Heidi.

"Sounds like she's going against her better judgment and suggesting a late-night rendezvous with the likes of you."

"One can only hope."

"You might want to think about changing. You know, at least wear a clean t-shirt, maybe shave."

"I was up and out early, checking out Lard Ass. I think he's going to be tied up for a day or two, so the timing on this meeting is perfect."

"You know it's probably best if I don't ask how or why he's going to be tied up. But a thought just crossed my mind."

"Oh?"

"You mentioned the other day that Tubby had you looking into Casper Trickle. Would this meeting be something he might find interesting? Maybe he received an email announcing the meeting, but maybe he didn't."

"And you're thinking I should call him?"

"What would it hurt? Even if he knows about the meeting, you'll still appear like someone who wants to be sure he's not missing out on some potentially valuable information."

I had to admit that didn't sound half bad. I pulled out my cell and called him.

"This is Mr. Gustafson's office," a pleasant voice said. Clearly, it wasn't Tubby who answered. For one thing, whoever it was sounded polite. Besides that, he didn't yell at me.

"I'd like to speak to Mr. Gustafson, please."

"Who may I say is calling?"

I knew for a fact he had my caller ID on a screen in front of him. "My name is Devlin Haskell. I have information for Mr. Gustafson regarding an investigation. He suggested it would be the wise move not to share this information with anyone other than himself."

"One moment, please, while I see if Mr. Gustafson is available." I heard a click, and suddenly I was listening to classical music. This was not the Tubby Gustafson that I knew. The voice was back thirty seconds later. "Please hold while I connect you."

"What in the hell do you want, Haskell?" Tubby growled into the phone. This was more like it, and I began to feel at home.

"Thank you for taking my call, sir. I just received a phone call from someone who informed me of a meeting at five this evening. The meeting is being conducted by a legal firm involved in a lawsuit dealing with Casper Trickle. I thought you might be interested in attending."

"There you go, trying to think, Haskell. Always a mistake on your part. No surprise. If I had to guess, I would say this is being conducted at the Gnome restaurant. Certainly, nothing will be discussed that I don't already know."

"Possibly, sir. I just thought you should know that—"

"And if you would recall my statement from five seconds ago, thinking is always a mistake on your part, Haskell." Click.

I picked up Liam for skating. Another day of obvious improvement, and I extended our time doing laps around the rink from fifteen to twenty minutes. He fell once or twice on each lap, but he had definitely increased his speed. I returned him to Melissa, who invited me to dinner.

"Oh, Melissa, thank you. I'd love to join you, but I've got a 5:00 meeting I have to attend regarding a case I'm working. Could I take a rain check?"

"Of course you can," she said, but given her tone, I thought it might be unwise to suggest I could show up with wine later on.

I picked up Morton at the office and hurried home to get cleaned up. I arrived in the upstairs room at the Gnome shortly after 5:00. Fortunately, the meeting hadn't started. Unfortunately, the room was full, and there was standing room only. I spotted Heidi in a chair up towards the front. Her back was toward me, so I couldn't get her attention. I did note that she had changed her hair color to a deep burgundy.

There was a bar off to the side with a line of people waiting to order a drink. I stepped into the line and was back leaning against the wall five minutes later with a beer in my hand. Fat Freddy and Tubby entered the room. They didn't see me and walked up to the very front. Two guys stood who had clearly been saving seats for them. The meeting got underway as soon as Tubby was seated.

There were a lot of questions asked that went right over my head. The anger in the room was palpable. Two people suggested the death penalty and received a round of applause. Heidi didn't ask any questions, but I noticed she was recording the entire event.

After ninety minutes, things began to wind down, and once the same questions were being asked for a third or fourth time, the meeting ended. I waited for Fat Freddy and Tubby to head for the door and met them at the staircase. "Pleasure to see you here, Mr. Gustafson."

Tubby shook his head. "Nothing's going to happen. The attorneys will sign up more clients for their class-action suit and prolong the case for years. I'll expect to see you at 10:00 tomorrow morning. Are you capable of driving yourself, or do I need to send someone so you arrive on time?"

"Oh, yes, sir. I can certainly drive myself. I'll be there at 10:00. You can count on me, sir. I'll be there."

"We'll see," Tubby said and slowly headed down the staircase.

"You better be there," Fat Freddy said just under his breath before he hurried down the stairs to catch up to Tubby.

Thirty

I walked back into the room to look for Heidi, hoping I might get lucky, but I couldn't see her. I searched for a while and eventually walked back down the block to my place. Just for fun, I drove over to Greasy's and checked the parking area in the back. The Camaro was still parked in the same place and definitely leaning to the left. It hadn't been moved, which meant that the soonest it could have new tires would be maybe noon tomorrow.

I was tempted to flatten the other two tires but then remembered the three bad actors inside Greasy's last night and thought it might be better to leave while I had the chance.

I drove over to Heidi's, hoping she was home, and we could maybe put the evening on a more interesting track. Her car wasn't parked in front, so I drove around to the back and parked. I opened her garden gate and peeked in the garage window. No car, but there were three boxes stacked against the far wall, and I remembered her comment about Cletus Devon and the nice clothes she offered.

Luckily, the side door was open, and I stepped in. The top box appeared to be filled with shirts, silk shirts. I tried on two, and they fit. I set the box off to the side. I opened the next box, trousers. Nice trousers. I pulled off my jeans and slipped on the top pair of trousers. They were a perfect fit. I tried on two more pairs, and both fit perfectly. I pulled off the current pair and was standing in my boxers and t-shirt when I heard a click and the garage door suddenly opened. Heidi's rental car pulled ahead maybe a foot. She saw it was me and turned on her bright lights. She lowered her window and shouted, "Don't let me stop you."

I stepped to the side and waved her in.

"How nice to come home to a strip show," she said as she climbed out of the car.

"I looked for you after that meeting at the Gnome but couldn't find you."

"One of the attorneys wanted to chat."

"I know how that can be. Say, as long as I'm here, maybe we—"

"Oh, sorry, Dev. I wish we could, but he's actually coming over here once he picks up dinner. We're, umm, going to discuss things further."

I had a comment on the tip of my tongue but decided it would be better just to shut up. "Well, let me just pack this stuff up, and I'll donate it for you."

"Maybe put your jeans back on before you leave. I need to hurry inside. I've got to get things ready."

"Don't let me hold you up."

"Just be sure to lower the garage door when you leave," she said and hustled toward the house. I thought about waiting around and decided that would be one of the dumbest things I'd done in a long time. I tossed all three boxes into the backseat and lowered the garage door. I drove around the block just as a black Mercedes pulled to a stop in front of Heidi's house.

I recognized the guy from the meeting as he climbed out of the car. I gave him the finger as I drove past. He didn't see it because he was pulling bottles of wine from the back seat. I watched in the rearview mirror as he headed up to Heidi's front door.

I drove home, stacked the boxes in the entry, and checked the time. It was still pretty early, so I put Morton in the car, and we drove down to The Spot. Louie was waiting with a handful of pork rinds when Morton came around the corner of the bar. "Oh, Morton, patience personified," he said as Morton licked his hand clean. "You go to that get-together regarding Casper Trickle?"

"Yeah, a lot of unhappy people. Thanks for the advice on calling Tubby. He apparently knew about the meeting, and he was there with Fat Freddy. I had the distinct sense the thing didn't start until Tubby arrived. I talked to him afterward, but he sounded less than impressed."

"Still, good you gave him a call."

Mike appeared with a beer for me and topped up Louie's drink. We chatted for nearly an hour. I had another beer and decided to head home. I took the long way home so we could drive past Trickle's house. I could see flashing lights from three blocks away. I stopped two doors before Trickle's and watched. He was on the front porch gesturing with his arms at white graffiti someone had spray-painted all over the front of his house. Two cops appeared to be taking notes and pictures. Arty and Jacob, the weightlifters, were standing off to the side with their hands in their pockets, staring at the ground.

I pulled back onto the street and slowly drove past the house. I read the graffiti as I passed. 'Payback!' 'Think it funy,' and then an image of a hand with the middle finger raised. It had to be Lard Ass. Who else would misspell 'funny'? But why would he do this? What did Casper Trickle do that— It suddenly dawned on me. The two tires I'd flattened last night, both on the left side, exactly like Lard Ass had done to Trickle's Mercedes. This was payback for me slitting the tires on Lard Ass's car. Thank God he hadn't spray-painted my name on the front of the house. I increased my speed and hurried home. I parked in the garage, and we went into the house.

I fell asleep at some point watching a boring movie. The TV screen was black when I woke, and Morton had already gone up to bed. I turned off the lights, looked out the windows for any sign of Lard Ass, and went upstairs to bed.

Thirty-one

Morton and I were down at the office before Louie arrived. I made fresh coffee, and then I sat and thought about the graffiti on Trickle's house until Louie showed up.

He wandered in, his usual red-faced self, a little after 9:00. Once he could finally talk, he said, "You look like you're deep in thought, Dev."

I told him about flattening Lard Ass's tires and the spray paint on Trickle's house.

Louie shook his head. "Smooth move, Dev. The thing I'd wonder about is, how did he get there? If his tires were flat, it's not like he could walk all that way. That's gotta be four or five miles. And then he's gotta walk home? I don't see it."

"I'm wondering if maybe he took a taxi."

"Oh yeah, and then he could tell the driver to wait while he spray-painted graffiti all over the front of that house. Of course, the meter would be running, but what would someone as charming as Jeremy Lawrence care? This was about sending a message. A misspelled message at that."

"Maybe he borrowed or stole one of the other cars parked in the back?"

"I suppose you could ask him," Louie said and laughed.

"I got a better idea. You going to be here for a bit?"

"I'm here until the noon hour," Louie said.

I wrote down Lard Ass's name and address and drove over to Trickle's house. There was a crew on the front porch. The windows and front door were draped in plastic. The work crew was up on ladders sandblasting the front of the house. I turned at the corner and spotted Arty and Jacob lifting weights. I parked and got out of the car.

"How's it going, guys?" I called as I approached.

"We've seen better days," Jacob said and sat up on the weightlifting bench.

"Yeah, what's that they're doing on the front porch?"

Arty shrugged. "Some irate investor spray-painted graffiti across the front porch. They've got to sandblast to get rid of the stuff."

"It's gonna cost Mr. Trickle an arm and a leg," Jacob said.

"Any idea who did it?" I asked.

"We got it on the security tape, but the guy was wearing a balaclava. All we know is he was a really fat bastard."

"You guys saw the tape?"

They both nodded.

"Would it be possible to view the tape? I might have an idea."

"I s'pose we could show it to you. You thinking of anyone in particular?"

"Yeah, but let me take a look at the tape before I say anything more."

They looked at one another. Jacob nodded and said, "You got time now? We made a copy of the tape. It's seven and a half minutes long. Come on in, and we can check it out."

I walked over to the gate and into the backyard.

"Security room is in the basement," Arty said, and they led me down a set of outdoor steps to the cellar entrance. The door was metal with a keypad. Arty entered a code, and as the door buzzed, he pushed it open. I followed them inside.

I expected a dingy basement with boxes piled on shelves and a workbench with rusty tools. Instead, we entered a well-lit hallway with white walls and framed contemporary artwork. There were three doors in the hall. We entered the first one. Another muscular guy was seated behind a desk. Four screens were on a counter behind him. He looked at us, studied me for a moment, and said, "What's up?"

"Jerry, this is the guy named Dev we were telling you about. Sorry, dude, I forgot your last name," Jacob said.

"Haskell, Dev Haskell. Nice to meet you, Jerry."

"He wants to see the spray paint tape," Arty said.

"I'm thinking I might have an idea of who did this."

"Another pissed-off client," Jerry said.

"Maybe, but I've got someone else in mind. I don't think he was a client."

"Perfect, another bunch that's pissed off at the boss."

"Let me view the tape before we jump to any conclusions," I said.

He pulled a laptop off a shelf and turned it on. After a moment, he typed in a code and turned the laptop toward me. The tape began to play. After a second or two, a very fat guy dressed in black and wearing a balaclava appeared. He quickly glanced around, uncapped the spray paint, and began. I recognized him within five seconds—Lard Ass with the cast on his right arm. The time displayed in the lower right corner read 02:23:16, sixteen seconds, and twenty-three minutes after two in the morning and counting.

Lard Ass proceeded to draw the hand with the extended middle finger. Only thirty seconds had passed, and I stopped the tape and said, "Okay, I've seen enough. I know who that is."

"You do? Are you sure? He's wearing that damn balaclava," Jerry asked.

"Yeah, I know him, or actually, I know of him. We've never formally met. He's that fat, and if you noticed, he's got a cast on his right arm, broken wrist or hand, I think. I've got a client he's been hassling for the past eighteen months. She's got a restraining order on him."

"And he's not one of Mr. Trickle's unhappy clients?"

"I don't know that for sure, but I'd be very surprised if he was. He doesn't have the dough. Here's what I think happened," I said and looked at Jacob and Arty. "When you guys drove me over here the other day to meet with Mr. Trickle, this idiot probably followed us. He figured I was a friend of Mr. Trickle, and that's why the spray-paint. He did the same thing to my house maybe a week or so ago. If you look closely, his right arm is in a cast. That's from me knocking the spray paint can out of his hand with a baseball bat. He's the same guy who slit the tires on the Mercedes. He drives a black Camaro."

"You got a name on this bastard?" Jerry asked.

"Yeah, Jeremy Lawrence. He's been living under the radar, but I was able to track him down. Lives over in the nine hundred block of Jackson Street above some sleazy bar named Greasy's. I think he's renting a one-room dive there."

Jerry turned the laptop around, studied the image, and slowly nodded. "Yeah, you're right. I thought it was some stupid spray painting glove, but it's a cast on his right arm. I don't know many guys that fat. What'd you say this piece of crap's name was?"

"Lawrence, Jeremy Lawrence. The address of Greasy's Bar is 980 Jackson Street. He lives in one of five units above that sleazy joint."

Jerry wrote down Lard Ass's name and address. "Thanks, we'll be sure to report this to the powers that be."

I took that to mean they weren't going to get the police involved.

"Glad I could help," I said. Jacob and Arty escorted me out of the basement. They said thanks, and I went back to the office.

Thirty-two

I had just climbed out of my car and was about to cross the street when a Cadillac Escalade screeched to a stop. Fat Freddy Zimmerman lowered the passenger window and said, "Haskell, you have once again disappointed his highness, Mr. Gustafson. Suffice to say, you're in one hell of a lot of trouble."

Oh, God. I'd completely forgotten about my 10:00 meeting with Tubby. "You mean he didn't get my phone call?" I asked. "I saw a child get hit by a sports car, and I took him to the emergency room. Don't know who the kid was. As soon as the emergency staff took charge, I thought the best—"

"Save it, dumb shit. Get in back and think about coming up with a better line. Go on, get in."

"Do you think this will take long? See, I've got—"

"Get your stupid dumb ass in the car, Haskell," Fat Freddy shouted. I decided that might be a good idea.

The ride to Tubby's was quiet. Thankfully, idiot Austin wasn't behind the wheel. No one said a word. Fat Freddy was busy sending a text message on his phone, so I took his advice and tried to come up with a better excuse. I never found one. I was searched by one of the guys outside front door and searched again by the guy just inside the front door. We walked down the hall. Freddy opened Tubby's office door as he knocked on it and pushed me in.

The massage table was erected just in front of Tubby's desk. Naked Tubby was stretched out on the table. I would normally have focused on the two scantily clad attractive women massaging Tubby's dimpled, hairy shoulders, but I couldn't take my eyes off his jiggling fat oozing over the side of the massage table. Fortunately, a large white towel was draped over his massive midsection.

"Umm, sorry I'm a bit tardy Tub—err, Mr. Gustafson. I saw a small child hit by a fire truck, and I—"

"Shut up, you nitwit. Suddenly it's a fire truck. You told Frederick it was a sports car not fifteen minutes ago. Lord, give me strength. I want an update on this low-life, Casper Trickle. Now, do you hear me? Now, damn it!"

"An update, well sir, let me see. Mr. Trickle's home had graffiti spray-painted across the front of it last night. He's got a crew removing it as we speak, sandblasting, actually. Other than that, with the exception of a guy with a leaf blower, there's been absolutely no activity at the Trickle residence."

"Someone with a leaf blower? For the love of God. Has he been paying his mortgage? Have his bank accounts been closed? Are they overdrawn? Any women spending the night?"

"I'm sorry, sir, but I don't have a handle on any of those circumstances, at least at the moment."

"Why am I not surprised? For the love of—pay attention, you nitwit. Here is what you are going to do, Haskell. I want a full report in the next twenty-four hours as to the status of this ne'er do well. If he is planning to leave town, I want to know. If he is going to fly to this mystery cabin of his—"

"The Gold Club, sir."

"Whatever, and don't interrupt me again. Frederick, if Haskell interrupts, you have my permission to cut off one of his fingers. I need to know what Trickle's immediate plans are. Do you hear me?"

"Yes, sir. Have you picked up on something I'm unaware of? Do you think he's going to be leaving town for a bit?"

"Leaving town for a bit? Are you listening? He is about to flee the scene, Haskell. His stock price has fallen forty-three percent just this morning, and it's not even noon. Leaving town? He'll probably flee the country. Go, you are through wasting my time. I want you to find out some current information for a change and report back to me no later than tomorrow, and God help you if you forget."

"I just wonder if—"

"Begone!" Tubby shouted. His chins wiggled back and forth, and his face was suddenly red. The two women massaging suddenly applied more pressure to his dimpled, hairy shoulders.

Freddy took hold of my arm and led me out of the room. Once he closed the door, we hurried to the front door. "I gotta ask you, Haskell. At what point do you start to cop on, or are you always this dense?"

"I know he's upset, but I didn't know why. I'll try to find something out. I would like to add that when he called me in on this, he specifically told me to find out personal information and not to worry about the financial and technical stuff because that was out of my element. Now all of a sudden, I'm supposed to come up with what went wrong with his financial plan."

"That's not what he said."

"Oh, really, so I must have misunderstood when he said the stock price has fallen forty-three percent, and it's not even noon, and I'm supposed to figure out if his bank account is overdrawn."

"Just find out whatever Trickle's plans are. How hard can that be?"

"Well, there you go. Nothing is impossible for the guy who doesn't have to do it."

"Get in the car, Haskell, and shut the hell up."

I climbed into the back seat. The driver held the door for Fat Freddy. Once he climbed in, the driver hurried around to his side and got behind the wheel. They drove me back down to the office. I climbed out of the car and knocked on Fat Freddy's window. He lowered the window, held up his hand as he shook his head, and said, "Don't say a word."

He raised the window, and they sped off up the street.

"Everything go okay?" Louie asked when I entered the office. He didn't bother to look up but remained focused on his computer screen.

"Two words, Tubby Gustafson."

"Oh, sorry to hear that."

I debated canceling the day's skating lesson, but in the end, couldn't bring myself to do it. I phoned Heidi and ended up leaving a message. I searched online for anything on Casper Trickle but, at no surprise, came up empty-handed. I decided to drive past Greasy's on my way to pick up Liam. I drove over to Jackson street. From three blocks away, I could see a smoke plume rising above the roof lines. When I went to turn at the corner, the street was blocked by two fire trucks.

I parked just past the front of Greasy's and made my way through the crowd of a half-dozen people holding drink glasses and watching as the fire crew extinguished the last of the fire behind the bar.

The old Ford station wagon with the fake wood panels and the white Mazda were gone. All that was left of the black Camaro was a smoldering car frame in a pile of foam. The vehicle and even the tires had been reduced to a pile of ashes.

"What the hell happened?" I asked the guy standing next to me.

He drained what was left of his drink, shook his head, and said, "I think it was a fire."

"Yeah, well, I gathered that. What caused it?"

He looked at me for a moment, then examined his empty glass and headed back into Greasy's. The rest of the crowd followed over the course of the next few minutes, and in short order, I was the only one left standing there watching.

One of the fire trucks loaded up and drove off down the street. There were four firemen left. Two of them were standing nearby chatting, and I walked over. "Any idea what caused this fire?"

They both looked at me, and one of them said, "Yeah, some idiot with a match. Lucky it didn't take down the entire building and everyone inside."

"Someone set it on fire? Any idea who?"

They shook their heads. "No idea and no security cameras to check. Someone with an ax to grind or maybe kids being stupid, who knows?"

"You know who owned that car?"

They both shook their heads. I pulled out my note with Lard Ass's name, phone number, and the license plate number on the car. "Here's the guy's name, Jeremy Lawrence, and the license plate number. The car was a black Camaro. I think a 2017. He lives up above Greasy's, and he's a real jerk," I said and nodded at the set of stairs going up the side of the building. One of the guys pulled a pen out of his pocket and wrote the information on the palm of his hand.

After a couple of minutes, I walked back to my car and drove over to the school. When I walked into the front office, Audrey looked up from her desk and actually smiled. "How are you this afternoon?"

"Been an interesting day so far. Any problems with the black Camaro?"

"No, thankfully. But I've mentioned it to the maintenance staff, and I phoned the police. We're keeping an eye out."

"Well, I wouldn't worry too much," I said and went on to tell her about the fire.

"Oh, well, my day has just improved. Does Melissa know?"

"No, actually, I just came from the scene. The fire department was getting ready to leave. There is absolutely nothing left of the vehicle."

"Oh, that's too bad," she said, meaning anything but. The bell suddenly rang, signaling the end of class, and a minute later, the noise level out in the hallway began to increase. "Well, let's get you down to the classroom, and you can give her the information. Oh, this is just wonderful. I can't tell you how happy I am to hear this."

"Fortunately, no one was hurt," I said.

"Mmm, too bad," she replied and led me out into the hall. She delivered me to Melissa's classroom and followed me in. Liam wasn't there yet, which was probably a good thing.

Melissa looked up and greeted me. "Hi, Dev," she said, then looked behind me at Audrey grinning. "Is there a problem?" she asked.

"No problem. Just a day brightener. Go ahead, tell her," Audrey said.

"What is it?"

"The infamous black Camaro is no more."

"What happened? Was there an accident? Did the dealer repossess it?"

"No. Apparently, someone set it on fire. It's completely destroyed, totaled."

Melissa raised her head toward the ceiling, grinned, and said, "Yes! Yes! Yes!"

I nodded and said, "It should give us a break for a bit. But sooner or later, he's going to get a check from his insurance company. It will no doubt be large enough to make a down payment on another vehicle."

"That would be true if he had car insurance, but I'm sure he doesn't," Melissa said and smiled.

"His car wasn't insured?"

"No, he thought insurance companies were scamming him. He paid for insurance just long enough to get the license plates and then canceled the policy."

Liam came into the room, and the subject changed, although Melissa couldn't seem to wipe the smile off her face.

Thirty-three

We moved to the next level in our hockey practice. I gave Liam a stick and a hockey puck and started him stick handling up and down the rink. It seemed to come naturally to him and our final twenty minutes doing laps as he stick handled went much better than expected. On the way to dropping him off with his mother, he asked me what she had been so happy about, and I told him I didn't know.

I dropped him off in Melissa's classroom then drove through the neighborhood just to be sure Lard Ass wasn't lurking around. I drove over to Casper Trickle's place and parked.

Arty and Jacob weren't out lifting weights. The sandblasting crew was gone. The plastic over the doors and windows had been removed, and the sandblasting dust had been swept up. I stepped onto the front porch and rang the doorbell. A brown leather computer bag and four suitcases were lined up on the porch. Two suitcases were black, and two were a cream color with shiny brass corner pieces. The word 'FENDI 'was embossed in the center of the cream-colored suitcases. The brown leather

computer bag was leaning against the black leather suitcases, close to the edge of the porch.

Arty answered the door a moment later.

"Oh, Dev. Umm, we're a little busy just now. Is
there a problem?"

"Actually, no, in fact, just the opposite." I went on
to tell him about driving past Greasy's and the car fire.

His reaction was about what I had expected. He
didn't seem the least bit surprised, which answered my
question. "Well, serves him right. Wish I knew who was
responsible. I'd like to buy them a beer."

"You guys heading out on a trip?" I asked and indicated the suitcases.

"Business trip. Mr. Trickle is heading up north to
umm, concentrate on some new opportunities that have
presented themselves. Jacob and I will make sure there
are no interruptions."

"Oh, up to Ash Lake then. You're leaving today?"

"Shortly, as a matter of fact. I should probably get
back to work, lots to do, and so little time. Thanks for
the update. I'll let Mr. Trickle know that you stopped
by."

"Yeah, please do and give him my best. Have a safe
trip," I said, but he'd already closed the door. I headed
back to my car. Against my better judgment, I drove to
Tubby Gustafson's mansion. I pulled up to the entrance,
climbed out of my car, and pressed the intercom button.

"Good afternoon. How may I help you?" a pleasant
male voice said. Once again, I was amazed. Someone

must have gotten to Tubby and told him to hire a pleasant individual. "Hello?"

"Oh, sorry about that. This is Dev Haskell. I've been working on a project for Mr. Gustafson, and he mentioned he would like the information I've discovered as soon as possible. I would like to see him if he is available."

"One moment, please, while I check."

I listened to pleasant, classical music while he checked. I thought the theme music from Jaws would be more appropriate for anyone waiting to talk to Tubby. The music suddenly stopped, and the polite voice said, "Mr. Gustafson will see you. If you would, please pull into the parking area." The iron gates suddenly began to open, and I hurried back into my car.

I pulled into the grounds and followed the drive up to the parking area. There were three cars and two Harley-Davidsons parked in the spaces. When I climbed out of my car, two armed guards were already waiting for me behind my car.

"Assume the position," one of them said in a tone that left nothing to question. The other guard patted me down, gave the okay, and they escorted me to the front door. Just like always, I was patted down once I stepped inside and then followed the guy to Tubby's office. He knocked on the door, opened it for me, and closed it behind me as soon as I stepped inside.

Fat Freddy was seated in one of the client chairs in front of Tubby's desk. There didn't appear to be any scantily clad women around, but then one could be waiting beneath Tubby's desk, and I'd never know.

Tubby looked up, took a deep breath, and exhaled as I approached. "All right, Haskell. State your purpose for placing a damper on my otherwise wonderful day."

"You said you wanted a current report on Casper Trickle by tomorrow morning, sir. I thought I would exceed your expectations and provide a report this afternoon."

Tubby glanced over at Fat Freddy and said, "Probably what they're going to have for dinner. Very well, Haskell, continue."

"I stopped by Casper Trickle's residence this afternoon, and there were suitcases lined up on the front porch. I interrogated one of his security staff. I threatened him if he didn't give me an answer, and he eventually informed me that they were leaving shortly for the property up in northern Minnesota."

"That place he calls the cold club?" Tubby asked.

"Actually, he calls it the Gold Club, sir. It's located on Ash Lake, and apparently, it's only reachable by plane. The nearest road is twenty miles away through the wilderness."

"How long do they plan to be gone?"

"At least three days, possibly longer, sir."

"Hmm, interesting. That would suggest the shoe is about to drop. No doubt the bottom is going to fall out of Trickle's company," Tubby said as he reached for the phone and punched in a number.

"I wonder, sir, if maybe—"

"Silencio, Haskell. I'm in the process of conducting business, and I…Yes, Desmond. This is Gustafson calling. My shares of Casper Analytics, I wish to sell them. No. I've currently got ten thousand shares. No, sell them all. Yes, immediately. I fear the company may be collapsing. No, nothing like inside information," Tubby said as he nodded at Fat Freddy. "This is more a case of having been booted around the block enough times that I suspect a collapse is on the way. Yes, I'm aware I'll take a loss, but let's limit the damage. No, I want them sold immediately. I'll deal with the damn loss. Let me know when this has been accomplished."

As Tubby hung up the phone, I said, "Glad I could be of service, Mr. Gustafson."

"Time will tell, Haskell. I have my doubts. Unfortunately, I find myself between a rock and a hard place. What's the world coming to when I'm forced to act on information you provide? Anything else?"

"No, sir. Just wanted you to know and thought it would be best to get this information to you as quickly as possible."

"Very well, Haskell. It pains me to say this but thank you."

"My pleasure, sir. Glad to be of service. Might I just say that—"

"Haskell, please see yourself to the door. Frederick, if you would be so kind as to see he doesn't get lost."

"I just thought that—" Fat Freddy was already on his feet. He grabbed me by the arm and led me out of the room. He opened the door, pushed me out into the hallway, and said, "Don't let this go to your head, Haskell." He shut the door, not quite slamming it closed but sending the message all the same.

Thirty-four

I drove out of Tubby's estate and headed back to the office. As I opened the door, Louie snapped awake and smiled. Morton opened his eyes, focused on me, and began to wag his tail, signaling a walk was in order.

"I'd better take Morton for a walk. You going to be here when we get back?"

"Actually, I was just resting up for my appearance over at The Spot."

"Appearance? Are you interviewing someone?"

"Yeah, Mike. I want to see which whiskey he recommends."

"We'll see you over there," I said. I turned off the coffee pot, clipped the leash onto Morton's collar, and we headed down the stairs. We took a nice long walk and were just about to head into The Spot when my phone rang. It was Heidi.

"Hi Dev," she said before I could say 'hello.' "Sorry it's taken so long to return your call, but it's been a crazy day. What's up?"

"I wanted to let you know I stopped by Casper Trickle's a while ago. He and his two security guys are heading up to his place on Ash Lake. This is the joint with no road access, so they have to be flying in. One of his security guys told me Trickle was going to concentrate on business opportunities. Just thought you should know."

"Interesting because the bottom has fallen out of his Casper Analytics stock. I just checked a little while ago, and it was down fifty-three percent."

"I told Tubby Gustafson about it earlier, and he got on the phone, called a broker, and told him to sell. Actually, he said he was aware he was going to take a loss, but he wanted to limit the damage. He said he had ten thousand shares."

"And when was this?"

"About ninety minutes ago. In fact, once he got off the phone, he actually thanked me for the information. Tubby Gustafson has never thanked me for anything, ever, in his life."

"Any idea why he decided to sell?" Heidi asked.

"No, except that the price had dropped, and his security guy told me Trickle was going to concentrate on some new opportunity. That could mean anything, including getting out before things get any worse."

"There's a rumor out there that he's looking to pick up a chip manufacturer," Heidi said.

"Chips? You mean like lime or BBQ flavored chips?"

"No, Dev. I mean the semiconductor chips we've been buying from China that we can't get now. The chips we can't get that have ended up costing car manufacturers two hundred and ten billion and counting. Those kind of chips."

"And some lunatic like Casper Trickle is going to begin manufacturing them? How in the hell is that going to work?"

"It will work well if he's merely funding the manufacturing startup. That's why his stock price is falling. He's sold all his stock. I'll bet he's going to take those funds and put them into semiconductor chip manufacture. That's who started the run on Casper Analytical, Casper Trickle himself. Dev, I'm smelling opportunity, big time."

"What am I missing here?"

"A brain, for starters. You don't get what you just told me?"

"I told you Casper Trickle is going to hide up in northern Minnesota, and you're seeing this as an opportunity to invest. The reason he's going to hide is because his stock is tanking."

"The reason his stock is tanking is because he's sold it. Now Gustafson is pulling out, and I'm sure a number of other large investors will see the decline and head for the hills. People like Gustafson have essentially created a run. The market is reacting because they only have half of the information. Hey, I've got to go and check some things out. I could kiss you for giving me the inside scoop."

"Kiss me? Is that all?"

"Yeah, yeah, not to worry. You'll get a lot more than that. Thank you. Thank you. Thank you," she said and hung up.

I stared at my phone for a long moment, then stepped into The Spot. Morton barked and immediately took off toward the far end of the bar, where Louie was seated reading the newspaper. He lowered the paper, saw us, and pulled a bag of pork rinds from the rack. As Morton came around the corner of the bar, Louie leaned down with a handful for him.

"Oh, Morton, yes, I know. Finally, someone who cares. Someone who knows what's important. Here you go. Dear God, you're beyond patient having to watch Dev all day, every day."

Morton inhaled the pork rinds in about two seconds. He lapped up the one that had fallen onto the floor and then sat staring up at Louie with a pleading look on his face.

"How was the walk?" Louie asked.

"Good. We took a nice long one. Got a call from Heidi just as we were about to step in here."

"Everything okay?" Louie asked and drained his drink just as Mike stepped over to us.

"I'll have a Summit IPA and better give Louie another," I said, and he headed back down the bar.

"Yeah, I think everything is okay." I went on to give him the short version of my phone call with Heidi just a few minutes ago.

"So she thinks Trickle is getting ready to move his business in another direction?"

"It sounds like that's what's already happening. Of course, a lot of guessing, and at the end of the day, we're not going to know until it's over. All I know is she couldn't wait to get off the phone with me."

"Interesting," Louie said and pulled out his phone. He set it down, then proceeded to drum his fingers on the bar, apparently deep in thought.

"Please don't tell me you're thinking of investing in Casper Analytics based on a two-minute conversation I had with one of Trickle's security guys."

"Not Casper Analytics. That's old news. I'm wondering what this new venture is going to be called."

"Look, I like the guy, I mean the security guy, but I'm not too sure about Trickle himself. He's in it just for him, and if you happen to get screwed, well, too bad. That wasn't his intent. I told you I went to that meeting of unhappy people who want to see the guy arrested and locked up for life. There's a number of lawsuits filed against him, but he still doesn't seem to have a problem finding investors. I don't get it."

"That's because you're not a financial guy, Dev."

"Yeah, probably, but if being a fan of the likes of Casper Trickle is what it takes to think financially, count me out. It's funny. Folks wonder how it is I can deal with someone like Tubby Gustafson, but they have no problem giving their hard-earned cash to the likes of Casper Trickle."

Louie seemed to think about that until Mike returned with another beer and a fresh drink for Louie. We toasted one another and changed the subject. I gave him the update on Lard Ass's Camaro and then told him about Liam's skating progress.

"The little guy is doing great. We started stick handling. He's a natural going up and down the rink. Be interesting to see how he does when there are guys trying to get the puck away from him."

"How are things working out with his mom?"

"You mean between the two of us? Well, there's been no time in the sack if that's what you're asking. That said, I've really enjoyed getting Liam lined up skating. The season starts at the end of next week, so we need to get him signed up and on a team. That will be the next big thing, getting him on a team and playing other teams. His mom, Melissa, is happy with it, and at this point, that's good enough for me."

"Well, you've certainly put in the time."

"Yeah, but it's been for the kid, Liam. I didn't do it to impress Melissa. She's got enough on her plate being a single mom and dealing with her jackass former husband. Speaking of which, I passed on his name and phone number to the fire department guys. Hopefully, they'll be one more group pressuring his dumb ass and trying to find out just what in the hell is going on."

"He's not working?"

"Not as far as I know, which doesn't mean he isn't. It just means I don't know. Quite honestly, the few times

I've seen him, he's so fat, I don't think he could do anything physical. Based on the little I know about him, I don't think you'd want him working for you. He'd make life miserable for all the employees around him. He's definitely got some issues."

We chatted for a while. Louie fed the remainder of the pork rinds to Morton, and we headed out the door. Even though I saw Lard Ass's Camaro burnt to a crisp, once we stepped out of The Spot, I still gave a look around just in case. All I saw was a couple of guys grabbing a quick cigarette before running back into the bar for another beer. I put Morton in the back seat, and we drove home.

I pulled into the garage, and we went in the back door. I made myself a chicken sandwich, and we settled in front of the TV. We watched a movie I'd seen before, but it was so long ago that it held my attention, and I didn't remember the ending until the very end of the movie when the woman came screaming out of the bathroom with an ax and pretty much split the bad guy in half.

Thirty-five

I woke to the sound of my alarm going off. Morton simply shoved his head under the spare pillow. I'd been downstairs for a good hour before he made his appearance. Once he was finished with his breakfast, we headed down to the office. For the first time in a long time, Louie was already at his desk, and a fresh pot of coffee was waiting for me.

"Morning court appearance?" I asked as I filled my mug.

"Yeah, in fact, I'm out the door in just a minute. Are you around for the day?" Louie asked as he stuffed a couple of files into his briefcase.

"I've got Liam skating this afternoon, but other than that, nothing is shaking."

"Wish me luck," he said and hurried out the door. I went online and checked out the Casper Analytics stock price, two dollars and eleven cents. One hell of a drop from the forty-nine bucks it'd been at just a couple weeks ago. I was tempted to call Tubby to see what he thought and quickly decided that would be a very bad idea. I phoned Heidi and ended up leaving a message.

"Yeah, Heidi. Dev calling. Just wondering how you're doing. I see Casper Analytics is just a little below a buck-fifty this morning. Give me a call when it's convenient. Time now is 9:05."

I finished another cup of coffee, put Morton in the car, and we drove over to Jackson Street. I wanted to see if the Camaro debris had been removed and if there was a new or different vehicle in its place. Not much had changed. The white Mazda and the Ford station wagon were parked on either side of the blackened Camaro frame. I didn't see anything that suggested Lard Ass had gotten another vehicle. I was about to leave when a woman stepped out of the enclosed staircase and walked toward the White Mazda. She was Asian, and when I made a quick u-turn and pulled in behind her car, she quickly opened the car door and got behind the wheel. I climbed out and hurried over just as she locked her car door.

I signaled with my hand for her to roll down her window. She lowered it no more than an inch.

"Hi. Sorry if I frightened you. My name is Dev Haskell. I watched them extinguish the fire here yesterday," I said and nodded toward what was left of the Camaro. "Do you know the owner, Jeremy Lawrence?"

She seemed to think about that. "I know who you mean," she said with an accent. "I don't really know this man. He lives to me next door. I don't talk with him, and he not talk with me. I find it is better if I stay away from him."

"I know exactly what you mean. Do you know if he got another vehicle?"

"A car? I would not know this. Like I say, I try to keep my distance. Try to keep him away. This is better for me. Yes?"

"Yeah, it probably is. Have you had problems with him?"

"That is something I should not say. I do not want anything to do with this person. I stay away from him. I do not want any trouble. I think that is all you need to know."

I nodded and pulled out a business card. "I'm a private detective, and I've been working with a client that Jeremy Lawrence has been stalking." I slipped my card through the one-inch opening in her window. "If I can be of any help or if you're feeling at all threatened, please don't hesitate to contact me. I've reported him to the police for harassment and for a hit-and-run accident. Fortunately, no one was injured in the accident, but two vehicles were severely damaged. Do you feel safe?"

She seemed to think about that and then nodded. "As long as I stay away from him, yes."

"Well, call me if there's a problem. I've taken up enough of your time. Thank you. Enjoy your day," I said. I hopped back in my car, drove down the alley, and headed back to the office.

Morton settled onto his pillow and closed his eyes. I called Junior Swindell. He answered just before I got dropped into voicemail. "Yeah, Dev," he said, then cleared his throat three or four times. I had the distinct feeling my call, at a few minutes after ten, woke him up.

"Thanks for taking my call, Junior."

In the background, a female voice said, "Come on back here. I'm not—" Whoever she was, and I guessed redheaded Mollie, she was cut off by a door slamming.

"I'm sorry, I missed what you were saying, Dev."

"Just saying thanks for taking my call. Hey, the reason I'm calling. Would you be interested in staking out a place today?"

"Yeah, sure, just tell me where and when."

"It's Lard Ass, actually." I went on to tell him about the car fire. I didn't mention the fact that I'd slit two of his tires. "I have a strange feeling he's got another set of wheels, but I can't spot them. If he shows up, see if you can get a license number and follow him. I'd be interested to see where he goes. Call me, and I'll meet you wherever you end up."

"Yeah, sure, I'm up for it. I'll head over there in a half-hour or so. Just gotta take care of something here."

I guessed he was going to return to whatever I'd interrupted. "Thanks, Junior, keep me posted," I said, but he'd already disconnected.

Another call came through before I set my phone down. "Hi, Heidi. Did you get my message?"

"I did, and I just checked the Casper Analytics price. It's at a dollar thirty-nine and falling. They're going to have to suspend trading soon."

"Any idea what his new operation is called?"

"I'm working on it," Heidi said. "If I can get in there on the ground floor, I'll make sure you get some, too."

"Thanks, Heidi. Let me see what I can find out here."

"Keep me posted," she said and disconnected.

I thought about calling Tubby Gustafson but just as quickly thought that wasn't the best idea. Morton was asleep on his pillow. I picked up the phone and placed a call to Aaron LaZelle. He answered on the second ring.

"Hi, Dev. I've got about ninety seconds before I have to head out. What's up?"

"Sorry to bug you. Anything happening with Jeremy Lawrence?"

"Jeremy Lawrence? Oh, the guy you called me about the other day. Look, Dev, you know how it works. I passed the information on. If they have time, one of the squads will check him out. But you know what's happening in town. We've got a mayor and a city council who are happy thoughts people, and they want to hire social workers instead of more officers. Our guys are exhausted from working overtime. The crime rate is up. Hell, we can't even answer all the 911 calls we're getting. We're short at least a hundred officers, and that's only going to get worse."

"Yeah, I know, and I get it. Just checking in. Someone set Lawrence's Camaro on fire early yesterday morning, burnt it to a crisp. I gave his name and license number to the firemen. Hopefully, they'll get in touch and start things rolling on that end."

"I wish I could do something for you, Dev, but we're dealing with shootings and carjackings at gunpoint in the middle of the day. Instead of hiring more officers, the city would rather spend their money adding more bike lanes."

"I get it, unfortunately. Look, if I come across something, I'll be in touch. Hang in there."

"Thanks, Dev. Gotta run," Aaron said and hung up.

Thirty-six

It was later in the afternoon when Junior phoned. I'd just gotten back to the office after dropping Liam off in Melissa's classroom.

"Hi Junior, anything happening?"

"Yeah, Dev, I'm following Lard Ass. He climbed in that station wagon just a couple of minutes ago. We're headed towards downtown now."

"He's driving that station wagon? That white thing with the fake wood panels?"

"Yeah, you got it. It's the Ford Country Squire that was parked in the back of Greasy's. He had the keys, climbed right in, and headed out onto Jackson Street. It's got a busted right taillight and pretty bald tires. The thing has to be over fifty years old. I'm surprised it can handle Lard Ass stuffed in behind the wheel, but that's what he's driving. Hang on. He just put the right blinker on. Okay, we're turning onto University, heading west."

"Keep me posted. I'm heading over to Jackson Street. That wagon belongs to the older woman living there. I wonder if she's okay."

"Anything happens, I'll give you a call," Junior said and disconnected.

"Come on, Morton," I said and grabbed his leash. I debated leaving Louie a note, decided against it, and we headed out the door.

I parked on the street alongside Greasy's. The only thing in the back parking area was the debris from Lard Ass's Camaro. I climbed up the stairs in the back. The door at the top was locked. I knocked on it a few times, each time a little harder than the time before. No one responded.

I went downstairs and headed into Greasy's. The one customer in the place was the bald guy who was usually passed out at the bar. Today, he was actually sitting up, watching some talk show on the TV. The same jerk as my two previous visits was behind the bar, apparently stuck on a crossword puzzle.

"You want something?" he asked, and just the tone in his voice set me off.

I took a deep breath and told myself to calm down. "Yeah, I'm checking on one of your residents upstairs. I want to see if she's okay. She's an older woman, drives that Ford station wagon. Would you be able to let me in up there? I just want to knock on her door and—"

"You know her name?"

"Know her name? Well, no, I don't, but I'm worried about her, and I was hoping you could give me a key to the door up there or even come with me, just to make sure she's okay."

"So, you don't know her name, and you want me to give you the key to her place. How dumb do you think I am?"

I thought it would be best not to answer that question. "Look, you can come up there with me if you want. It will only take a minute."

"Yeah, and I'm running a business here. I can't just walk out when I feel like it."

Yet another reason not to leave my gun in the car. I thought about going out to get it and coming back in but figured that would be the one call the cops would be able to answer right away. I pulled out my wallet and checked out the cash. A ten-dollar bill was all I had.

"I've got ten bucks. Give me two minutes of your time."

He seemed to think about it, grabbed the ten-dollar bill from my hand, then looked down the bar at the only guy in the place. "Soaky, keep an eye on things. I'll be back in a minute."

The guy mumbled something unintelligible, and I followed the bartender out the door.

"Sorry, but I didn't catch your name," I said as we climbed the stairs.

"Not telling you," he said as he reached the top of the stairs. He pulled out a key ring and unlocked the door. "Which unit is she in?"

"I'm not sure."

"What's her name?"

"Well, umm, I told you, she drives that Ford station wagon."

"So you don't know her name. You don't know which unit she's in, and you're gonna check on her? You trying to play me? I tell you what. Why don't you turn around and get the hell out of here before I call the cops."

"Look, can't we just check to see if she's okay?"

"Her car isn't even parked out back. She's probably running errands or driving around town visiting girlfriends or her grandkids."

"No way. You know who's driving her car right now? That lard ass, Jeremy Lawrence. The big fat guy who lives up here. He's driving around town in her car right now. His Camaro goes up in flames, and suddenly, he's got the keys to her car. I just want to check on her, is all. Can't you just knock on her door? Please?"

He swore under his breath, shook his head, mumbled, "Jesus Christ," and headed down the dim hallway.

I followed right behind him. The hall was painted a light gray color. I could smell the two trash bags that sat outside the door at the far end of the hall. There was a six-inch-wide line of grime along both walls, no doubt from people over the years running their hands on the walls. We stopped at the third door. He shot me a vicious look and rapped on the door three times. Nothing happened.

"There, happy? Now let's get the hell out of—" I reached over and pounded on the door. "What the hell do you think you're doing? All right, that's enough. You're out of here."

"Wait. Hold on. Can't we just see if she's home and okay?"

"No, because she ain't home, dumb shit. If she was, she would have answered when you pounded on the door. So turn around and get the hell out of here."

"But can't you just see if—"

"No, I can't just see if she's home. If she was home, she would have answered the door by now. Get it? So turn around and get out of here."

"But we—"

He pushed me, not too hard, but he pushed me. "I'm warning you. Don't do that again."

"I'm telling you nicely to get your dumb ass out of here. I mean it. Get moving," he said and pointed to the stairs.

No matter what I did, he wasn't about to change his mind. I walked back down the stairs and headed out the door. He locked the door at the top of the stairs and hurried down.

"If something happened to her and it turns out she's up there on the floor with a broken hip or bleeding to death, it's gonna be on you," I said.

He didn't say anything. Instead, he walked to the bar entrance, flashing me his middle finger along the way. "Don't hurry back," he called as I crossed the street to my car.

I climbed in behind the wheel, drove down a block, and stopped. I pulled my phone out and called Junior.

"Yeah, Dev, What's up?"

"That's what I was going to ask you."

"I'm sitting at the McDonald's on University watching your pal inhale a pre-dinner snack of two Big Macs, fries, and a large chocolate shake. They knew him when he stepped up to the counter. Called him by his first name, Jeremy."

"He's not meeting anyone or making a phone call?"

"Nope. He seems quite comfortable being up close and personal with those big Macs."

"Okay, keep an eye on him. Call me if he heads down Melissa's way."

"Yeah, okay. Catch you later," he said and disconnected.

I headed back to the office. I let Morton out of the car, and we went for a short walk. Louie was at his picnic table desk when we walked into the office.

"How'd things go in court?" I asked as I unclipped Morton's leash.

"The usual, we've got an appearance scheduled for a month from now. That gives my client time to get his act together, start attending AA meetings. If he gets that going, it's his first and, hopefully, last time in court, and that'll be it. He screws up again, and he'll pay the price. All well on your end?"

"I'm a little concerned with whatever Lard Ass is up to. Not much I can do about it other than worry." I went on and filled Louie in.

"You think maybe the guy didn't have the key to her unit, and that's why he left?"

"No, I think he was just being a jerk and decided he'd done his bit. I'm wondering if I should go back and wait for the woman in the Mazda to show up."

"You should have gotten her phone number."

"With me suddenly appearing, giving her a card, and asking about Lard Ass, I don't think she was in the mood to give me her phone number."

"Well, if she finds something wrong, she can call the cops, or she's got your number. That's about all you can do at this point."

"I just wish that guy hadn't been such a jerk, but I suspect he's like that all day, every day."

"You know what might help?"

"No, what?"

"A relaxing evening at The Spot," Louie said and turned off his laptop. He placed it in his bag, zipped it closed, and stood. "In fact, that sounds like such a good idea, I think I'll partake. Care to join me?"

"Yeah, I'll be over in a bit. I'm just going to make a phone call."

"I'll save you a place at the bar," Louie said.

I watched out the window as he waddled across the street and stepped into The Spot.

Thirty-seven

I settled in behind my desk and phoned Heidi. After three rings, I got dumped into voicemail. "Hi Heidi, it's Dev. Just checking in. Nothing new on this end. You learn anything else on Casper Analytics?" I disconnected and glanced out the window.

A black Cadillac Escalade was just pulling up across the street behind my car. I recognized the driver from the other day, but I never learned his name. At least it wasn't that brute, Austin. The back seat appeared empty, so Tubby wasn't in the car. That probably meant Fat Freddy was in the front passenger seat, although I couldn't see him to be sure.

I clipped the leash onto Morton's collar, stepped out of the office, and locked the door. We went down the hallway past the hairdressers and a couple of offices. We took the back stairs down to the first floor and hurried out the rear door. We walked down a block, over another block, and back up to the main street where we crossed. I walked up the alley to the backdoor of The Spot and knocked. The door opened almost immediately.

"Oh, Linda, hi. Thanks for letting us in."

"Who are you two hiding from?"

"Oh, we were just on a walk, and this seemed like the logical way to come in."

She shot me a look that said she wasn't buying it and closed the door behind us. Once she locked the door, she looked out the window to see if anyone was following.

Louie was seated on his usual stool with his back to us, reading what looked like the obituaries in today's paper. Morton gave a little bark as we stepped alongside.

Louie looked down and said, "Oh, Morton, sorry, I was just checking to see if they had me listed. Looks like I'll be coming into work tomorrow," he said as he pulled a bag of pork rinds from the rack.

Morton's tail began to wag and bounce against the side of the bar as Louie opened the bag and poured a handful into his hand. Morton devoured them in a half-second. Louie sat up and said, "What's with the secret entry?"

"Fat Freddy's sitting across from the office in the Escalade."

"You want me to go out and see what's up?"

I shook my head and said, "No, I think I'll have a beer first, and then we'll go out there. They can follow us home, or they can go ahead to my place. Either way, I'm going to have a beer."

Mike arrived and took our order. He was back a minute or two later, and I said, "Thanks, Mike. I got this, Louie."

Just as I opened my wallet, I remembered it was empty after giving my last ten bucks to that jerk bartender at Greasy's. "Give me a minute. I gotta hit the ATM."

I was back with a twenty and handed it to Mike. He smiled and headed down the bar. I chatted with Louie for twenty minutes. Morton devoured the rest of the pork rinds, and we headed out to the car. As luck would have it, Fat Freddy was still waiting in the Escalade.

I put Morton in the back seat and walked over to the passenger side of the Escalade and knocked on Freddy's window. He lowered the window and said, "Your presence is requested. Don't even think about saying no."

"Okay, not a problem. I'm just going to take Morton home. You want me to follow you to the mansion?"

"No, we'll take you."

"You sure? If I drive, that saves you the hassle of having to bring me back."

"No, we'll take you there, and if you're a problem, we'll make you walk home, or you if you're a bigger problem, you'll get a ride in the ambulance. Your choice."

"I'll see you at my place," I said and went back to my car. I was wondering what in the world Tubby wanted now. I told him about Casper Trickle flying up north to the Gold Club. I couldn't think of any other information he would be interested in. I parked in the garage, gave Morton a biscuit in the kitchen, and headed out the front door to the Escalade and Fat Freddy.

Just like before, no one said anything as we drove to Tubby's. I was patted down outside the mansion and once again when I stepped inside. Fat Freddy dutifully knocked on the door to Tubby's office, pulled it open, and we stepped inside.

Tubby was dressed and standing in front of his desk, sipping a glass of red wine. He was watching a news report, actually a market report, on TV. "Good evening, Mr. Gustaf-"

"Shut the hell up, Haskell. I want to hear today's numbers." Tubby listened to the report, took a couple of sips of wine, and then pushed the button on the remote, turning the TV off.

"Sit down," he said as he walked around the desk and settled into his chair.

Once I was seated, I thought it might be a good idea to begin on a positive note. "How is that therapy working on your cardiac condition, sir?"

Tubby shot a look at Fat Freddy and then curled his lip in an attempt to smile. "It's an ongoing process, Haskell. Have you heard anything from Casper Trickle?"

"Trickle? No sir, nothing at all. I didn't expect to. As I mentioned earlier, he and his security team are up north at the Gold Club. That's his getaway place up on—"

"I know what the hell it's called Haskell, and I know damn well where it's located."

"He wouldn't be contacting me, sir. I've only met him one time. I do know that his stock has fallen substantially since you sold your shares."

"I had a very decent ride and made it out by the skin of my teeth. I'll expect you to keep an ear to the ground and find out what his next undertaking is going to be. The little I know suggests to me he's already got something in mind. The question is, what? And more importantly, how do I get my share?"

"If I learn anything, you'll be the first person I call, sir. It's just that I have no way of contacting anyone, and even if I could, anything they tell me would be pure speculation on their part."

"Not good enough, Haskell. I'll need information from Trickle sooner rather than later. I do not intend to be making my decision based on information released to the general public. That's where you come in. This is your opportunity to prove you're not as worthless as everyone suggests."

"I'll do my best, sir."

Tubby looked at me, shook his head, and then moved his hand back and forth as if he was brushing crumbs from a table. "Get him out of my sight, Frederick. I can't be bothered." As Freddy led me out of Tubby's office, I heard the TV come back on.

The Escalade had just pulled to the curb in front of my house when my phone rang. I automatically pulled it out and checked the screen. Heidi calling.

"You going to answer that?" Fat Freddy asked.

"I'd rather hear a final word from you. How'd I do tonight?"

"You never fail to disappoint, Haskell. Now get out," he said.

I climbed out of the Escalade and waved goodbye. As they pulled away from the curb, Fat Freddy gave me the finger.

I hurried inside and returned Heidi's call.

"Dev?"

"Sorry I couldn't take your call. I was driving," I lied.

"I don't suppose you were listening to the news."

"No, I wasn't."

"No surprise. Casper Analytics has ceased trading. Let me rephrase that. They've basically gone bust. Are you sure you can't reach your contacts with Casper Trickle?"

"Heidi, they're up in northern Minnesota, in the middle of nowhere."

"That's not what I asked."

"Oh, sorry. No, I can't reach them."

"Let me know if you hear from them. I'll call you tomorrow morning," she said and disconnected.

I phoned Junior Swindell. He answered on the third ring. "How's it going, Junior?"

"The guy finished his Big Macs about an hour ago, stopped at a bakery on the way home, and now he's back in his place above Greasy's."

"I don't see him doing much else. You might as well knock off for the night," I said.

"Any chance I can get paid?"

Not what I wanted to hear, but he had kept an eye on Lard Ass the entire day. "How 'bout you meet me at the bank ATM? I'll get you paid, and you can enjoy the evening."

"That's exactly what I intend to do. I'll see you at the bank."

"Hey, Junior. Before you go, can you write down the license number on that station wagon for me? I'll pass it on to the powers that be."

"Not a problem. See you in fifteen minutes."

Morton had settled onto his pillow in the kitchen. I took a biscuit from the jar, tossed it to him, and headed back out the door. I was just finishing up at the ATM when Junior pulled in front of the bank. I walked over, climbed in the passenger seat, and handed him the dough.

"Here you go, Junior. Once again, I appreciate you helping out on short notice."

"Happy to do it, Dev. This makes for a good night," he said and waved the handful of twenty-dollar bills. "Oh, here's that license plate number you wanted," he said and handed me a yellow cheeseburger wrapper from McDonald's. The license plate number appeared to be underlined by a ketchup stain.

"Thanks for this. If you don't mind me asking, does Mollie ever give you a freebie, or do you always have to pay?"

"It's more subtle than that, Dev. I take her to dinner. I buy her a new top. We go out for the night. That sort of thing. Hey, we're both happy and getting what we want. End of discussion."

"Believe me, I get it," I said.

Thirty-eight

I decided to sleep in and didn't bother to set the alarm. So, of course, I was wide awake at 6:30. I'd been downstairs for an hour before Morton wandered in. I let him out, fried up some bacon and eggs for me, and filled Morton's food and water dishes. We were down in the office before 8:00. Louie wouldn't be in for at least another hour. I made fresh coffee and checked Casper Analytics online. Heidi had been right, trading was suspended. I placed a call to Trickle's security guy, Jacob Hammen, and left a message.

"Yeah, Jacob, Dev Haskell calling. Just checking in to make sure you guys are doing all right. Give me a call when it's convenient. Catch you later."

I grabbed my binoculars and checked out the apartment across the street. Nothing was happening. I drummed my fingers on the desk, debated going past Greasy's to see if the station wagon was there, and decided that would be a waste of time. Louie pulled in across the street a little before 9:00. I had a fresh mug of coffee waiting for him when he stepped into the office, red-faced and breathing heavily. If you didn't know, you'd swear he'd run a half marathon instead of just climbing stairs to the second floor. He gave his standard wave upon entering, pulled the coffee mug toward him, and then focused on a few sips before he said anything.

"So, what's the word?"

"Talked to Heidi last night. Trading was suspended late yesterday. I'm just waiting for him to start up the new company, and I'm going to jump on board."

"You're going to invest in the stock market?"

"Well, actually, Heidi said she would do it for me."

"And you've set aside funds for this?"

"Mmm, I kind of worked out a deal with her, and I—" My phone rang. "This may be her calling now." I pulled out my cellphone. The screen said, 'Number Unknown.' I answered anyway.

"Haskell investigations."

"Mr. Devlin, please," a woman with an accent said.

"Yeah, you got him."

"Mr. Devlin, I Chai Shinawatra." Her voice sounded somewhat panicked and maybe a little familiar, but her name wasn't ringing a bell, and then there was the accent. "We speak yesterday. You give me this card with your number for the phone."

There it was, the Asian woman in the white Mazda. "Yes, thank you for calling. Is everything all right?"

"This I think not. I afraid. I hear her crying last night, my neighbor, and then all is quiet. This fat man is in her apartment. He is never there before, but I hear him. This is not good."

"Did you call the police?"

"This I cannot do."

"Do you need their phone number? You can just call 911, and they'll—"

"No, you do not understand, I think. It is not safe for me to make this call."

It suddenly clicked inside my thick skull. "I understand. Is Lawrence there now?"

"I know not what you mean."

"The fat man, is he there now?"

"No, I watch. He go in her car. I knock on door, but I do not hear her. I not see her go, so she is here. This is what I think."

"Tell me your name again," I said slowly.

"My name is Chai."

"Okay, Chai. I'm going to come over. I will be there in ten minutes. When I knock on the door, will you let me in, please?"

"Yes. This I can do."

"You stay in your apartment until I come. Wait until I call your name and you hear me knock."

"I do this."

"Okay. Goodbye," I said and waited until she hung up.

"Everything okay?" Louie asked as I unlocked the bottom desk drawer and took out my pistol in the sticky holster. I tucked the holster in my belt and headed for the door. "You going to be here for a bit?" I asked.

"I'm here all day. Go on, stay safe."

"Thanks, Louie." I went down the stairs two at a time and dashed out the front door. Fortunately, there were no cars coming. I ran across the street and hopped in my car. I was speeding up the street toward the interstate entrance a moment later. Morning rush hour was ending, but it was still busy on 35E. I made my way into the fast lane and stepped on it. I took my phone out, pushed the speed dial for Aaron LaZelle, and put the call on speaker. I zipped back into the middle lane, sped past two cars that were doing maybe five miles over the limit, and shot back into the fast lane.

Fortunately, Aaron answered. "Yeah, Dev. Hey, I checked. You were wrong. It's your turn to buy. How does next—"

"Aaron, listen up. I just got a call. It sounds like a possible kidnapping or hostage situation."

"Don't joke, Dev. You know—"

"I'm not joking, man. I just got a call from a frightened woman. I'm headed there now if these bastards would get the hell out of my way." I leaned on the horn for a long moment until the guy pulled into the middle lane. He gave me the finger as I shot past him.

"Address?" Aaron said.

"980 Jackson Street. It's the apartments above Greasy's Bar."

"Back in a second," he said.

I cut across three lanes of traffic and took the Cayuga exit. It basically made a three-hundred-and-sixty-degree turn and had me headed toward Jackson Street three blocks away. I was racing in the oncoming traffic lane leaning on the horn as I shot past a half-dozen cars. I checked Jackson Street as I screeched around the corner and sped up. At this hour, most of the traffic was headed in the opposite direction into downtown. Greasy's was eight blocks away.

Aaron came back on the line. "Dispatch has two squads in route. One coming from the Midway area, the other from Lake Phalen. They're maybe eight or ten minutes out."

"I'll be there in two, Aaron."

"Wait for them, Dev."

"Aaron, this is some senior woman. I don't know her condition, but she was heard crying last night. The guy is this lard ass, Jeremy Lawrence. His ex-wife, Melissa, has a restraining order on him. He's been stalking her. I'm turning onto Jenks Street now and going in. I'll be in touch."

"Damn it, Dev. Will you just—"

I turned off my phone and ran across the street. The Ford station wagon was nowhere to be seen. Hopefully, Lard Ass wasn't around, but I wasn't going to take any chances. I shoved the phone in my pocket, put my right hand on my pistol, and charged up the stairs.

I pounded on the door and called, "Chai. Chai. It's Dev Haskell. Open the door. Chai?" I heard a door close and then footsteps, hurrying and getting louder. A moment later, the lock clicked, and the woman from the

Mazda yesterday morning opened the door. Her eyes were red and puffy, and she had clearly been crying.

"Chai, are you okay?"

She grabbed my hand, held on tight, nodded she was all right, and then pulled me down the hall. We stopped at the third door. The same door the jerky bartender had knocked on yesterday. She knocked on the door, and we waited, but nothing happened.

"What's her name?" I asked.

"Is John?"

"You mean, Jane?" I asked.

She nodded. "This is it, Jan."

"I'll try Jane. Jane. Jane," I called and pounded on the door. We heard what sounded like a bump from inside and then another. "Stand back," I said and moved Chai off to the side. I stepped in front of the door, leaned back, and kicked, planting my foot just to the right of the brass doorknob. The door flew open. I pulled my pistol and stepped inside.

Thirty-nine

The room was small, with a tiny kitchen area off to the right. A large, empty pizza box and a half-dozen empty beer bottles sat on what passed for the kitchen counter. There was a black and gray braided rug on the floor. A worn, brown wingback chair was on the far side of the rug, and an older, gray-haired woman with two black eyes was taped to the chair. She wore blue jeans and what looked like a red fleece top. Her legs were taped to the front legs on the chair. The tape appeared to be two-inch wide blue masking tape.

Chai gave a shriek and ran to her. I hurried behind the chair and into the bedroom, looking for anyone hiding. The bedroom and the bathroom were empty. Chai was carefully removing the tape from around the woman's head. I stepped into the kitchen area, pulled a knife from the rack next to the pizza box, and proceeded to cut the tape around her legs. I pulled the tape from her legs and then sliced the tape wrapped around her upper body that was holding her arms against her chest.

Chai was on her fourth or fifth unraveling of tape around the woman's head and covering her mouth.

"Oh, God. Oh my God. Thank you. Thank you. Please hurry, he might come back. Please," she pleaded just as we heard a distant siren.

"He won't be back. You're safe, Jane. Is it Jane? Your name?"

She nodded and squeaked out a hoarse, "Yes. The bathroom. God, I need to use the bathroom."

I helped her out of the chair, and she held onto my arm as we headed to the bathroom. Her legs and upper body still had lengths of blue tape attached. "Are you all right? Can you make it on your own from here?" I asked and held the bathroom door open.

"Yes, thank you, just give me some private time," she said and closed the door behind her. The siren was loud and sounded as if it was right outside and then stopped.

"Chai, the police are outside. I'm going to let them in. I'll be back in a moment."

She gave me a worried look but didn't say anything and nodded. The door at the top of the stairs was open. As I stepped into the hallway, two officers were running up the stairs.

"In here, guys. I think she's okay. My name is Dev Haskell. I phoned Aaron LaZelle in homicide, and he—"

They hurried past me and into the apartment. "Yeah, we heard from him. He's on his way. Are you the victim?" one of them asked Chai.

She shot me a worried look.

"No, her name is Chai, and she called me. She's the one who suspected something was wrong."

"And she didn't call 911."

"She was concerned because her English isn't that good. We just got in here a couple of minutes ago. The victim was taped in that chair. I had to kick the door in to release her. She's in the bathroom now. Her name is Jane, and I would guess she's late seventies. Bloody nose, black eyes, she was clearly beaten. But she seems okay. It would probably be a good idea to call the EMTs though."

"They're on the way," one of the cops said just as we heard another siren.

The other cop stepped off to the side and spoke into the radio attached to his shoulder.

There was a small Formica topped table with two chairs positioned in front of a window. A pile of mail was on the table. Once the cop finished his radio call, he rifled through a couple of envelopes and then carried one over to the bathroom door and knocked softly.

"Ms. McCarry, this is Officer Gibson," he said, reading her name off the envelope. Are you all right?" He waited a moment and glanced over at his partner. "Ms. McCarry. Can you hear me?"

"Yes, yes. If you'd give me a minute, I'm just freshening up."

"There's a medical team on the way. No makeup, please. They'll want to check you out and then take you for a thorough examination."

"I'll be out in a moment," she said just as another siren pulled up outside and stopped. I heard footsteps on the stairs again, this time not charging up. One of the cops stepped into the hallway and called, "In here. She's in the bathroom at the moment," he said just as the bathroom door opened and Jane McCarry stepped out.

Both eyes were black and swollen. The right eye was nearly swollen shut. Her nose and the right half of her upper lip were swollen. Her nose had a bloody split across the bridge, suggesting it might be broken. Bloodstains were on her red fleece top.

"Please sit down, Miss McCarry," one of the cops said and nodded toward the wingback chair just as two more cops stepped into the room.

"Oh, anywhere but there," she said, shaking her head at the wingback chair. She settled onto a small loveseat against the wall.

More footsteps were on the staircase, and a moment later, two EMTs stepped into the room. There were now nine of us in the room, probably more activity than the place had seen in years.

"Officer," I said to one of the first guys on the scene. "Maybe we could step into Chai's unit and give the EMTs some room. I'm sure you have some questions."

Chai gave me a frightened look.

"That might be a good idea. Which unit is yours, ma'am?"

Chai pointed into the tiny kitchen area and said, "Next door."

She led us out of the apartment and into her unit. It was even smaller, much smaller. Basically, a room with a single bed, a wooden chair, and a bathroom. What served as the kitchen area was an antique refrigerator and an electric burner resting on the top of a small bookcase. There weren't any windows, and I was pretty sure there was a laundry list of city code violations.

I sat next to Chai on the bed. The cops asked her most of the questions and took notes. I filled in a couple of gray areas, like my visit with the jerk bartender the day before and information on Lard Ass. I told them about his hit-and-run and Melissa's restraining order, then gave them the yellow cheeseburger wrapper from McDonald's with the license number.

"Oh, hey L.T.," one of the cops said as Aaron stepped into the room.

"How's it going?" he asked.

"You see the woman next door?" one of the cops asked.

"Yeah, they're getting ready to take her down to Regions Hospital for a more thorough examination. She seems okay, other than the bruising, but they want to be sure. Any idea where this guy is right now?"

"Haskell gave us the license number of the car we think he's driving." The cop waved the McDonald's wrapper. "They just put out a BOLO on it."

"If you're finished with us, I'd like to head over to Melissa's school, just in case he decides to show up there. Even if he's unaware we're here, sooner or later, he's going to get desperate."

The cops looked at one another and then at Aaron, who just nodded and said, "I think that's probably a good idea."

I stood and indicated with a nod of my head that Chai should follow me out. Everyone exited the room. Chai locked the door behind her and hurried down the hall. I followed her out of the building and walked her to her car. "Chai, don't worry, they're not going to arrest you. Do you still have my card?"

She nodded.

"If you need a place to stay tonight, call me. I have a room you can use. I think it would be a good idea if you did not go back there until they have arrested Jeremy Lawrence." She gave me a confused look. "The fat man. Do not go back to your apartment until the police have him. Do you understand?"

She nodded and said, "I have girlfriend I stay with."

"Okay, good. Call me if you have a problem."

"Yes, yes. I will. Thank you," she said, then stood on her tiptoes and gave me a kiss on the cheek. She quickly packed a bag and I followed her outside.

I held the car door for her as she climbed into her Mazda. She waved once she backed up and drove off. I went back up to talk with Aaron and to thank him for getting things moving.

The EMTs brought Jane McCarry down to their vehicle. They left with lights flashing but no siren. I filled

Aaron and the cops in on my bogus visit to the apartment with the bartender the day before. Two of the cops headed down to the Greasy's, they did not look happy. I talked with Aaron for a few more minutes and then drove over to Melissa's school.

Forty

I did a quick check of the immediate neighborhood and then pulled into the school parking lot. I entered the building and made my way to the front office. There was a kid in the office seated on the couch. He was probably nine. Whatever the reason he was waiting outside the principal's office, he looked guilty. I was reminded of me at the same age, having yet another meeting with the principal.

"Dev? You're here early. Everything okay?" Audrey asked and stopped typing on her computer.

The principal's office door suddenly opened, and a nice-looking guy stepped out. "William Porter," he said and pointed to a chair in the office. The kid on the couch did not look happy. He swallowed and walked into the office with his head hung down. The door closed behind him.

"What did he do?"

Audrey shook her head. "He had a little rubber ball that amazingly just happened to bounce into the girls' bathroom, and so he went in there after it."

"I got nailed for something similar at the same age."

"I'm not surprised. What brings you in here this morning?"

I went on to tell her about Jane McCarry and that Lard Ass was the primary suspect. "I told the cops I was coming over here. I'm sure they'll probably be doing drive-by's for the rest of the day, but I figured you should know about this. It doesn't have to be right this minute, but at some point, I'd like to let Melissa know what's happened."

Audrey stood up from her desk, shaking her head. "Let me just lock the doors. I'd say I can't believe this, but unfortunately, I can. Oh, poor Melissa, she doesn't need this. Nobody does."

"Well, this is a big enough incident that hopefully something will be done about it. The guy is clearly a nutcase."

Audrey hurried out of the office with a ring of keys. I settled onto the couch just as my cellphone rang. "Dev Haskell," I answered.

"Hi, Dev, Terry Hogan at the rink. Hey, just wanted to let you know, registration has opened up. If you want that kid you've been teaching to get on a team, now is the time to sign him up. How old did you say he was?"

"Thanks for the call, Terry. He's eight."

"If you want to stop in the office this afternoon, you can get him registered. Cost is four hundred bucks. That includes a jersey and socks."

"Four hundred bucks?"

"Yeah, that's the mites league. Like I said, you get the jersey and socks."

"Four hundred bucks? When did that happen? I was thinking it would be fifteen bucks or something."

"You're thinking back in the dark ages when we were kids. Four hundred for the season. You can do monthly payments if you want. It doesn't have to be all at once."

"No, just caught me off guard, is all. Can I stop in the office this afternoon?"

"I'll be here," Hogan said.

"Thanks for the call, Terry," I said and hung up just as Audrey stepped back inside the office.

"There, we're all locked down. Let me just send the word, noon and our fifteen-minute afternoon recess will be indoors today. You said you haven't spoken to Melissa regarding this latest incident?"

"That's correct."

"I'll have her stop in here during the lunch hour. You can update her then."

"Good, and then if it's okay, I'll just remain here until the end of the school day when I take Liam skating. I don't expect any problems, but I'd like to be here just in case."

"I think that would be a wonderful plan. Thank you."

Melissa stepped into the office a few minutes after the bell rang, signaling the lunch hour. "Dev, what are you doing here?"

"Something's come up, and I just wanted to let you know. I don't think Jeremy will show up, but I wanted to be here just in case."

"I've locked the doors to the school. It's why noon recess has been canceled," Audrey said.

"What's happened? What did he do?"

I went on to give her the update. As I explained the situation, her eyes grew wide, and she stood there listening with a shocked look on her face and her mouth open.

"You're telling me he held this woman hostage, beat her, and stole her car?"

"It certainly appears that way. She was taped to a chair in her apartment. He had wrapped tape around her head so she couldn't call out for help. I'm guessing he ate the takeout pizza and drank the half-dozen beers. The EMTs took her to Regions Hospital to get checked out. They'll probably have her spend the night. Police will be driving past the school from time to time to make sure everything is okay. I wanted to be here just in case he does something stupid."

"Does Liam know?"

"No, I mean, how could he? I'm certainly not going to tell him. In fact, I got a call from a pal who manages the rink we've been practicing at. I can sign him up for the league today, and he'll be placed on a team for the season."

"Really? Do you think he's ready?"

"Oh yeah, and frankly, he's at the stage where he'll learn just as much if not more from teammates and a coach."

"So you're going to sign him up?"

"Yeah, as long as it's okay with you. He's put a lot of time and effort into this. It would be a shame to stop it after he's come this far. You might find yourself taking him to games and some of the practices but being on a team would be really good for Liam and the next big step. He's earned it, Melissa. He really has."

"Yes, okay, sign him up this afternoon. As far as Jeremy goes, I'm not going to mention it to Liam unless I absolutely have to. He's got enough pressure and bad experiences without having to pile these charges on top of everything else. Does he ever ask you about his father?"

"No, he's never brought the subject up, even once. Now, I'm going to sit in the office here and keep Audrey company until school lets out this afternoon. Do you want to bring Liam up here after class?"

"Yeah, sure. I can do that. Thank you for being here and thank you for making sure we're all safe." Melissa said and gave me a kiss on the cheek. I grinned, thinking, two kisses in one day, not bad.

Forty-one

I phoned Louie and told him I wouldn't be in the office until sometime after 4:00. I phoned Heidi and ended up leaving another message.

"Yeah, Heidi, this is Dev. Just checking in. Call me when you've got time."

I spent a half-hour or so scrolling through messages and Google posts on my phone. I must have drifted off to sleep because when Heidi's call came through, it woke me up.

"Hi Heidi, thanks for calling me back."

"I've only got a minute, Dev. Listen to this. Casper Trickle is going ahead with helping to fund a semiconductor chip manufacturing facility. We have an opportunity to invest, the two of us. The group will be called Trickle Down, and the initial investment isn't small. They're looking for a quarter of a million."

"A quarter of a million? That's how many of these chip things they're going to make?" Heidi didn't say anything for a long moment. "Heidi?"

"Yeah, I'm here. No, Dev, you misunderstood me again. The quarter of a million refers to dollars, as in we would invest a quarter of a million dollars."

"I don't think I could come up with that kind of cash. In fact, I know I can't."

"I'm aware of that, Dev, no surprise. I'm thinking we work out a deal. Say I loan you ten grand. You work it off, and then presumably you'll make a profit, and that will serve as a nest egg that will allow you to get started and make future investments."

"And you're okay with that?"

"It goes against my better judgment, but yeah, I'm fine with it, Dev, as long as you use it for its intended purpose and you're not taking a hundred bucks out every weekend because you've got a hot date or you want to fly down to Chicago for a baseball game. The path to success here is to stay focused and involved. Do you understand what I'm saying?"

"Yeah, yeah, I get it, and it sounds like a great idea. I'm on board."

"All right. I'll draw up a contract and—"

"A contract? You know how I hate all that formality stuff."

"Yes, and you know how I insist on it. Since I'll be running the show, we're going to be doing it my way. Any further questions? No? Good. I'll let you know what you've signed on to. Thank you, goodbye," she said, never giving me the opportunity to get a word in edgewise.

Two-thirty couldn't come soon enough, but finally, the bell rang, signaling the end of the school day. Audrey hurried out of the office with her keys to unlock the doors. Melissa delivered Liam to the front office ten minutes later.

"Hey, there he is. You ready for practice?" I asked. He grinned and nodded. "Good, let's get going. We should be back at the usual time. Feel free to call if anything is happening," I said to both Melissa and Audrey.

As we headed out to my car, I looked around but didn't see anything like the Ford station wagon. We parked at the rink and carried in our equipment. "Let's stop in the office for a second," I said to Liam. The rink was empty, so we'd have the whole thing to ourselves. Nets were set up at both ends of the rink so we could practice stick handling and shooting.

Terry Hogan was seated at his desk when we stepped into the office. "Hey, guys, you ready to sign up?"

"You bet we are. What do you say, Liam? You ready to play on a team?"

"A team? Really? You mean it?"

"I sure do. Terry, sign him up. Liam, you'll have to give Terry your phone number and address. You take a personal check, Terry?"

"We do, four hundred even and make it out to St. Paul Mites Hockey League," he said.

Liam gave Terry his address and Melissa's phone number while I wrote the check. Heidi's voice was ringing inside my head, 'You're not taking a hundred bucks out every weekend, blah, blah, blah.'

We were out on the ice fifteen minutes later. We skated back and forth. Liam worked on stick handling and shooting the puck. It took some time, but by the end, he was doing reasonably well. When I took him back to school, Melissa met us at the door.

"Everything go okay?" she asked.

"Yeah, fine. Everything all right here?"

She nodded and said, "Yeah, just nervous after your earlier news. No sign of any problems here."

"Good. I'm going to leave Liam in your capable hands. I'll drive past your place just to make sure everything is okay. I told you Jeremy's driving a white Ford station wagon with fake wood panels on the sides. I really don't think you're going to see him. If the police don't already have him, it wouldn't surprise me at all if he's left town, maybe even the state."

"I'm afraid you're giving him too much credit," she said.

"We'll see. Any problems or concerns you call me and don't be afraid to call the police. They're looking for him."

"God," she said and shook her head. "How did it ever come to this?"

"Just be glad you did the right thing and protected yourself and Liam."

"Thanks," she said and gave me a peck on the cheek.

I did a quick drive around the school and didn't see anything. No sign of Lard Ass along Melissa's route home. I stopped at her house and did a walk around the place. Everything appeared to be in order, so I drove down to the office.

Morton met me at the door. Louie was leaning back in his office chair, snoring. I grabbed the leash, and we went for a walk. Louie was just waking up when we returned.

"Oh, there you are," Louie said and followed up with a yawn. "Just closed my eyes a minute to rest up before I headed over to the spot."

"You were snoring when we left for our walk twenty-five minutes ago. You've been out for a while."

"Well, that just goes to show I must have really needed it. I'm going to head over now. You going to make an appearance?"

"Yeah, I've got a couple of phone calls to make, and then we'll catch up."

"See you over there," Louie said as he buckled his computer bag closed and headed out the door. I watched him cross the street and go into The Spot. Once he disappeared, I settled in behind my desk. I sat and thought about Heidi paying ten grand for me in Casper Trickle's new Trickle Down venture. She was smart. She'd made a lot of dough investing, but the idea of owing her ten grand just didn't sit very well with me. And what about Tubby Gustafson? He wanted inside information on

Trickle's next venture. Did I tell him about Trickle Down? If I told him and Heidi ever found out, she'd kill me and then send me a bill for ten grand.

I sat there for a long time, trying to come up with a good answer. It never happened. Eventually, Morton and I headed over to The Spot. I looked up and down the street for Fat Freddy in the Cadillac Escalade or Lard Ass in the Ford station wagon. The coast was clear.

We stepped into The Spot. Louie was seated on his stool, reading the paper. Morton gave a bark as he strained on the leash, pulling toward Louie. Louie was ready with a handful of pork rinds as Morton came around the corner. There was already a fresh beer waiting for me at the bar. I figured things were beginning to look up.

That's when my phone rang. Melissa.

I let go of Morton's leash. "Is everything all right?" was how I answered the phone.

"No. He's following us."

Forty-two

I grabbed Morton's leash, and we hurried out the door, leaving my beer on the bar. "Where are you, Melissa?" I asked.

"We're at the Mall of America. I'm driving through the parking ramp looking for security, but I can't find anyone."

"Is Liam with you?" I asked.

"Yes."

"In the back seat?"

"Like always."

"Does he know what's happening?"

"I don't think so."

"Do you know what your license plate number is?"

"My license plate? No, I mean it's from Minnesota."

"Okay, don't worry about it."

"I want you to head back into town. Take Highway 5. It goes through Fort Snelling, and it turns into West Seventh Street when you take the bridge across the river. Do you know where I mean?"

"Yes. Yeah, I know the area."

"Okay, at the first stoplight, I want you to take a left. That's Davern Street. Follow that for a couple of blocks until you get to a stoplight. That's St. Paul Avenue. Keep going straight. You'll go up a big hill with a patch of trees on the righthand side. I'll be behind you, but if he's still following, I'm going to stop him. Don't you stop, no matter what. You two just get home, okay?"

"Take a left at the first stoplight," she said.

"Yeah. Now, if he's not following, I'll get behind you anyway and follow you home just to be sure."

"Yeah, yeah. Okay. I'm going to pull out of the parking ramp in just a minute."

"I'll be waiting for you. Don't worry."

"Thanks, Dev," she said and hung up.

I opened the rear door of my car, and Morton hopped in. I jumped in behind the wheel, and we took off up the street. I slowed for the red light at the entrance to 35E heading south. No cars were coming, so I ran the light and accelerated down the ramp. West Seventh was the first exit about a quarter-mile ahead. I sped up the exit, slowed to check traffic, and screeched around the corner onto the street. I ran the next two stoplights just as they turned red. Davern was maybe a mile and a half down the road. I was doing fifty in a thirty-five zone. Luckily it was dinner time, and traffic was light. I turned onto Davern Street, drove for two blocks, and pulled over.

From where I parked, I could see the cars in my rear-view mirror as they took a left-hand turn off of West

Seventh and drove past me. I'd been waiting almost ten minutes, and I was thinking of calling Melissa when I saw her silver Ford C-Max make the turn. I pumped my brakes three times. Melissa drove past a few seconds later, but if she knew it was me, she gave no indication.

A car with its blinker on was waiting to make the same turn. Three, four, and finally, a fifth car drove through the intersection in the opposite direction before it was able to turn. I saw a white antique station wagon with wood panels. Lard Ass.

I waited for him to pass. There was no other traffic, so as soon as he passed, I pulled back onto the street.

Melissa slowed for the red light on St. Paul Avenue. Luckily, it turned green before she came to a stop. The street is four lanes with a boulevard in the center. The steep Davern hill begins on the far side of St. Paul Avenue. Melissa accelerated slightly to climb the hill. The space between her and Lard Ass in the station wagon grew. At the top of the hill, she seemed to accelerate some more, creating a greater distance between her and Lard Ass.

That was my chance to pull past him. I accelerated and zipped past. A quick glance on my part confirmed it was him. I pulled back into the lane and pulled up close to Melissa, flashed my headlights, and slammed on the brakes. I put the car in reverse, shouted, "Down Morton, down."

Morton laid down on the back seat as I accelerated in reverse. By the time Lard Ass realized what I was doing, it was too late. He attempted to pull to the right and over the curb, but he'd barely begun to turn when I slammed into him at maybe forty miles per hour. Whatever my speed, it set off his airbag.

Morton bounced off the back seat and onto the floor. My head bounced off the steering wheel and the driver's window. It took me a second to get my bearings. I pulled my keys from the ignition, slid out of the car, grabbed my pistol, and charged toward the station wagon.

Lard Ass was still wedged behind the steering wheel. The driver's door was buckled, but I was able to pull it open. I grabbed a handful of his dark curly hair and pulled, only to find out it was a toupee. I looked at it in my fist for a moment, then tossed it onto the roof of the station wagon. A car driving in the opposite direction pulled over and lowered the window.

"Everything okay?" the guy asked and then focused on my pistol.

"You got a cellphone? Please call the police. This guy is wanted on an assault charge."

"Assault?"

"Call the police. I'm a private investigator."

He nodded and pulled out his cellphone. Lard Ass moved slightly from side to side, but he was still held in place by the steering wheel. I noticed the number thirteen tattooed onto the back of his neck was gone. I took hold of the steering wheel and moved it ever so slightly. Lard

Ass began to wiggle toward the passenger side. He had a bloody nose, and his eyes were focused on my pistol pointed at him.

"I want you to slide out of the front seat very carefully. You try anything stupid, and I will shoot you more than once."

"Cops are on their way," the guy yelled from his car.

"Thank you," I called back, but he was already pulling further down the road. I watched until he stopped around the corner.

Lard Ass looked at me and said, "You, you, tried to kill me. Running into me with that car of yours. I'm gonna sue your ass and—"

I took a deep breath. Placed the pistol in my left hand, wound up, and gave him a solid punch right between the eyes. The blow knocked him back onto the bench seat. His bald head landed on top of a large red container of McDonald's French fries.

"Shut the hell up, Lard Ass. You are done making life miserable for people. You're just damn lucky the cops are on the way. Now get out of this car and sit your fat ass on the ground."

He groaned as he sat up. Blood was running from his nose. He attempted to slide past the steering wheel.

"Not that way, dumb shit. Slide out on the passenger side. I'm warning you. Try to get away, and I'll shoot your fat ass." In the distance, I could hear a siren. A half-minute later, I saw a set of flashing lights.

As the cops pulled up, I slipped the pistol back in the sticky holster. Based on the way they climbed out of the squad car, I figured the guy who called the cops also mentioned I had a gun. The cop in the passenger seat stepped out and stood behind the open passenger door. The driver was out of the car, but he didn't move beyond it. Both had their hands on their weapons.

I couldn't blame them. A report of an accident, an armed individual, and an injured party, even if it was Lard Ass, put things up in the air.

I raised my hands and said, "My name is Devlin Haskell. I'm a licensed P.I. I have a conceal and carry permit. The individual on the ground is Jeremy Lawrence. There is a BOLO out on him. He's wanted on hit and run and assault charges, and kidnapping a woman named Jane McCarry. Officer Gibson and Lieutenant Aaron LaZelle were with me this morning when we rescued her. I think you'll find this vehicle is owned by Jane McCarry and was stolen by this piece of shit," I said and nodded at Lard Ass seated on the ground.

"If you would move away from the vehicle, sir. Keep your hands where we can see them."

I moved away from the station wagon and raised my hands over my head. Two cars had pulled to the side to watch. Another set of flashing lights was just turning onto Davern Street from West Seventh.

"Turn around, sir, and place your hands behind your back."

I did that and was now facing away from the police car.

"Kneel down, sir."

I knelt down and heard footsteps hurrying toward me. Handcuffs were suddenly slapped on my wrists.

"I've got a pistol tucked in a sticky holster in the front of my belt here. You'll want to grab it," I said.

The cop stepped in front of me, pulled the sticky holster out, and asked, "Anything else?"

"Just a set of car keys, and my Golden Retriever is in the back seat of my car."

"I think we'll just leave him there for the time being. I'm going to help you up and walk you to the back seat of our squad car. Okay?"

"Yeah, sure. If you check out this Jeremy Lawrence, you'll see he's wanted for an assault and a number of other charges."

"We're checking it. All right, now, if you'll stand up," he said and helped me to my feet. He walked me to the squad car and placed a hand on my head as I sat down in the back seat and then swung my legs in. He closed the door and went to join his partner.

Forty-three

I sat in the back seat of the squad car for what felt like hours. In reality, it may have been about forty-five minutes, tops. There were now three police cars, an unmarked car, and an EMT crew checking out Lard Ass. Oh, and Aaron LaZelle, eventually showed up. He climbed in the backseat of the squad car with me.

"Hi, Dev. Hey, how's it going?"

"Are you kidding me? Come on, man. My back is killing me with these cuffs on. I've been sitting back here for hours while Lard Ass is getting special treatment."

"He's got a broken nose, Dev. Severely broken."

That brought a smile to my face. "Yeah, well, he was stalking my client, Melissa Donnelly, and her son Liam. Following them around the Mall of America. This is the guy who beat up that older woman above Greasy's and stole her car. You saw what he did to her this morning."

"Relax. We get it. Look, they're just checking him out to make sure we can lock him up tonight. Here, turn around. Let me get these cuffs off you. In case no one mentioned it, thanks for finding him." He unlocked the cuffs, and slowly but surely, my arms began to come back to life. "I would have been here sooner, but I'd just ordered a delicious pasta dish, and well, since it was you, I knew you wouldn't—"

"Are you kidding me? I've been—"

He laughed and then said, "Come on, slide out, and let's get some information."

Just as I began to slide out of the squad car, my cellphone rang. It stopped after two rings and dumped the call into voicemail. "You mind if I make a quick call back? That's probably Melissa, and she's worried. I had five or six calls come through while I was handcuffed. Let me just tell her I'm okay, and I'll join you. Only take a minute."

"Yeah, sure. Don't take too long," he said as a tow truck suddenly drove up the hill and pulled in front of my car.

I took out my cellphone. I'd gotten five calls from Melissa.

"Dev?" she answered.

"Hi, sorry it took so long. I've been tied up working with the police. They have Jeremy in custody. He has a broken nose, but that's about it, so I'm thinking he'll most likely be spending the night in jail."

"But you're all right?"

"Not to worry, I'm fine. I've got to get back with the police. They've got a lot of questions. But can I ask you something?"

"Okay," she said, not sounding too sure.

"I thought Jeremy had the number thirteen tattooed on the back of his neck. But now it's gone."

"Oh, God, that's him trying to look tough. It's not a tattoo. He uses those kids' washable tattoos. You buy the numbers zero through nine on a sheet. I think they're just a dollar. He used to tell me it was a joke, but he was actually trying to look like a bad guy. Just one of the many things about him that made the breakup easier."

"Liam's okay?"

"Fine. He wasn't aware of anything happening, which is good."

"Good, listen, don't worry. I think this is going to bring the stalking and harassment problems to an end."

"Thank God. You're okay?"

"Yeah, I'm just going to be tied up for a while. If it's not too late, I'll call you when we're finished."

The EMTs gave the okay to lock up Lard Ass. Since my car was being towed, Aaron gave Morton and me a ride down to the police station. I gave him what information I had on Lard Ass along the way and then sat in a viewing room, and we watched as two officers interrogated Lard Ass.

Basically, he accused me of a hit-and-run. He wouldn't admit to stalking Melissa and insisted there was no restraining order filed against him. He swore he'd never met Jane McCurry. Fortunately, the officers had more than enough information. They locked him up, and Aaron gave Morton and me a ride home.

It was close to 11:00 by the time we were home, and I figured it was too late to call Melissa. Instead, I sent a text message to Louie, asking him if I could get a ride in the morning, and then Morton and I hit the sack.

We were both up early the next morning. I let Morton out and then hit the shower. We ate breakfast, and then I sat on the front porch waiting for Louie to give me a ride down to the office. He was only forty-five minutes late, not that it made any difference. I gave him the update on Lard Ass along the way. He dropped me off at the office and drove down to the courthouse.

I phoned Heidi around 10:00, ready to leave a message. Amazingly, she answered. "Don't tell me you've heard," was how she answered.

"I haven't heard anything. Yesterday was a little crazy. What are you talking about?"

"Rumor has it Casper Trickle is going to be indicted."

"Indicted? What does that mean for the investment?"

"It means it's not going to happen. I'm just glad I didn't already send him the funds."

"Well, he'd have to return them. Wouldn't he?"

"Yes, he would be required to return the funds. But that doesn't mean he necessarily would return them, and even if he did, it might be a long time coming."

"So just a hypothetical question here. Suppose Tubby Gustafson sold ten thousand shares of Casper Analytics and was going to invest that money in Trickle Down. Where does that leave him?"

"Well, if he hasn't invested yet, he's fine. If, on the other hand, he has already invested, thinking the sooner, the better, mmm, he could be in for a long wait."

"Oh boy."

"Dev, no offense, but a successful criminal like Gustafson, I'm pretty sure he's waiting to see what happens before he purchases."

"I don't know, Heidi. He seemed pretty anxious to—" As I spoke, I turned in my desk chair and casually glanced out the window. A black Escalade was just pulling to the curb. The Escalade had barely stopped when it shook from side to side as Fat Freddy slid out on the passenger side and waddled across the street.

"Sorry, Heidi, I've got to go. Bye," I said and disconnected. I ran out the door and down the stairs just as Fat Freddy entered the building. "Oh, Freddy, great to see you. I just got some inside information for Mr. Gustafson. My car is in the shop, and I was going to taxi. You think you could give me a lift?"

Freddy looked confused but nodded and said, "Yeah, yeah, sure. Come on. Let's go."

Forty-four

Once again, no one said anything on the ride, which was just fine with me. I was busy trying to come up with a way to tell Tubby about the indictment without getting blamed for his investment in the first place.

I was searched twice, just like always, and then Fat Freddy led me into Tubby's office. Tubby was standing in front of his desk in a pair of black silk boxers and knee-high stockings held up by leather sock garters.

A topless woman in a black thong was sitting on the floor. Her legs were spread, and a white plastic cup was on the floor between her legs. Tubby was attempting to putt a number of golf balls into the white plastic cup. From what I could see, it looked like he'd missed every putt thus far.

"Good morning, sir," I said in the middle of Tubby's backswing. The golf ball rolled off to the side and bounced off the woman's foot.

"Damn it, Haskell!" Tubby said and slammed the putter on the floor twice. On the second strike, the shaft bent.

The woman quickly placed the golf balls in the plastic cup and stood. She took the bent putter from Tubby's hand and hurried out through a paneled door in the far corner. It didn't appear to be the first time she'd done this.

"Do not ever mention that worthless activity to me again, Frederick."

"Bit of a golf problem, sir?" I asked before I could stop myself.

Tubby's eyes flared. "As if the day hasn't been bad enough. No, Haskell. Actually, you're the problem, and it's not even noon. Just what the hell do you want?"

"Sorry to interrupt your practice, sir."

"Were you listening, Haskell? I asked you what in the hell you want."

"Just picked up some information, sir, and thought you should be the first to know. Casper Trickle is going to be indicted."

"Really?" Tubby said, sitting down at his desk. He picked up a cigar from a crystal ashtray, lit it with a lighter, and proceeded to build a cloud of smoke around his fat head. "Did you hear that, Frederick? Casper Trickle is about to be indicted. Interesting. Just how did you happen to come across this information?"

"The way it was presented to me was that it was a rumor, sir. But I thought you should know immediately."

"And just what do you think I should do with this information, Haskell?" He drew out the word, 'information' suggesting I was presenting anything other than new information.

"That's for you to decide, sir. Obviously, you know way more than I could ever hope to learn about the market and investments."

Tubby puffed his cigar, smiled, and said, "You are so right, Haskell. What I would suggest is that you get out of my sight as quickly as possible."

"I'm only trying to help, sir. I wouldn't dare to suggest I know more than you. It's just that—"

"Silencio," Tubby yelled. "Fredrick, remove him from the premises."

Tubby didn't have to tell me twice. I hurried to the door. Fat Freddy followed me out the door and back to the front entry. Two guys were in the process of carrying luggage into the mansion. One carried two black leather suitcases and set them down against the far wall. The guy behind him carried two cream-colored cases with shiny brass corners and the logo 'FENDI' emblazoned on the side. I thought it strange. They looked like the same suitcases that I'd seen on Trickle's porch.

Fat Freddy stopped and asked one of them, "How did the trip go?"

"Not a bother, lovely campfire," the guy said, and they all laughed. One of the 'FENDI' cases had what looked like the corner of a hundred-dollar bill hanging out the side. I wondered what the odds were that there were four Fendi suitcases in town. By the time I climbed into the Escalade, I was pretty sure those were the same suitcases that had been sitting on Casper Trickle's front porch the other day.

I had another quiet ride in the Escalade. Louie's car was parked on the street, and Fat Freddy's driver pulled in behind it. "Thank you for the ride," I said as I climbed out. I closed the door behind me, put on a fake smile, and gave a wave.

Fat Freddy cracked an evil grin and said, "Remember what he told you, Haskell. Silencio!" Just like before, he gave me the finger, and I watched as they drove up the street.

Up in the office, Louie was on the phone. I turned on my laptop and Googled the name 'FENDI.' It turned out to be an Italian company that made everything from shoes to jewelry, ski wear, purses, and suitcases. The suitcases that matched the two at Trickle's and today at Tubby's were priced at five grand each. Yeah, five grand for a suitcase. I remembered the corner of the hundred-dollar bill sticking out of one of the 'FENDI' suitcases.

Louie hung up the phone and looked at me. "Everything okay? You seem deep in thought."

"Just trying to figure something out. You have any lunch yet?"

"No, I've been dealing with a client all morning," he said and shook his head.

"If I can borrow your car, I'll grab something for us at Roosters. I want to drive up to my place and let Morton out of the house for fifteen minutes."

Louie tossed me his car keys and said, "I'll take the BBQ pork shoulder and fries."

"Back in a half-hour or so," I said and hurried out to Louie's faded Ford Fiesta. It took three tries, but I finally got it to work. Just as the engine came to life, there was a huge explosion. I looked in the rearview mirror as a black cloud floated down the street. I drove home, let Morton out, and filled his water dish. After ten minutes, I coaxed him back inside with a biscuit and drove over to Trickle's mansion on Summit Avenue.

I parked in front of Trickle's and headed toward the porch. As I drew closer, I spotted the brown leather computer bag hanging from the hedge in front of the porch. I grabbed the bag and rang the doorbell a couple of times. No one answered. I checked the mailbox. It was empty, which probably meant Trickle had halted the mail.

I picked up the bag and walked around to the back. I pounded on the door leading up to Arty and Jacob's unit above the garage. I didn't get an answer. I walked over to the stairs leading down to the cellar and the security room and pounded on the door. No one answered the door, so I tossed the computer bag in the car and headed down to Roosters.

I parked across the street from the office. I grabbed two BBQ pork sandwiches, fries for Louie, the brown leather computer bag, and headed up to the office. We ate in relative quiet until Louie finally said, "Something's bugging you, Dev. What is it?"

I was about to open up and then remembered Tubby and Fat Freddy's warning, 'Silencio.' "Oh, nothing, just a lot of things up in the air at the moment. Thinking about what the repair on my car is going to run."

"Never fun," Louie said and shook his head.

I sent a text message to Melissa, telling her my car was in the shop and I wouldn't be able to pick up Liam after school. She called just before 3:00.

"Hi, Melissa, did you get my text message?" was how I answered her call.

"Yeah, Dev. Not a problem. Liam has his first team practice tonight at 5:00. I can take him. He's all excited."

"He should be. He's worked very hard to get there."

"I can't thank you enough for everything you've done, Dev. I, umm, got a call from the police this morning. We talked for quite a while. Audrey had to watch my class for over an hour. Jeremy is going to remain in jail for the time being. He's been identified as the assailant by Jane McCarry. I'm hoping that under the circumstances, there won't be bail, not that he'd have the funds to pay for it anyway. We, umm, we need to talk, you and me. You've really been a big help."

"Not necessary to thank me. Just glad I could help. I'm more or less stuck until I can get my car out of the shop. Hopefully, they'll call this afternoon and tell me what it's going to run."

"Well, I should get back to work. I have a lot to catch up on after missing more than an hour this morning. Let's plan on touching base tomorrow."

"Yeah, you bet. Talk to you then," I said, and she hung up.

Years of experience had taught me that when a woman said, 'We need to talk.' It never, ever, went my way. Just to cap off the day, my car repair guy phoned around 4:00. He gave me a laundry list of items that had to be replaced or repaired on the car. He promised to get used items when possible. Bottom line, the work would take two days and run me $4,300.

There wasn't much I could do. I couldn't get another vehicle at that price, so I said, "Yeah, okay. Go ahead, and thanks for the call, Sam."

Forty-five

Louie gave me a ride home. I took Morton for a walk. We settled in front of the TV and went up to bed around 11:00. We both slept through the night, although I dreamt about a fat guy chasing me with a giant French fry. I was up before Morton. I had breakfast and let him out once he came downstairs. Louie picked us up just before 9:00, and we headed down to the office. Over the course of the morning, I left two messages for Heidi. I phoned Melissa just before 3:00 that afternoon.

"Dev?" was how she answered.

"Hi, Melissa. Just touching base. My car is going to be ready sometime tomorrow, and I was wondering if we might get together for dinner tomorrow night. I know a nice, quiet little spot and—"

"Oh, Dev, thanks. That's really nice of you, but we're going to be out of town."

"Out of town? Is everything okay?"

"Better than okay. I'm putting the house on the market. We're driving to Austin tomorrow. I'm interviewing for a job teaching first grade down there."

"You're driving to Texas?"

"No, Dev, Austin, Minnesota. I've got cousins down there. We can stay with them until the house up here sells. It's all happening so quickly, and I—"

"Well yeah. I mean, don't you want to think about this for a bit? What about Liam? He just made the hockey team. Wouldn't it make sense to—"

"Dev, Jeremy's arrest was on the news this morning. They didn't mention his name yet. But that's probably going to happen within the next twenty-four to forty-eight hours. I don't want Liam to have to deal with that. Based on how my interview goes, I can start in Austin in a week. The school here has a substitute teacher lined up to step in, so the class won't miss a day. I was hoping to be able to tell you this in person, but everything is suddenly happening at breakneck speed, and you don't have a car."

"I just told you I'll be getting the car back tomorrow."

"Yes, and I told you we'll be out of town. Were you listening?"

"Maybe I could watch Liam. You can check out this new school and your cousins, and I could get him to practice. We could take a taxi if my car isn't ready in time."

"Oh, that's nice of you, but he gets along great with his cousins, and the sooner he begins to adjust to Austin, the better it will be for him. Besides, I want to get him away from any of the Jeremy news."

"Well, I guess there's not much left to say except to have a nice trip. Can you give me a call when you get back?"

"I think so. Thanks for understanding."

"Yeah, well, I didn't have much—" but she'd already hung up.

"You okay?" Louie asked.

"I think I just got dumped."

"That wasn't Heidi, was it?"

"No, Melissa. She's apparently got a teaching job waiting for her down in Austin, and she wants to get Liam out of town before the news breaks about Lard Ass assaulting that woman."

"Well, you can't blame her for that. You okay?"

"I guess, maybe. Right now, I don't know. It all happened so fast."

"Might be for the best, Dev."

I placed a third call to Heidi and left another message. "Heidi, it's Dev. Don't bother to call me back."

I pulled the binoculars out of my desk drawer and focused on the empty apartment across the street for the next hour. No one was home. Just after 4:00, Louie suggested we head over to The Spot. I grabbed Morton's leash, took him for a long walk, and we joined Louie a half-hour later.

"Wasn't sure you guys were going to make it," Louie said as he pulled a bag of pork rinds from the rack. Morton's tail started banging against my leg, but I didn't really notice.

"Get you a beer, Dev?" Mike asked as he set down a fresh drink in front of Louie.

"You know, I think I better take a pass, Mike. Thanks anyway."

"Suit yourself," he said and headed down the bar toward a couple just settling in.

"Dev, come on, man. You need to snap out of this. You're turning into a real downer here."

"It's going take a while, Louie. I had high hopes for Melissa. I really enjoyed teaching Liam how to skate, and all of a sudden, she's leaving town. Between this and Tubby always yelling 'silencio' at me, life is suddenly looking pretty grim, man."

"You feel like just heading home?"

"Would you mind?"

"No, as a matter of fact, I'll be happy to drop you guys off. It's been a long day for both of us, Dev. I hope things look better for you in the morning."

Ten minutes later, Louie pulled to a stop in front of my house. "Thanks for the lift, Louie. You know, I think we might just take a break tomorrow. I need a day off."

"I can pick you up tomorrow, Dev. No problem."

"No, thanks, but a day off might be just what I need."

I planned on sleeping in and didn't set the alarm. Of course, I woke the following morning at sunrise. I hit the shower and dressed in one of the silk outfits I grabbed from Heidi's garage. I was watching the news while eating a dish of cinnamon ice cream for breakfast. They were covering a story about a fire up in northern Minnesota. I was more focused on the ice cream until they mentioned that the fire was on Ash Lake, and four individuals were reported to have died.

Ash Lake and four individuals. I immediately focused on the TV, all the while thinking, Casper Trickle, Arty, Jacob, and Jerry. The guy at Tubby's with the suitcases the other day told Fat Freddy they had a lovely campfire. Was he actually telling Fat Freddy something else?

I was online the rest of the day, trying to find anything I could on the Ash Lake fire. It turned out to be a futile search. I had a bottle of Pinot Noir for dinner and fell asleep on the couch.

I sent Louie a text message asking him to pick me up in the morning then headed up to bed.

Forty-six

Louie arrived just before 9:00. I was waiting for him on the porch. I hurried to his car.

"Where's Morton?" he asked as I climbed in.

"I'm hoping to get my car back sometime today and figured he'd be happier at home. You in court this morning?"

"Yeah, in fact, after I drop you off, I'm heading down to the courthouse."

"Oh, you should have said something. Sorry to be a hassle."

"Not a problem, Dev. You'd do the same for me."

"Yeah, but I never have anything going on."

"Not true, and stop beating yourself up. That's my job."

Louie dropped me off, and I went up to the office. I turned off the coffee, dumped the scorched remnants down the sink, and made a fresh pot. I pulled the binoculars from my desk, and the woman across the way was on the phone, sipping coffee and wearing a smile. Maybe things were going to get better.

Sam called me just after ten. "Yeah, Dev, we've got everything put back together. I can bring the car down to you. Have to pick up another not too far away, so it's no hassle."

"That would be great, Sam. I'll keep an eye out for you."

"Be down there in about a half-hour. If you can have that check ready, forty-three hundred bucks, that would be great."

"Yeah, I'll have the check ready for you," I said, thinking I'd have to date it for about two months from now.

I got back on my computer and checked out the four victims of the fire up on Ash Lake. No news update. The image of the suitcases at Tubby's kept going through my mind, and I suddenly remembered the brown leather computer bag from Trickle's front porch. It was on the floor next to my desk. I placed it on top of the desk, said a quick prayer, and opened it up. I stared at the contents and then dumped them out onto my desk.

Five bundles of ten-dollar bills. Each bundle was wrapped with a yellow-colored currency band labeled $1000. The bills were crisp, unwrinkled, and felt real. Five bundles added up to a five grand, and it fell off the front porch?

I didn't think very long before I pulled a manila envelope from my desk. I picked up a bundle, counted out thirty ten-dollar bills, and stuffed them with the four, thousand dollar bundles, in the manila envelope.

Sam pulled up in his flatbed tow truck twenty minutes later. I grabbed the manila envelope and ran outside as he was lowering my car onto the street. It only took about four minutes to unhook my car. It was washed and looked almost brand new.

"What do you think, Dev?"

"Sam, it looks great. Thanks so much."

"My pleasure, sorry about the cost. I knocked off ten percent, and we changed your oil for free."

"I appreciate it. Here you go. Thanks again," I said and handed him the envelope.

He opened it up. His eyes grew wide, and he looked from the envelope to me and back to the envelope. "How in the hell did—"

"I ran out of checks and had to get cash. I didn't want to pay five bucks for a cashier's check. Hope that's okay."

"You kidding? It's great. Twenty percent discount next time you need work done," he said and shook my hand.

"No offense, but let's hope there isn't a next time."

Louie showed up just before noon with a large take-out pizza. "Hey, I didn't think your car would be back so soon, so I picked up lunch. Looks like they did some nice work," he said, tossing a couple of napkins my way. He opened the pizza box and let me take the first piece.

"Thanks, Louie, but you didn't have to go to all this trouble."

"No trouble, I have to eat, too."

It was close to 4:00 when I saw the first news report on the Ash Lake fire identifying two of the victims. Casper Trickle and Jerold Schneider. I figured it was a pretty sure guess that Arty and Jacob were the other two victims. Officially, a gas leak was suspected as the cause of the fire. Based on the four suitcases I saw at Tubby's mansion, I had my doubts. Along with photos of Trickle and Jerry, there was a picture of what was left of the structure. From the look of the foundation, it had been a very large place, now reduced to a pile of ashes.

I was just getting ready to head home when my cell-phone rang. Heidi.

I debated answering for a second or two and then picked up. "Hi, Heidi."

"Hi, Dev. Thanks for taking my call. I'm sorry about last night. Believe me, I would have enjoyed your company a lot more."

"Not a problem, as it turned out, I had something going on anyway."

There was a momentary silence, and I was just about to say something when Heidi said, "Well, I was just calling to see if you had time to come over for dinner. Nothing fancy. I have some leftover roast chicken from last night and plenty of wine."

"Yeah, sure, can I bring anything?"

"Just yourself, come whenever you can."

"I'll be there within the hour," I said.

"Sounds like things might be looking up," Louie said.

"One can only hope. I'll see you in the morning, and thanks for putting up with me the last couple of days."

"Just glad things are getting back on track."

I hurried home, let Morton out, and hopped in the shower. Just in case, I grabbed a couple bottles of wine at Solo Vino and hurried over to Heidi's. She answered the door in a red silk kimono and tossed my wine bottles on the couch. "We need to talk, but that can wait," she said and led me into her bedroom.

Epilogue

I spoke with Melissa a few times on the phone, but without actually saying it, she made it clear she didn't want to see me again. The following week she moved down to Austin, a hundred and twenty miles to the south. Four weeks later, I received a UPS package at the office. It was wrapped in brown paper and addressed to me. As I unwrapped it, it became obvious the brown paper had originally been a grocery bag. The box was small and square and apparently had held a scented candle at one time.

I opened the box and pulled out a handwritten note on a piece of paper torn from a spiral notebook. The printing was large but pretty good, considering the age of the sender and the misspellings.

'Dear Dev, I wnat you to have this. It's from my first goal and we won 1 to noting. Thank you for yur help. I love hocky. Yur pal forevr Liam.'

The hockey puck had clearly seen a number of games. God knows he probably stole it after the game. But to send it to me was very special.

"Hey, Dev. You okay?"

I sniffled, wiped the tear from my eye, and cleared my throat. "Yeah, look at this, Liam's first goal. Wish I could have been there."

"You were there, Dev. You'll always be there with Liam."

"Hey, Louie, Silencio," I said, and we both laughed.

The End

Thank you for taking the time to read **Silencio!** If you enjoyed the read please take a moment and leave a review. Even if it's just a word or two, it really helps.

Don't miss the sample of **Surprise, Surprise!** The next work of genius in the Dev Haskell series.

Surprise, Surprise!

Second Edition

MIKE FARICY

Prologue

Damien Dambella refilled the crystal wine glass almost to the rim and handed it to the sultry blonde stretched out on his bed. "Enjoy the wine, Phoenix."

She adjusted the pillows behind her and reached for the glass. She took a sip, smiled, and then studied his backside while he topped up his glass. He'd probably been an athlete a thousand years and forty pounds ago. That was okay. The bank accounts more than made up for it. He held out his arm and clinked the crystal with her before he climbed back into the four-poster bed.

It wasn't lost on her that his glass was barely half-full, not that it made any difference. Her husband was working late, again. If he did happen to arrive home before her, she'd just tell him she'd been doing a late-night workout, which in a way, wasn't far from the truth.

After a couple of sips and some idiotic comments, Dambella set his glass on the bedside table, raised his eyebrows, and slid beneath the sheet. Phoenix continued to sip. She occasionally let loose with a false moan and more encouragement. She checked the digital clock on the chest of drawers. After a few minutes, she drained her glass and set it on the bedside table next to her. It was time to bring things to a close. She moaned loudly, rolled onto her side, and groaned, "Oh my God. Oh my God."

The wine bottle was empty. Dambella had shoved it into the silver ice bucket upside down. They'd been involved in post-coital chatting for the past thirty minutes, and he had just said, "It's too bad you're married. Think of all the fun we could have together."

She thought for a long moment, *'The bank accounts, his Victorian mansion, the Florida Keys, trips to Europe. Yeah, I can fix that,'* and she proceeded to consider how, exactly.

One

It was going to be another warm summer day, and I was sipping coffee at my desk. My officemate, Louie Laufen, had a court appearance this morning. My golden retriever, Morton, was ensconced on his pillow gnawing on his rawhide bone. At the moment, I was staring through my binoculars at the apartment across the street. The shade was up on a third-floor bedroom window. I'd been enjoying the view as a woman took her time getting dressed.

As I set the binoculars down when she left her bedroom, I noticed the blue BMW convertible pulling in behind my car parked across the street. A very attractive blonde climbed out of the car. She was wearing a short black skirt and a white top. She removed her sunglasses, placed them in her purse, and waited for a bus to pass. Once the street was clear, she strutted across as if she was on a fashion show runway. A car drove by and tooted its horn as she stepped onto the sidewalk.

I figured she must be headed for the hairdressers just across from our office. A moment later, I could hear the stairs creak ever so slightly. I thought I'd been right about the hairdressers when suddenly there was a knock on the office door, and it slowly opened.

The same attractive blonde peeked around the door and said, "Hi, umm, sorry to bother you. I'm looking for Dev Haskell, the private investigator."

"Oh, yeah, that's me. Please, please come on in," I said, standing up behind my desk. I quickly slipped the binoculars into a drawer and closed it with my knee.

The blonde was even more attractive close up. She flashed a sexy smile of sparkling white teeth and extended her hand as she walked toward me. "Hi, I'm Phoenix Starr. I got your name from a friend." As we shook hands, a wonderful perfume scent drifted over me. She gently rubbed her thumb a couple of times over the back of my hand and smiled.

"Please, have a seat, Phoenix. Nice to meet you. Can I interest you in a coffee?"

"Only if you have it made. I don't want to put you to any trouble."

"No trouble at all. I've got a fresh pot on," I lied. I grabbed my mug and headed toward the coffee. Fortunately, there was enough left from yesterday for two cups.

Morton was up off his pillow. He wandered over to Phoenix and sniffed. She reached down and scratched him behind the ears, which gave me the opportunity to empty Louie's coffee mug from yesterday and refill it.

"Here we go, fresh coffee. You take it black?"

"Yeah, that's perfect," she said, which was good because we didn't have any cream or sugar. "What a nice doggy. What's his name?"

I set Louie's refilled mug in front of her. "That's Morton, and now that you've given him a scratch behind the ears, he'll be your friend for life. Please, have a seat. How can I help you?" I said and nodded toward the client chair in front of my desk.

She sat down, took a sip of coffee, and slid the mug off to the side at an arm's length. I noticed a very large set of diamonds on her left hand. She slowly crossed her legs and smiled. "Well, I got your name from Monica Dolan. We both belong to the Town and Country Club."

"Oh, yeah, I've known Monica since we were kids." Which was true since we went to the same grade school. I'd asked her out a half-dozen times in high school. She always said no. I hadn't seen her in at least fifteen years. The two of them belonging to the Town and Country Club put them on a much higher social level than me drinking at The Spot bar.

"Monica suggested you might be able to help me. I'm afraid I've got an embarrassing situation."

"Phoenix, I deal with all sorts of situations. Please, don't feel embarrassed. I had a client once who insisted his neighbor could turn invisible and was knocking over the trash bins. Turns out it was just the wind, but the guy still believed it was his invisible neighbor."

She flashed a quick smile, took a deep breath, and said, "Well, I'm pretty sure my husband is having an affair."

"Oh, I'm sorry to hear that. Can you tell me why you think this?"

"Well, he's always working nights, just about every night. He comes home late, ten, eleven, sometimes even midnight. How can I put this? No matter what I do, he seems to have lost all interest in me," she said and let that last statement just hang out there for a moment.

Based on her appearance, I figured the guy was nuts. "I see. Any idea who the other party might be?"

She shook her head.

"Tell me about your husband. What does he do?"

"He's an accountant. Has his own accounting firm. He's invested heavily, and, I have to say, successfully, in stocks and a couple of start-up companies. He's always been a workaholic, but something's changed in the last year or so, and I'm pretty sure I know what it is. He's found someone else."

"Other than working late, do you have any evidence? Phone calls? Emails? Text messages? Does he come home smelling of perfume?"

"Well, actually, no. There's been nothing of that nature. But then he's always been boring."

"Do you have any children?"

"No. We decided on a childless marriage. It's part of our contract. Sterling Kozlow is my husband's name. We've been married for almost five years."

I grabbed a pen and a legal pad. I pulled off the top sheet where I'd written my grocery list, tossed it in the wastebasket, and began taking a few notes. "And you kept your maiden name when you married?"

"Yes, I did. Phoenix Starr, two 'r's' in my last name."

"Are you living in town?"

"Yes, we have a home on the River Boulevard," she said, mentioning one of the nicer streets in town. Unfortunately, it was also the same street where Tubby Gustafson, the city's local crime lord, resided.

"What would you like me to do?" I asked.

"Well," she said, slowly uncrossing and then crossing her legs again. Out of force of habit, I took a quick glance, red lace. "I'd like you to confirm if Sterling is having an affair. I can pay you, and I'd, well, I'd be *very* grateful." *Did she just raise her eyebrows, or did I imagine that?*

"What kind of car does your husband drive?"

"A red Mercedes. He's told me a million times what kind it is, but I can never remember. A bunch of letters, ABC or something like that. It's a very nice car."

"And you said he has an accounting firm?"

"Sterling Kozlow Finance. Here's his business card," she said and handed me a card.

I recognized the address. The office was in a 1950s strip mall down on West 7th Street, just a couple of blocks from Highway 5 heading out to the airport. Not exactly what I would call high price space, but then maybe that was typical of an accountant.

"I'll check this out and get back to you. My rate is two-fifty a day, plus expenses. I usually ask for two days up front, but how about I check a few things out, and we can discuss what I think this might run in a day or two?"

She smiled and nodded. "I'm sure we'll be able to work something out. Give me that business card back for a minute," she said, then reached into her purse and took out a pen. She wrote down her phone number and an email address on the back and returned it to me. She'd drawn a little heart next to her email address.

"Thanks. Is it all right if I phone or email you?"

"Absolutely. That's my cellphone, so Sterling will never answer. The email address is very private. You can tell me anything. I'll look forward to hearing from you," she said then stood and picked up her purse.

"Very nice to meet you, Ms. Starr," I replied and held out my hand.

"Oh, please. Call me Phoenix, baby. I'm sure we'll be working very closely," she said and this time definitely raised her eyebrows. I followed her to the door and opened it for her. "Oh, you're so kind. A perfect gentleman." She leaned against me, gave me a peck on the cheek, then stepped out of the office and headed down the stairs. I watched her go halfway down the stairs, then closed the door, and hurried to the window. A hint of her lovely perfume still hung in the air.

My office mate Louie had just parked his faded red Ford Fiesta in front of my car and climbed out. He headed across the street, nodded as he passed Phoenix, and then turned and stared. She climbed into her convertible, put her sunglasses on, and started the car. Louie stood on the sidewalk and watched for a long moment as she drove off.

I heard the stairs creaking as Louie made his way up to the office. The door opened, and where sexy Phoenix Starr had kissed me a moment earlier, now a red-faced Louie stood, gasping for air. He stopped, sniffed, and asked, "Was that hot-looking blonde up here?"

TWO

Sterling Kozlow Finance was located in Sibley Plaza, a shopping center developed back in 1955. The center was actually two one-story structures featuring a total of twenty-one different suites, twelve of which were vacant. A large parking lot was in the front of the buildings. The office of Sterling Kozlow Finance was set between a Dollar Store and a vacant unit with a large **For Rent** sign.

I was parked in the parking lot, three lanes away from Kozlow's office. I was on my second McDonald's cheeseburger and halfway through my strawberry shake. Other than three employees leaving at the end of the day, there had been no other activity in the office. At exactly 6:00, a guy I pegged at maybe mid-fifties with thinning gray hair stepped out of an office and locked the front door. His tie was loosened, and the sleeves on his white shirt were rolled up to the elbows. If he was Kozlow, he looked old enough to be Phoenix Starr's father. He turned the lights off in the front office and stepped back into what I presumed was his office. A red Mercedes CLS was parked just in front of the office. I presumed that was Kozlow's car and had copied the license number.

I sat in my car for the next three-and-a-half hours, and nothing happened. I drifted off to sleep for maybe a minute or two but woke when my head bounced off the steering wheel. The Mercedes was still parked in front, and light was still drifting out of the open doorway from what I presumed was Kozlow's office.

It was after 9:30 when he finally turned off the light and stepped out of the office. He locked the front door, climbed into the Mercedes, backed out of his parking place, and drove off.

I followed at a respectable distance. He came to a complete stop at each of the four stop signs along the route. He drove up St. Paul Avenue to Cleveland, Cleveland to Randolph, where he took a left turn and headed down to the River Boulevard. He took a right and pulled into a driveway a half-block later.

One of the automatic garage doors on the attached three-stall garage rose as he approached. He drove inside and disappeared. The two-story house, at least from the street, was dark on the first floor. What appeared to be a bedroom light was on in a second-floor room. A minute later, light drifted out through the living room lace curtains. I waited another thirty minutes. Apparently, Kozlow was home for the night. I yawned and headed to my place. Morton met me at the front door. I let him out back for fifteen minutes, and we headed up to bed just after 11:00.

We drove past Sterling Kozlow Finance at 7:30 the following morning. The large parking lot was empty with the exception of Kozlow's red Mercedes and two taxi cabs in front of a coffee shop. I parked at the far end of the parking lot, clipped the leash onto Morton's collar, and we headed toward Kozlow's office.

As we walked past the office, I glanced in through the floor-to-ceiling windows. The front room had a reception desk, four chairs against a wall, and a coffee table with three magazines. No doubt the magazines would be months old. I didn't see Kozlow, but the light was on in the same office from last night. I figured he was already at his desk.

We walked past his car and then stepped into the parking lot. I had a piece of white chalk in my hand, and as we walked alongside the Mercedes, I leaned over and drew a vertical line down the rear tire on the passenger side. If he drove anywhere during the day, the chalk line would be in a different position the next time I was here. We walked back to our car and headed to the office.

I made a fresh pot of coffee, and at one minute after 9:00, I phoned my friend Denny in the department of motor vehicles. "Dennis Glazier," was how he answered the phone.

"Hey, Denny, you're sounding cheerful for first thing in the morning."

"Hi Dev, you just getting home from last night?"

"I only wish. Wondering if you could check a license for me. I've got a client who's looking to buy a car from a private party. I just want to make sure the sale is legit and not something that's going to come back and cause a bunch of problems."

"What's the license number?"

"Minnesota plates," I said and gave him Kozlow's license plate number. "It's a red Mercedes CLS." I could hear the keyboard clicking.

"Yeah, here it is. Actually registered to a company, Sterling Kozlow Finance. A red 2021 Mercedes CLS. Strikes me as strange someone would be selling that privately."

"Oh, it's some sort of shirt tail relative. I'm not sure what the deal is. I just wanted to be sure the deal is legit, and it sounds like it is."

"You owe me a beer for my effort," Denny said.

"You got it, happy to pay up. It's been too long since we were last together."

"Oh man, between work and getting the kids to swimming lessons, the boy's baseball practice, my daughter to ballet, we're exhausted by the end of any given day."

"Well, give my best to your wife. She's obviously very patient and still has a lot of work to do on you."

"Ain't that the truth. Good talking to you, Dev."

"Thanks, Denny, I…" but he'd already hung up.

Louie wandered in about twenty minutes later. I heard the stairs creaking as he slowly climbed up to the second floor. I grabbed his coffee mug off my desk. Lipstick from Phoenix Starr was still on it, and I wiped it off, and filled it just as he stepped into the office. As always, you'd think he ran a couple of miles based on his red face. He gave me a nod and settled in at his picnic table desk. I placed the mug in front of him. He stared at the steaming mug for a minute or two, eventually took a sip, and said, "So what's going on in your world?"

"Not a heck of a lot. I think I did pick up a new client yesterday."

"Don't tell me it was that hot-looking blonde who drove off in the convertible yesterday. Well?" he said after a long moment.

"You told me not to tell you."

"So she was in here. I thought so."

"Yeah, she seems really nice. Thinks her husband might be having an affair."

"Well, based on what I saw, if he's having an affair with someone, he's missing more than a few brain cells."

"I'm going to watch him over the next couple of days and see. She certainly wasn't hard on the eyes."

"Remember to use your brain and charge her the full amount. No discount just because she's hot looking."

"I've already given her my daily rate plus expenses, so you don't have to worry."

"Just make sure you stick to it," Louie said.

I spent the next hour checking out Sterling Kozlow Finance online. There was a website that had, among other things, a number of reviews, all five stars. Three employees were mentioned. Two of whom, a man and a woman, I'd seen leaving the office just after 5:00 last

night. I wrote down their names along with the five people who left reviews. I made calls to the reviewers and
left four messages. The fifth and last person answered on
the second ring.

"Jason Corbin."

"Hi, Jason. Thanks for taking my call. My name is
Dev Haskell. I have a small company, and I'm looking
for an accountant. I saw the review you wrote on Sterling
Kozlow Finance. Have things worked out well for you
there?"

"With Kozlow Finance? Yeah, very well. They
know what they're doing. What I like about them is they
give me options and explain what to expect, given the
choices I make. I run a sales firm. I've got eleven employees. We're all hustling. We do a lot of traveling. We
have a lot of expenses. With the exception of two office
workers, the rest of us are on commission, so there are a
lot of gray areas. They really helped out. It seems like
one of us is getting audited either by the IRS or the state
every other year. I haven't had to pay a fine since I
moved my account to Kozlow."

"Pretty good endorsement. You actually deal with
Sterling?"

"Yes, although I've had some interaction with Mar-
shal Jones there too. But the vast majority is with Kozlow. I could say he can be boring as hell, but the guy is
an accountant. They're all boring. I just want him to keep
my ducks in a row, and he does that."

"You know anything about him socially?"

"Socially?"

"Yeah, does he play golf, or fish, follow sports, that kind of thing? Is he a party animal?"

"I've no idea. Well, except I think I can state for a fact he's probably not a party animal. He strikes me as a one glass of wine type of guy. I'm paying him to handle my financial stuff and protect me from getting audited. That's all I care about. I do know that he's married. In fact, he has a photo of his wife behind his desk. I just presumed it was a picture of his daughter and said something to him once. When I found out it was his wife, I was more than a little embarrassed. Anyway, the guy is good at what he does, damn good. Hope I've been some help."

"Yeah, you have. Business good for you?"

"Hey, we're in sales here. There's always something more you can do. No complaints, I can pay my bills and put a little aside."

"Well, Jason, I appreciate your time and recommendation. Wishing you continued success."

"And same to you. Good luck," he said and hung up.

Three

Two of my four messages were returned early in the afternoon. Both with solid reviews on Kozlow. No suggestion of the guy being wild and crazy or a womanizer. But then, if he was involved in an affair, he'd probably be keeping it very quiet.

Louie had a court date at 11:00 and promised to return with some BBQ sandwiches from Roosters. He didn't return until just after 2:30. As I opened the food tray, my stomach growled.

"Yeah, I get it. Sorry I was so late. Some earlier hearing got held up and knocked everyone back a good hour and a half. It was in Devitt's courtroom. He was not a happy camper," Louie said. He draped his tie over his shoulder and took a large bite from his sandwich. BBQ sauce immediately shot onto his chin and then dripped down the front of his white shirt. He looked at the BBQ stain, shrugged, and kept eating.

I had just finished my sandwich when my phone rang. "Good afternoon, Dev Haskell," was how I answered, figuring it was another one of the folks returning my phone call. Wrong, unfortunately.

"Haskell. Get your dumb ass out here. Mr. Gustafson would like a word with you."

I turned in my chair and looked out the window. A black Cadillac Escalade was parked behind my car. I could just make out the rather large image of Fat Freddy Zimmerman in the front passenger seat.

"Actually, Freddy, not that I wouldn't like to see Mr. Gustafson, but I'm working a case right now. How 'bout I give him a call and stop over later this afternoon. Would that work?"

"In a word, no. Bad idea. A really bad idea. I need to see your dumb ass out here in about sixty seconds, or I'm going to send Happy up there to get you. Let me warn you. He was out last night, and he's nursing a hangover. It would not be a pleasant visit."

Happy Hoffman, Fat Freddy's driver. Not a guy to mess with, especially if he had a hangover. "I'll be down in just a minute," I promised and hung up.

"That didn't sound like it went your way," Louie said. At the moment, he was dabbing at the BBQ stain on his shirt with a wet paper towel, which only seemed to be making the stain larger.

"Fat Freddy is out on the street. He wants to take me to see Tubby. God only knows what that will be about."

"You don't know what he wants?"

"I don't know and really don't care. But things will get even worse if I don't go. You going to be around this afternoon?"

"Yeah, I'm here for the rest of the day. If you're not back before 5:00, Morton and I will be over at The Spot."

"Thanks," I said, took a deep breath, and headed down the stairs. As I walked out of the building and crossed the street, Happy Hoffman stepped out from behind the wheel and opened the rear door for me.

"Thanks, Happy. How's the head?"

"I was home watching the game last night. He was just pulling your leg," he said under his breath.

"About damn time," Fat Freddy growled as I climbed in. I took his greeting to mean he was the one nursing the hangover. The trip to Tubby's mansion proceeded in silence. Once Happy turned onto the River Boulevard, I could see Tubby's mansion on the next block. Phoenix Starr and Sterling Kozlow's home was just two blocks behind us.

The iron gate opened automatically as we approached. Happy drove along the circular drive and stopped opposite the front door.

"Let's go. Move it," Fat Freddy snarled as he climbed out.

"Good luck," Happy said under his breath as I climbed out of the back seat. He drove over to the parking area as a security guy named Billy approached me.

"Hold your arms out to the side, and I'll check you. You carrying?" he asked as he waved a handheld metal detector over my left arm and down my side.

"No, I'm not carrying. I've got a strip of metal in my wallet and a pen in my pocket."

Billy nodded and a moment later, the wand beeped as it ran over my wallet.

"Let me see what you've got in your pocket," he ordered.

I pulled my wallet out and handed it to him. "Oh yeah, one of them Dango's," he said, eyeing the wallet. He glanced at the two one-dollar bills behind the black rubber strap and shook his head. "Figures," he said.

"Haskell, are you through screwing around? Come on, you're keeping the boss waiting," Freddy yelled from the front door.

I hurried toward him. A guy on a short three-step ladder was washing the windows and using a squeegee. Freddy held the door with a disgusted look on his face. Once I stepped inside, another security guy set his comic book on his chair and patted me down. "Okay," he said and returned to his comic book.

I followed Freddy across the entry and down the hall toward Tubby's office. A woman was busy mopping the floor in the entryway, and another woman was vacuuming the staircase leading up to the second floor.

Freddy stopped at the office door, took a deep breath, and knocked as he opened the door. Tubby was seated at his desk, wearing a suit, a tie, and a starched white shirt. Instead of a drink, there was a coffee cup and a saucer. Fresh cut flowers, daises, were in a vase on the fireplace mantel. The office smelled of polish and Windex. The usual cadre of semi-naked women giving neck rubs and a lot of attention to Tubby was nowhere to be seen.

"Nice to see you, sir. I get the feeling there are some changes going on. All the cleaning, cut flowers, you're all dressed up. I mean more than you usually are, and let me just say you're always looking good, sir."

Tubby shook his head and mumbled something I probably was better off not hearing. He cleared his throat a couple of times and said, "I'm going to need your help, Haskell."

"My help?"

"It would seem I have a guest arriving tomorrow."

"A guest?"

"Yes, my sister."

"Oh, I guess I didn't know you had a sister, sir. Well, I hope you have a nice visit. Do you see her very often?"

"As little as possible, Haskell, and that's where you're going to come in."

"Me? I'm not following, sir."

"Oh, yes, you are, Haskell. I suspect you're following quite well. Quinnie is arriving at noon tomorrow. Let me thank you in advance for making her trip so enjoyable."

"Enjoyable?"

"Haskell, I'm a busy man. I don't have time to waste like you do. You will mind Quinnie, take her to dinner, show her the town. Drop her off here at night. She'll be staying in one of my guest rooms. I want her to be busy

from sunup to sundown, and that task has fallen on you."
"Me? Look, Tub, err, Mr. Gustafson. I'm in the process of working on a case for a new client. It's going to keep me busy until late every day. I'll be doing stakeouts, eating meals in my car, and—"

"No, you won't, Haskell. Oh, and thank you for reminding me. I'll expect you here at 9:00 tomorrow morning. If you're not here, just drive to the emergency room at the Regions Hospital. It will save you the trouble of calling an ambulance. You will be here at 9:00 sharp. You'll trade in that dreadful vehicle you drive, and I'll loan you one of mine. Quinnie will be arriving at the airport on a 10:00 flight from Los Angeles. Thank you in advance for meeting her at the airport. I will be otherwise detained for the entire day. I'll have a schedule and a list of places the two of you can visit."

"Mr. Gustafson, I'm sorry, but I really can't do this. I'm just beginning work for a new client and—"

"Frederick, would you please summon Breaker? It would appear we have an issue here that is going to have to be dealt with, and I—"

"Wait a minute, sir. You don't have to bring Breaker into this. I'll attempt to adjust my schedule and—"

"Attempt?" Tubby said and glared.

"I look forward to being here tomorrow morning and meeting your sister, sir."

"Much better, Haskell. Oh, and if you wouldn't mind. Perhaps something a little more presentable," he said and nodded at my faded t-shirt featuring the Rolling

Stones distressed tongue. "Something a bit more appropriate."

"She doesn't like the Rolling Stones?"

Fat Freddy grabbed my arm and pulled me toward the door.

Tubby glared and pointed. "Out! Remember what I said, Haskell. 9:00 tomorrow morning, and for God's sake, wear something appropriate."

Four

Fat Freddy pulled the door closed behind us and shook his head. "What the hell is wrong with you?"

"Pardon me, gentlemen," a woman said. She hurried past, pulling a vacuum cleaner.

As we followed her down the hall, Fat Freddy proceeded to lecture me. "Do you have any idea how crazy things are around here? Take a damn look. The entire place is getting scrubbed within an inch of its life. You screw this up, and there will be nothing anyone can do to save you. I'm not kidding, Haskell. This is serious. His sister is a major pain in the ass, and he doesn't want anything to do with her. Let me warn you. You goof this up, and the emergency ward is going to look like a vacation spot."

We walked across the entryway and stepped outside. A taxi driver was in front loading three large suitcases into the back of the taxi. Three Asian women were all smiles as they watched their luggage being loaded into the taxi. I recognized them as the women in thongs I'd seen giving Tubby his massages along with other, more personal attention. Who knew they actually owned nice clothes?

Three of the security guys were focused on the women and didn't even notice Fat Freddy and me. One of the guys opened the taxi door, and the women began to slide in. Just the exercise of climbing into a taxi seemed to make them appear super sexy. Once the doors were closed, the taxi slowly made its way around the circular drive. A back window was lowered, and one of the women waved goodbye and blew a sultry kiss. The three security guys all waved back.

"Where are they going?" I asked.

"A three-day work trip in Las Vegas. It's a pity, really. We're all going to be tip-toeing around here for the next few days, and that's where you come in, Haskell. You gotta keep Quinnie out of here."

"Why do I have to—"

"Stop. Do not say another word," Fat Freddy said just as the Escalade pulled up. Happy was behind the wheel. Freddy opened the front passenger door, climbed in, and looked at me. "Get your dumb ass in back," he said, shaking his head and mumbling something I couldn't quite make out.

It was a quiet ride back to my office. Happy pulled to the curb in front of the building and came to a halt at the bus stop.

Fat Freddy turned partway in the passenger seat, but he was so fat, he couldn't face me seated behind him. "Let me just say it one more time, Haskell. For your own

good. You screw this up, and there will be nothing anyone can do to save you. So, let's pretend your worthless
life depends on it. Be there tomorrow morning at 9:00
and not a minute later. Now get out."

I hadn't quite closed the door when Happy took off
down the street. The door was yanked from my hand and
slammed shut. I watched them disappear and then just
stood there on the sidewalk, shaking my head. I climbed
the stairs up to the office. As I stepped inside, Morton
opened one eye, saw it was me, and went back to sleep.
Louie was snoring lightly in his desk chair. I walked over
to my desk and sat down. I debated calling Phoenix Starr
and telling her I would be otherwise detained for the next
two or three days. But then, the more I thought about it,
the more I decided it really wouldn't matter. I could
check out Kozlow tonight, and if nothing happened, I'd
call her tomorrow and tell her I was going to back off for
a couple of days just so he didn't spot me.

The more I thought about it, the more I decided that
would not only work, but it sounded like a great plan. I'll
show what's-her-name, Tubby's sister, around town. Get
a handle on what she's interested in, and Tubby will end
up owing me a favor. I input Phoenix Starr's phone number on my contact list.

"Rumph, rumph," Louie mumbled and moved from
side to side in his chair. "I must have closed my eyes for
a moment. You been back long?"

"Not really," I said and noticed that the BBQ sauce stain on his formerly clean shirt was now about the size of a dessert plate.

"How did things go with Mr. Gustafson?"

"A pain in the butt, but I can deal with it. I have to keep his sister busy for the next couple of days. She's coming in from L.A."

"His sister? Why do you have to do that?"

"I'm guessing because the two of them don't get along. Could you imagine having someone like Tubby for a brother? Or, for that matter, what kind of family raises a kid that grows up to be Tubby Gustafson?"

"Well, yeah, I mean, I get that, Dev. But why do you have to—"

"Oh, it's really simple. If I don't, Tubby is going to have one of his thugs, a guy called Breaker, put me in the hospital. That pretty much got me on board."

"He threatened you?"

"No, it was more of a promise. Anyway, I gotta be at his place tomorrow morning at 9:00. Get this, he's going to loan me one of his cars, and I'm supposed to dress up. So I look nice. If nothing else, it'll be interesting to see what his sister is like. Who knows, maybe I'll learn some deep dark secret about Tubby."

Louie shook his head and turned on his computer. I took Morton for a walk around 4:30, and we met Louie in The Spot. I wanted to check out Sterling Kozlow, so I took a pass on having a beer. Louie fed Morton a bag of pork rinds. We chatted for about ten minutes, and I took

Morton home. I drove over to Sibley Plaza and parked a couple of lanes over from Kozlow's Mercedes. Based on the chalk line I'd left on his rear tire, the car had been in the same place all day.

Once again, Kozlow walked out of his office at 6:00, locked the front door, and went back into his office. He didn't reappear until almost 9:30. I followed him home, watched his house for a half-hour, and then drove back to my place. I let Morton out the back door, ate some leftover pizza from earlier in the week, and we went up to bed at 11:00.

I was up early the following morning. I showered, shaved, and made breakfast. Once I'd eaten, I hurried upstairs and dressed in a nice pair of slacks and a shirt I'd only worn once since it came from the dry cleaners. I thought about a tie; I had three, but they were all Christmas ties and played a carol when you squeezed them, so I took a pass.

I left Morton in the backyard and drove back over to Sibley Plaza. I parked in the almost empty lot at the opposite end from Sterling Kozlow Finance. Kozlow's car was already parked in front of his office. Just like yesterday morning, I walked past his Mercedes. I left a chalk line on his rear tire and headed back to my car. I drove to the office and left Louie a note reminding him I was involved in Tubby Gustafson duty for the day and then headed over to Tubby's.

To be continued . . .

Thanks for taking the time to check out the next book in the Dev Haskell series, **<u>Surprise, Surprise!</u>** Better grab your copy!

Books by Mike Faricy
Crime Fiction Firsts

A boxset of the first four books in four crime fiction series:

Russian Roulette; Dev Haskell series
Welcome; Jack Dillon Dublin Tales series
Corridor Man; Corridor Man series
Reduced Ransom! Hot Shot series

The following titles comprise the Dev Haskell series:

Russian Roulette: Case 1
Mr. Swirlee: Case 2
Bite Me: Case 3
Bombshell: Case 4
Tutti Frutti: Case 5
Last Shot: Case 6
Ting-A-Ling: Case 7
Crickett: Case 8
Bulldog: Case 9
Double Trouble: Case 10
Yellow Ribbon: Case 11
Dog Gone: Case 12
Scam Man: Case 13
Foiled: Case 14
What Happens in Vegas… Case 15
Art Hound: Case 16
The Office: Case 17

Star Struck: Case 18
International Incident: Case 19
Guest From Hell: Case 20
Art Attack: Case 21
Mystery Man: Case 22
Bow-Wow Rescue: Case 23
Cold Case: Case 24
Cash Up Front: Case 25
Dream House: Case 26
Alley Katz: Case 27
The Big Gamble: Case 28
Bad to the Bone: Case 29
Silencio!: Case 30
Surprise, Surprise: Case 31
Hit & Run: Case 32
Suspect Santa: Case 33
P.I. Apprentice: Case 34
Rebel Without a Clue: Case 35
Puppy Love: Case 36

The following titles are Dev Haskell novellas:
Dollhouse
The Dance
Pixie
Fore!
Twinkle Toes
(*a Dev Haskell short story*)

The following are Dev Haskell Boxsets:
Dev Haskell Boxset 1-3
Dev Haskell Boxset 4-6
Dev Haskell Boxset 7-9
Dev Haskell Boxset 10-12
Dev Haskell Boxset 13-15
Dev Haskell Boxset 16-18
Dev Haskell Boxset 19-21
Dev Haskell Boxset 22-24
Dev Haskell Boxset 25-27
Dev Haskell Boxset 28-30
Dev Haskell Boxset 1-7
Dev Haskell Boxset 8-14
Dev Haskell Boxset 15-19
Dev Haskell Boxset 20-24
Dev Haskell Boxset 25-29

The following titles comprise the Jack Dillon Dublin Tales series:
Welcome
Jack Dillon Dublin Tale 1
Sweet Dreams
Jack Dillon Dublin Tale 2
Mirror Mirror
Jack Dillon Dublin Tale 3
Silver Bullet
Jack Dillon Dublin Tale 4
Fair City Blues

Jack Dillon Dublin Tale 5
Spade Work
Jack Dillon Dublin Tale 6
Madeline Missing
Jack Dillon Dublin Tale 7
Mistaken Identity
Jack Dillon Dublin Tale 8
Picture Perfect
Jack Dillon Dublin Tale 9
Dublin Moon
Jack Dillon Dublin Tale 10
Mystery Woman
Jack Dillon Dublin Tale 11
Second Chance
Jack Dillon Dublin Tale 12
Payback Brother
Jack Dillon Dublin Tale 13
The Heist
Jack Dillon Dublin Tale 14
Jewels To Kill For
Jack Dillon Dublin Tale 15
Retirement Scheme
Jack Dillon Dublin Tale 16
The Collector
Jack Dillon Dublin Tale 17

Jack Dillon Dublin Tales Boxsets:
Jack Dillon Dublin Tales 1-3
Jack Dillon Dublin Tales 4-6

Jack Dillon Dublin Tales 1-5
Jack Dillon Dublin Tales 1-7
Jack Dillon Dublin Tales 6-10

The following titles comprise the Hotshot series;
Reduced Ransom! Second Edition
Finders Keepers! Second Edition
Bankers Hours Second Edition
Chow Down Second Edition
Moonlight Dance Academy Second Edition
Irish Dukes (Fight Card Series)
written under the pseudonym Jack Tunney

The following titles comprise the Corridor Man series:
Corridor Man
Corridor Man 2: Opportunity knocks
Corridor Man 3: The Dungeon
Corridor Man 4: Dead End
Corridor Man 5: Finger
Corridor Man 6: Exit Strategy
Corridor Man 7: Trunk Music
Corridor Man 8: Birthday Boy
Corridor Man 9: Boss Man
Corridor Man 10: Bye Bye Bobby

Corridor Man novellas:
Corridor Man: Valentine
Corridor Man: Auditor

Corridor Man: Howling
Corridor Man: Spa Day

The following are Corridor Man Boxsets:
Corridor Man Boxset 1-3
Corridor Man Boxset 1-5
Corridor Man Boxset 6-9

All books are available on Amazon.com
Thank you!

Contact the author:
- Email: mikefaricyauthor@gmail.com
- Twitter: @Mikefaricybooks
- Facebook: Mike Faricy Author
- Website: http://www.mikefaricybooks.com

Published by

MJF Publishing